NO ONE
LEFT
BUT
YOU

NO ONE LEFT BUT YOU

TASH McADAM

Published in the United States by Soho Teen
an imprint of Soho Press, Inc.
227 W 17th Street
New York, NY 10011

Library of Congress Cataloging-in-Publication Data

Names: McAdam, Tash, author.
Title: No one left but you / Tash McAdam.
Description: New York, NY : Soho Press, Inc., 2023. | Audience: Ages 14 and up.
Audience: Grades 10-12. | Identifiers: LCCN 2023015380

ISBN 978-1-64129-489-8
eISBN 978-1-64129-490-4

Subjects: CYAC: Murder—Fiction. | Interpersonal relations—Fiction. |
Transgender people—Fiction. | Mystery and detective stories. | LCGFT:
Detecive and mystery fiction. | Novels.
Classification: LCC PZ7.1.M3997 No 2023 | DDC [Fic]—dc23
LC record available at https://lccn.loc.gov/2023015380

Interior design: Janine Agro
Butterfly illustration: vahlakova, iStock

Printed in the United States of America

10 9 8 7 6 5 4 3 2 1

For the lost

NO ONE LEFT BUT YOU

AUTHOR'S NOTE

IN THIS STORY, I was unable to find a way for Max to thrive without transition-related healthcare support—frankly, because that support is life-saving, life-affirming, and without it many people do not survive, let alone thrive, and this story was walking closer to that line than I wanted it to in its earlier iterations.

Transgender rights are in crisis around the globe.

Trans teenagers are particularly at risk, as they do not have autonomy to make their own informed decisions. Trans teens are at incredibly high risk of mental health issues. A 2022 PubMed study[1] shows 82% of trans people will consider suicide and 40% have attempted it, with suicidality highest amongst youth. It does not have to be this way.

---

1 Austin A, Craig SL, D'Souza S, McInroy LB. Suicidality Among Transgender Youth: Elucidating the Role of Interpersonal Risk Factors. J Interpers Violence. 2022 Mar;37(5-6):NP2696-NP2718. doi: 10.1177/0886260520915554. Epub 2020 Apr 29. Erratum in: J Interpers Violence. 2020 Jul 29;:886260520946128. PMID: 32345113.

Make no mistake: it is possible to be a happy, healthy, empowered trans individual when supported by our communities, our families and our legal systems.

We need that support now. We are watching bills be passed against our existence and hate speech being publicised and engaged with as if it's reasonable. We are so, so tired. We are losing hope, we are losing lives.

My cisgender readers, contact your representatives, MPs, etc. We need your voices in this fight now.

To my trans family around the globe, be strong. Be brave. There is love in this world waiting for you to find it; there's a sunrise every day, and most of them are beautiful.

A NOTE ON CONTENT WARNINGS

Dear Reader,

This is a messy book about messy people in messy situations. My intention is never to hurt my readers, or shock you (besides with a plot twist!), and I have endeavoured to be thoughtful and gentle around challenging topics. A detailed and expanded list of content warnings can be found on my website, but please be aware that this novel contains on-page depictions of the following:

alcohol (use, abuse)
drug (use, abuse)
violence
anxiety
depression (references to suicidal ideation, depressive episodes)
homophobia (verbal, implied violent)
bullying
transphobia (misnaming, off-page deadnaming, misgendering)
child abuse, neglect

Take care of your mental health, friends! (and enemies, and those yet to be classified)

Tash McAdam

AFTER

1

PASSING STREETLIGHTS BATHE the back of the car in sharp, unnatural orange and make the blood drying on my hands look fake, but it's not. It's real.

So are the handcuffs.

The police station is awash with noise, the world thin and unreal, too distant for me to hear what anyone's saying; there's a song stuck in my head.

you and i curled in the safety of the deep leaf shadows

A woman speaks to me gently, her words drifting past without meaning, but all the other voices are loud and angry. My wrists ache. I'm handcuffed to a metal table in a small room that smells of sweat and something worse. Fear, maybe. Or hopelessness.

our mouths lodestones, forever drawn to each other

They take samples from my hands, then clean me up and

stitch the cut in my palm. There's a tideline of rust-red in my nail beds. I get stuck looking at how whole the flesh there is; it's been so long since I chewed my skin off in meaty chunks. Now, I can smell his blood on them.

I'll never bite my nails again.

BEFORE

1

"MAX."

The sound of my name makes me look up from my work, and I can't suppress a wide, face-splitting grin. I changed it over seven months ago, right before year thirteen started, but it'll never get old. My dad did so much work, leveraging his friends in the fire services and their connections, to get my name change sorted and my medical care organised. It's the only fight he's ever stood his ground for, but it's the most important one.

Max. It rolls off the tongue. Sounds like me. Like the boy that's been fighting to climb out of his girl-skin since birth.

My maths teacher is staring at me, waiting for me to zone back in. She squints in the thick stripes of March sunshine pouring through the blinds, but the affection on her face is clear. She likes me. Most of the teachers do . . .

Or did, I guess. A lot of them got weird this year when I came out. Started tripping over my name and pronouns, stumbling through conversations like they needed a map for how to speak to me. As if they thought I had changed instead of their perception of me. Not Ms. Hennessey, though. Even when she was adjusting and slipped on my pronouns or name, she corrected herself and moved on instead of apologising and making me reassure her.

Now, her eyebrow twitch implies she's going to wait for me to stop daydreaming and verbally respond. I find my voice after a moment. "Yeah?"

She inclines her head towards the door. Is it time to pack up? No, that's wrong, school hasn't even started yet. I'm the only one in here, revising instead of messing around outside on the sun-slicked fields, reluctant to come in for the first day back after Easter break.

It's easier to avoid Danny if I stick to classrooms or the library. Less chance he'll "accidentally" shoulder me into a wall in the corridor or loudly brag about all the girls who want him when I happen to be nearby.

A woman steps into the room, and my ribs constrict, talons around my lungs. Breathtaking—I understand the phrase for the first time. She has a long, rich swathe of probably dyed red hair furling down a silky blouse and green, piercing eyes. A new student teacher? I squirm, confused and uncomfortable with their focused attention.

"Max, this is Emily. She's going to be joining our class for the last few months of school, and she's also ahead. I thought you could work together. She's new to town, from London. Maybe you can show her around."

Sour saliva gathers under my tongue. I finished the advanced level year twelve book last spring, and now I'm working on some more interesting stuff as an independent project. Ms. H—as everyone calls her—never made me join in with the main lessons. Now, she's trying to force someone to join me at the back of the room. She probably thinks she's helping me make friends.

Until this year, school wasn't so bad. Better than home, anyway. I was a loner, but mostly by choice, and I never had to give myself a power up talk to get through the doors in the morning. Not like it's been since summer and Danny. These days, I don't have any energy left over for anything except surviving the hole he left in my chest.

"Sure." I fail to sound welcoming. With Emily assessing me, I'm an insect under a microscope and can't stop myself from squirming. This girl isn't small-town pretty, she's big city. She's one of the sunshine people, the type that glides through life in their own perfumed bubble. They don't have to wade through the shit, so they don't believe it exists. Her straightened hair and sticky pink lips are so shiny the lights reflect off them, as if she's made of precious stones. It's hard to look right at her.

"Gloss." The random word drips out of a heart-shaped mouth. She has light eyes, like a cat. They laser into me, scanning me from head to toe. Judging my beat-up Chucks and my chewed raw nails.

Finding me wanting, like the rest of the world. Like Danny. I force myself away from the thought of him.

My island of isolation at the back of class suits me just fine. I don't need an interloper, especially one who probably wants to get vaccinated before sitting next to me.

"What?" I trip over the question and let my fluffy, dark fringe flop in my face. I'm sure my cheeks are flushed, highlighting my inflamed skin in all its hideous glory.

"Call me Gloss," she says to both me and Ms. H. It's a decree that brooks no argument. "Everyone does."

"Uh . . . Okay. Welcome to Ridgepoint." What am I, a butler?

I swallow, needlessly moving my textbook over and knocking my phone off the table in the process. Ms. H chuckles, and it's thunder in the silent room. The sun that was warm and pleasant has become oppressive while I was distracted, burning my back through my thick hoodie as I scramble to pick up my phone. There's a fissure across the middle of the screen. Great.

"Nice to meet you, Max."

Gloss's sugar-sweet drawl seizes me by the intestines and squeezes, and the cracked screen doesn't matter anymore. My name in her unplaceable accent echoes in my ears. I shove my phone in my pocket to avoid her gaze, and the bell rings, saving me from having to unclench enough to respond. Students shove their way through the narrow doorway, drawing the weight of attention away from me. I can finally inhale.

"All right, all right. Daniel, sit down! Ashdeep, give Devon's bag back. Lina, his lap is not your seat." Ms. H does her level best to herd the animals while I wither into myself, trying to avoid catching Danny's attention.

Gloss takes the chair right next to me, all precise angles and lustrous hair. Focusing on details helps me ward off panic. Her skin is as smooth and pale as creamy paper, her white shirt almost sheer. The artfully puffed sleeves turn into tight cuffs halfway down her forearms. They're fastened with miniature gold buttons. Black lines peek out from under a matching gold watch on her delicate wrist. A tattoo? Or a doodle? She doesn't seem like a doodler. I tug my ragged sleeves over my hands and poke my thumbs through the strategic rips to keep them there.

Making the mistake of glancing across the room, I catch Michelle's eye. She flashes me a quick smile, which drops off her face when Danny flops down next to her, slinging his arm across the back of her chair. She leans into his side with a little pout. I struggle to drag my gaze away. Luckily, Gloss leans over, reaching out with one manicured finger towards my ragged fringe, jerking my attention back to her.

"You need a haircut," she tells me, cool and collected as if she's commenting on the weather.

My throat closes so my indignant, defensive response comes out as a strangled squawk. My mother is always telling me I need a haircut to get the fringe out of my eyes. It's her favourite line—when she's not telling me I should grow it out to look more feminine.

And then Gloss drops her hand and touches my chest, brushing her fingertips against my "he/him" pin. Electricity jumps into my sternum. "You need a haircut. This is a butch lesbian haircut. Not a young man's haircut."

I choke on my own spit, distracting me enough that I miss his approach.

"He is a butch lesbian."

My spine stiffens. I don't need to turn around to know that Danny's looming over my desk, but I do anyway, forever unable to resist him. Paper crinkles as he leans against the poster-covered wall. The sight makes me want to reach out and push him away from the work he's casually ruining. The way he ruined me.

His long blond hair is perfectly scruffy, and the stubble on his cheeks sparkles, gold glittering in the sun. He's bronze after spending the last two weeks surfing in Newquay. Can I smell the salt? I wish I didn't know what he looked like laughing in the waves, hadn't checked his socials forty times a day over the holiday, torturing myself. Is it still misgendering if someone uses male pronouns but calls you a lesbian? Does he know how ridiculous it is for him, of all people, to call me a lesbian? If I was brave, I'd raise an eyebrow at his belt buckle and make him remember the very unlesbian things we did together under the summer sun. But I'm not brave. I stare fixedly at my pen, squeezed in my hand. The plastic creaks, splitting under the pressure. I focus on the crawling sensation as the crack works its way through the shaft, under my sweaty fingers.

Danny smirks at Gloss. "Hello, gorgeous. What's someone like you doing back here with the cryptids?"

He's drawling the way he does when he wants to impress someone, when he thinks he's extra cool. My stomach does that frustrating melt-and-slide into warmth. I scowl. The pen snaps in my fist.

Gloss inhales softly. She turns her laser eyes on to him, drags them over his body like she did to me. He preens; he knows his thin white T-shirt makes him look like a Greek god, all golden skin with a six-pack you can see the shadows of through the fabric. He makes Primark look like Gucci. I stare at my ink-stained hands. I don't want to watch the car crash of Gloss teaming up with him to torment me.

"Yes, I'm sure it's a vast shock to discover that I might choose to spend time with someone thoughtful and intelligent instead of an arrogant asshole with the emotional range of a Bop It."

It takes me a moment to catch up, to believe she hasn't giggled and flicked her glorious wave of hair over her shoulder to look up at him in feminine awe like every other girl and a good number of the boys at school.

"Go away, you spoilt toddler, the adults are talking," she says, dismissing Danny with a sneer that makes my skin crawl.

My eyes dart up without permission to watch Danny as he registers what Gloss has said. He looks confused, almost hurt, for a moment. Like a kid who's dropped an ice cream and is staring at the empty cone trying to work out what's happened. Then his face hardens, and his summer sky eyes go flat and cruel.

"Whatever, bitch. Catch you later, Maxipad."

My heartbeat spikes, tears prickle my eyes. I should take a deep breath to try and ward off the anxiety attack threatening to burst open in my chest, but I can't. My body's stuck.

Gloss turns to me, putting her back to Danny as though

he no longer exists. I'm not sure I've ever seen anyone ignore Danny. I didn't know it was possible.

"You working on stats right now, Max?" She pulls my stats textbook over, and a waft of strawberries and clean linen teases me; I can breathe again.

Everything outside us fades away.

THE MINUTE I'M THROUGH the music room door, Mr. Murti gives me the eyebrow. I grimace and reach into my pocket, accepting the inevitable.

"All right! Max, my guy!" He chortles happily as I hand over the USB stick containing the rough copy of my album project. Six songs, every single one of them about last summer. About finding a whole world in someone's eyes and never being allowed to look into them again.

After he listens, I'm going to get called into the counsellor's office, guaranteed. They made me go twice a week all through the first term, to "support me" in my transition. Like I want to sit and explain myself to some old cis guy with a rainbow flag on his desk. As if taking deep breaths can fix this fucking town, this hateful world.

"I knew you'd come through. I can't wait to listen." Mr. Murti has enough enthusiasm for five people, and he always tries to lend it to me through sheer force of will. It's a losing battle, but I appreciate the effort.

"It's pretty emo," I warn him.

"I'd be shocked if it wasn't." He chuckles. I roll my eyes, which makes him laugh more.

The rest of the music students are waiting behind me. Mr. Murti jerks his head at me to accompany him to one of the small "soundproof" rooms I helped install in year eleven. The cork- and egg-carton-enclosed space relaxes me—until I see that Mr. Murti has followed me in. Dammit, I thought I was getting a time out. My forlorn hope that he'd just take the digital copy at this point vanishes. He closes the door, leaning his shoulders against it. "Take it away, kiddo."

He waves a hand, all too pleased with himself. Glowering, I pick up my guitar from where it's leaning against the table. He planned this ambush, and I should have seen it coming. I've never been late with anything before, but this work is so private I've been avoiding him. It seems my reprieve is over. Bracing myself—physically against the wall, and mentally with the thought that he's always been supportive of my originals—I check the tuning. It's not like I have the guts to play in front of anyone else, and songs are meant to be heard.

His brown eyes are steady and warm, his smile encouraging. I can do this.

"This one's called 'A Cruel Chrysalis,'" I say.

Mr. M gives me the finger gun that means "nice" because he's a weird dude. I wait for the twisting in my belly, the sick sadness that comes with letting myself enter the pain that fills this song. But instead, I find myself thinking about her.

The way her hair fell past her jaw when she turned to me, a curtain between us and the world. The peach lacquer on her nails, smooth and even, like rose petals.

The calluses on my fingers catch the strings. I press into the first chord before starting to sing.

well i told you that i was a butterfly boy
but all you could see was the seams
where i sewed on my wings

but i showed you my heart
in the wrecks of my hands
and oh how i begged you to see

i'm all out of guts and my tongue's falling off
my bones break and rot
my skin's sloughing rough
i'm who time forgot
i'm who time forgot

yeah i told you that i was a butterfly boy
and you just wouldn't listen to me
the chry-

sa-

lis
that i made for myself
was the wrong kind of fabric you see
the map i was given was riven with lies
the names written backwards
the seas in the skies
if only i could just change and take flight
then of course i would
but wings run on hope
and i'm dry

i'm all out of luck and my heart's a dumb bitch
my fists shake and snap
my soul slides and slips
this meat doesn't fit
this meat doesn't fit

i'm who time forgot
i'm who time forgot

but now's all that i got
it's all that i got
i'm all that i got

THE REST OF the morning trickles by, shapeless and confusing. Singing six songs about my broken heart should wreck me, leave me exhausted and empty. Having a panic attack or a panic nap, or a lovely pairing of both. I'm not, though. There's the seed of a melody twitching in my brain, but I can't catch it. I don't have a class after lunch. Usually, I'd revise or read, maybe work in the music rooms. I start and abandon a dozen activities and end up lying under a tree on the edge of the field with my backpack for a lumpy pillow, annoyed at my inability to *do* anything. I can't even zone out on my phone, barely managing to text my dad back in reply to his latest shift update.

> Breaking News: Stefford managed to break the station deadlift record.

Stefford is six foot seven and set that record himself. Dad only ever tells me shit like that. What they had for lunch, or who's done something stupid and is in trouble with the chief. Not about the calls, never about all the horrific ways he could die and leave me all alone with the vicious ghost that used to be my mother.

Scattered students yell and throw things at each other on the field. It's all laugh-shouts and squeals, like children. I half-heartedly watch a terrible game of frisbee, wishing I had the guts to skive off school properly, leave and skate to clear my head. Danny has his design technology block after lunch. He wouldn't miss that. I could go to the skatepark . . .

A window creaks open. The sound draws my eye down the grassy slope, past the cracked basketball court and to the sprawling buildings. The pitted walls are grey and dull in the brightness of the day, the windows loamy holes in the grave-yard of teenage hopes and dreams. I imagine the hundreds of students inside, snoozing away the hazy warmth of climate change spring afternoon classes, and droning teachers bored of their lives.

A bag swings into view from the newly opened window in the humanities block. It's black leather with shining metal on the front, and a pale hand holds the strap. One long leg, then the other, appears over the sill. I recognise those ridiculous heeled boots even from this distance.

Why is Gloss climbing out a window on her first day of school?

My pulse throbs in my throat. I'm over-caffeinated, though it's been hours since my cup of shitty vending machine coffee.

Gloss pauses on the window frame, then gracefully slides out. It makes no sense that such a polished person would climb out a window, that an advanced-placement student would leave class without permission. My tentative assessment of her crumbles again, and while I'm trying to stick the pieces back together, she sashays across the court—ignoring the two boys playing illegal shirtless one-on-one—and picks her way up the hill.

Towards me.

For a breathless moment, I imagine she's going to lift one heeled boot and place it on my sternum. My heart rate doubles. Triples? A hummingbird beats its wings in my chest. She sits down next to me, heedless of the grass that will ruin her clothes, and pulls out a shiny gold vape.

Her voice is light and easy, her accent refined but not English. "So what's the deal with you and that shit kebab from math?"

The insult makes me do an embarrassing snort, and I respond quickly to try and cover it. "What do you mean?" I think it's a valid question. Guys like Danny step on people like me, and not in a fun way. It's the way things are. It's a microcosm of what rules the entire world. Everything from seat belt design to history textbooks prioritises people like him. He's the pinnacle of what society has been told is perfect, and I'm . . . not.

Surely, Gloss understands that. Or perhaps not, which would explain why she's willing to be seen talking to me.

"Why do you look at him like you want to lick his stomach when he's a skid mark?" she elaborates, perfect pink mouth exhaling a cloud of thick white.

I hunch my shoulders away from her question, and she huffs. "Stop doing that."

Invading my space, she puts her fingertips under my chin. For a wild moment, I think she's going to kiss me, and my stomach flips over. Bubble gum fills my lungs. I've always been quiet, too in my own head, but since Danny and I exploded, I'm close to silent. At home, I'd been doing my best impression of someone who wasn't there for years, so it wasn't a huge step to disappear at school too. But she saw me. She's touching me, and it shakes everything inside me loose, even the words. "Stop what?" I ask.

"Stop hiding. If you hide, then the world will walk all over you. It's not fair, but people treat you the way you demand to be treated. You deserve better, so try acting like it. What's the worst that could happen?"

I flinch away from her hand, my nascent facial fuzz brushing against her skin. It's so soft I doubt she'll notice, but the sensation sings through my spine and puddles, hot in my belly. It's been a long time since anyone touched me. A memory surfaces of Danny's fingers roughly grabbing the nape of my neck, pulling me around to kiss him. I remember how much I wanted it, his frantic lips driving mine open, and shiver. Gone now.

He's not queer.

"Why are you doing this?" I ask.

Gloss licks her square, white teeth, blinks long lashes at me and smiles, slow and predatory, before sitting back and leaning against the tree, relieving me of the overwhelming weight of her attention. "Bored of this town already. I need a project."

The sun drapes us in gold heat, beating my bones molten until I have to pull my jumper off or leave. I don't want to leave. I want to stay with Gloss in this thick silence, clouded by sweet air that tastes like sugar-covered promise. She teases at the worn fabric of my backpack strap, eases the threads back down flat where they're puffed free. There's an echo of her hands on me, soothing my rough edges into order. A project.

I don't even notice the bell—just the change in mood of the teenagers dotting the field as they plod towards the building, their joy evaporating as class rears its tedious head. I have English, by far my worst subject, and I should definitely go, but I'm stuck to the grass beneath spreading boughs and blazing sky. My heels dig into the cushy ground, divots cradling my shoes.

Gloss places her hand right above my belt. "May I?"

"Yeah," I blurt, even though I have no idea what she's asking. In that moment, with the heat of her palm somehow burning me through the fabric of my sunbaked black shirt, there's not a "no" inside me. I'd jump off a bridge. I wouldn't even look before I leapt.

She lies down and lifts her hair so it drapes over my hip before resting her head on my stomach; this girl has no concept of personal space. I don't know what to do with my arm, so I hover it, the grass tickling my hand, before digging my fingers into the ground. Gloss shifts, tilting her head up so she can see me.

"Tell me about him."

There's no need to ask who. I lick my lips, searching for the right words. They spool up in my throat, getting tangled in each other. But she waits for me, no impatience on her face.

"He lives in the Crescent, near the skatepark. He never really noticed me in school, we didn't have any classes together until this year, but I skate there. A lot. For years. I guess he watched me sometimes or whatever. Last summer, he started coming to sit on the ramp. He thought it was cool that . . ." I trip over it. "That a girl could skate."

I clear my throat, looking up. The light slaps the leaves neon, so bright it's hard to see. It's better that way. "He'd wander out with Cokes for us or a beer." My voice breaks. I don't know if it's puberty or emotion. Both.

"Did he hurt you?"

There's real feeling in her voice for the first time, a hard and brittle edge.

"No, fuck, no!" The denial bursts out of me, thick and hot. "It wasn't like that."

She weaves her fingers on her white, white shirt. "What was it like?"

"It was like . . ." But everything is too weighted, has been turned into angst-laden lyrics too many times. "It was like being set on fire. Warm and good, then hot, then agonising."

It's the best I can do to explain how it was without getting too detailed, too personal. Because even though there's a drive inside me to share with her, I'm not going to show her my open wounds without being sure she won't pour salt in them. The last time I let someone get close to me they ripped my heart out.

She laughs, but there's no humour in it, only acid. It's not for me, though, and she doesn't move from my stomach. "You're a poet."

"Lyricist, actually." I have no idea where this courage comes from, the desire to tell her something about me that isn't sad and pitiful. I don't want her to pity me. I'm not sure what I do want, but not her pity.

"Oh yeah?" She sits up, and I immediately miss her against me. Without her weight, I'm drifting off the grass and everything is oversensitive. I'm thrumming with awareness of her body. Tuned to her; GlossTV. Her hair swings behind her, so red it burns glitter into my vision. I know I'm staring, but I can't stop.

She rummages in her leather bag and pulls out sunglasses. Big, black frames, like a Kardashian. When they're settled on her face, she lies back down, resting her head against me with an airy sigh. I'm pinned. My back's damp under my shirt and oh no, I hope I don't smell. Did I put on deodorant this morning? Pre-testosterone I didn't sweat much, and sometimes I forget those days are over and I am now a sweaty teenage boy.

She tilts her chin up. The freckles scattered on her nose are like miniature golden coins. "What kind of music are you into?"

"I play guitar." The words tumble out. I want to impress her, and I sound like an overexcited idiot, but she just flashes her dimples at me, as if I'm cute. "Mostly old acoustic emo stuff. Bright Eyes, Bon Iver kind of vibes. I listen to a lot of punk, though."

She beams, and it's brighter than the sun. Her nose has a little wrinkle in it. "A tortured youth. I never would have guessed."

"No!" The grass gives under my clenching fist. "Well . . . maybe."

"It's cool, suits your aesthetic."

Now I know she's teasing me, and I smile at her for the first time. "Angsty emo kid loathes popular crowd?" I joke, though it's not really a joke, even if it's more longing than loathing. Wanting to unlock the secret of how easy it is for them, how their worlds make sense and fit with each other. To understand why I never fit. I settle my head back on my bag and look through the branches. There's a flock of birds flying far in the distance.

"I'm the popular crowd, and you don't loathe me."

She's self-possessed in a way that sounds too adult for a secondary school student. Everything about her seems too adult for a secondary school student. Who is she? What has she seen to make her so worldly? I wouldn't be surprised if it turned out she was anything from an undercover police officer to a princess attempting to get "real" life experience.

"Danny's king of the school." I think I'm warning her, but my voice gives away the pleasure I took in her cutting him down.

"Sweetie, I'm the emperor." She loads it with too much drama, and we both laugh at the same time, but I believe her.

I've only known her for a few hours, and I can already tell her power isn't limited to teenage boys. If it was, the head teacher would have been out here moments after she absconded from class. And the way she shut Danny down earlier. I shiver.

I should wish he and I had never happened, but I only wish he didn't hate me. I wish I could go back to the glorious moment where we kissed and smiled into each other's mouths. When he leapt off the side of the kid's play castle and punched the sky in happiness on his walk home, his whole body screaming how perfect that kiss was. I would stay there for the rest of my life. It's the best I've ever felt. The best anyone could ever feel.

Gloss reaches over her head and curls her fingers around my wrist, bringing me back into my body. She takes my hand out of the grass and laces our fingers, heedless of the dirt smudging my tattered nail beds. I don't know what to do, my sweaty fingers don't fit with hers, but she bullies my hand how she wants it, and I let her. When I relax, it's comfortable. We rest our joined hands on her stomach, and I pray to a god I don't believe in that I won't leave stains behind.

"So apart from fucking with Danny, idiot king of the fools, what is there to do around here?"

She brushes her thumb over the base of my palm. Lightning dances up my forearm, making my arm hairs stand up. She doesn't comment, but the corner of her mouth quirks like she's noticed.

Discomfort rolls through me as reality hits. I'm holding hands with a girl I met this morning. From no friends to physically intimate in hours. Could this be a trick somehow?

Even if it's no prank, Gloss could change everything. Danny's angry and awful, but he's not clever. People follow him because he's beautiful, and magnetic, and has that stupid athlete's natural leadership thing going for him. What if Gloss decides it's better to be on his good side? She has a terrible potential energy humming around her. I've known her for less than a day but already, I know it in my bones: If she wanted to, she could destroy me.

Head spinning, I try to free myself. She tugs back, play-fighting me for possession of my fingers and not giving up, no matter how I twist. Finally, I let her take my hand back to her stomach, but this time our knuckles are coiled into a shared fist. My heartbeat thrums in my wrists.

"Uh, not much." If she cares how long it's been since she asked what there is to do around here, she doesn't show it. Her smile is so approving the last of the tension drains out of my spine into the springy grass. "There's the skatepark, the river-bank, the library." I cringe. The *library*.

"Mmm, I was hoping for something a little more . . . exciting. Where do people drink?"

She reaches for her vape again, and this time, when she exhales, I dare to point at it with our joined hands. She passes it to me as the bloom of smoke drifts up into the reaching tree branches. I inhale, tasting the sweet pink, feeling the low buzz.

It steadies the nervous energy that always jangles inside me. Maybe I should start smoking.

"There's a couple of pubs that aren't too strict on ID, and a place I go to for gigs that serves me, but it's in the next town over." Though I haven't been since summer and by now, Mandy's probably forgotten all about the shy trans kid she let use the employee washroom at punk gigs. We texted a bunch at first, but then Danny happened, and I stopped replying, and finally, she gave up.

"The music man." Gloss taps a made-up beat on her thigh with her free hand, making me refocus on her instead of another failed attempt at a friendship. "Should've known you were into live music."

"I'm into a lot of things," I tell her, and I've never felt so brave.

She laughs, and it's a bell, floating through the leaves and up into the sky. "Give me your phone."

I dig it out of my pocket, and she flicks it to the camera. She takes a selfie so perfect it could have been selected from dozens, edited and filtered.

"Here, now you have a pic for my contact info."

I grin a Max-sized grin and let her put her number in. She calls herself, then saves me in her phone as Max MusicMan.

When the end-of-day bell rings, we unpeel ourselves from the ground and return to the world. She kisses my cheek at the double doors to the science wing, and I blush scarlet, have to duck inside to hide from her affectionate laughter.

I peek through the glass pane in the door to see her walk away. There's not a mark on her shirt.

AFTER

2

MY DAD BURSTS through the holding room door at the police station, shouting. He's ashen, with deep purple smears underscoring his eyes. I got my mother's black hair and pale skin, but I always looked more like my dad, even before the hormones. The way I hold my face, the way I duck my chin. The way we both slide away from confrontation.

He pulls me into his chest hard enough that the handcuffs dig into my wrists. He moves us closer to the table to relieve the strain, still yelling. I'm lost in a rushing ocean of noise, and all the while, a song plays in my mind.

our bare skin touched / i discovered electricity

My brain isn't working. I'm not sure if it's the drugs—fuck, what did I take? I'm not even supposed to drink on my mental health medication, and I did a lot more than drink. There are no words left inside me except the song.

The kind woman who's been with me since I arrived at the station takes my dad's arm and speaks to him. Pressure expands in my chest and explodes out of my chapped lips. "Dad." I'm too quiet, broken. Have to try again and cough up the word like a hairball. "Dad." The sound of my voice snaps the rest of the world back into focus. The song vanishes.

He spins back to me immediately, his large hands fluttering around my face, taking my chin, looking in my eyes. "Max. Buddy. I'm here, it's okay."

I laugh in his face.

My dad recoils like I've stung him but then swallows hard and gestures angrily at the police officer, who loosens the handcuffs but doesn't take them off. My fingers tingle as blood starts flowing again. There are purple dents in my narrow wrists where the metal was.

"Max, son. You need to tell the police what happened at the party. Just exactly what happened. It's okay, it's all going to be okay," he repeats.

It's not okay. Nothing will ever be okay again.

Danny's dead.

BEFORE

2

AFTER SPENDING THE last four hours with Gloss, I can't bear to be weighed down, so I leave my guitar with Mr. Murti and grab my skateboard. A steady trickle of students filters down the corridor, leaving school, and I slip into it with my trucks between my fingers, holding my board by my side like a shield.

All I can think of is her. She fills my head, pounds in my chest. Her hand on my hand, the residual heat where she kissed me. There must be lipstick, at the least. The urge to scrub at my tingling cheek fights with a fierce want to parade through the school with her mark on me. I can imagine the pink stain perfectly: a cupid's bow of scalded skin. The desire to show the world that at least one person doesn't find me repulsive wins out. I march through the hallway with my head up and my shoulders back, wearing the print like a medal.

Outside, I fly down the road faster than I ever have before, invincible and enormous. Concrete races past, and I duck and dive around old ladies running errands, dart through crowds of rowdy primary school kids. My wheels rattle with every bump but never stick or stutter. On the hill down to my house, I spread my arms like wings and shout into the wind.

My good mood collapses as soon as I walk inside.

"Bring me some wine, you angel," my mother calls from the living room.

Cigarette smoke is foul in my throat, and I have to swallow a cough as I rush past the door. She's sprawled in front of the TV, as always. My dad's at the firehouse, so my mother is free to be her worst self. I dread the days he's away, but even if I could find the words to explain to him what it's like here without him, what could he do? Quit the job he loves so I don't have to be alone with her?

I ignore her, thundering up the stairs to the solace of my room. Black painted walls and poster-layered-over-poster darkness envelop me. The teenage cave is a classic for a reason. Clothes folded or hung in the wardrobe contrast with the piles of scribbled lyrics and books threatening to collapse my straining desk. Home. Mine.

Slamming the door behind me, I exhale, imagining my anger floating out of my lungs, and strive to recapture the magic of the day. When I face the mirror, there's a small smile tucked in the corner of my mouth and light in my eyes. I look alive.

The faint remnant of Gloss's kiss glimmers in the light from the window, invisible to anything but a close inspection. No one will have seen it, but I don't wipe my cheek.

Will she kiss me goodbye tomorrow? Will she even speak to me tomorrow? I have to believe the way we connected today isn't something ephemeral that will shimmer away overnight. But still, the intrusive thought keeps presenting itself. What if she's only interested in me because of Danny? If she wanted to get his attention, what better way than to push back against what he expected from her?

My mind drifts to Michelle. "Sorry, Max, but he's ... Danny. I liked you, but he doesn't want us to be friends anymore."

Our seedling friendship—my first ever, really, because Danny was never a friend—slotted into the past with her mild regrets. Leaving me alone, again.

Like most evenings when my dad is on shift at the fire station, the evening spreads out into a string of loud music and writing. But my insides are itchy, I can't focus, I want to skate, but the skatepark ...

I haven't been back since summer. With that thought, my room starts crushing me. I'm starving, but if I go downstairs, my mother will follow me from room to room until I end up bursting out the front door. Instead, I open my window. The evening is cool and clear, sunset spilling egg yolk over the red-tiled roofs of the nearby houses. I breathe in, letting the crisp taste of cut grass and blooming flowers calm me.

Around Christmas when I was eleven, my mother was screaming through my bedroom door, trying to kick it in so she could yell in my face. I was so scared I climbed out the window. I swung myself out and around, my small hands slipping on the drainpipe. I thought I'd fall, which was still better than staying inside. I forget what that argument was about, but I'm grateful it gave me this escape.

I'm bigger now. Stronger and taller. My shoulders opened six inches in two weeks after my first shot of testosterone. It's an easy stretch from the sill to the pipe, to the lip of the roof. Up and over, my stomach muscles burning in the best way as I pull my feet up, brace on the wall and wriggle over the edge on my belly. I settle on my back with my hands behind my head. The rust-red tiles hold the heat of a long day and warm me. My knobby knees poke through the rips in my black jeans, the skin pressed white and pink by the tight strings.

Above, the stars pop out one by one, marking time while

I scroll through Gloss's Instagram, analysing every post. Her account only goes back until last May, but she has over seventy thousand followers. People from school have already started following her, commenting on her gorgeous pictures of spectacular vistas and mouthwatering meals. It doesn't hit me until I'm scrolling back up that there's not a single photo of her with another person.

When I'm riddled with pins and needles from the hard tiles, I go back inside. Sleep has never been a friend of mine; usually, bedtime is something to put off in the hopes I'll be too tired for my brain to replay the Max Files: Embarrassing All-Star Moments. But today, I fall facedown on the bed without even brushing my teeth.

THE TEXT FROM Gloss is the first thing I see the next morning after I grope my screaming phone off the bedside table to make it shut up.

> Pick me up @ Denevue and 3rd.

I stare at it. It was sent half an hour ago. Did she mean right away? What if Gloss has been waiting there for half an hour already? What if she thinks I ignored her? What if she hates me now? How does she even know I have a car when I didn't take it yesterday?

I dress even faster than usual, shoving my feet into Vans to save the thirty seconds pulling on Converse would cost me. I poke myself in the eye with my car keys trying to finger comb my hair on the way out the door, and it's red and weeping when I catch a glimpse of it in the rearview. Great. The perfect accessory to a dishevelled look.

My beat-up Jetta is my second home, but I'm not very house proud. I'm so distracted by trying to clean up the front seat that

I scrape a new line onto my bumper going through the old stone arch. It's a lost cause, anyway—crisp packets, chocolate bar wrappers and paper coffee cups sprinkle the floor out of my reach, even with acrobatic driving. I pull in at Tesco to fill up with exactly four pounds fifty worth of petrol—all I could find in mum's handbag—and then spend ten frantic minutes trying to make my car look like an adult owns it instead of a teenage dirtbag.

The streets are quiet and still. I can see three church spires from here, and this morning, instead of annoying me, they're beautiful. I lose another minute staring at the grey and tan stone steeples, spotted pink and white with old lichen, catching the richening light.

Denevue and Third turns out to be the new development of massive condos for the commuting London financier with money to burn and a desire for country town living. The buildings are out of place among the old—sometimes centuries-old—terraced houses that make up most of Ridgepoint. The historical society was furious about it. Pulling over, I park and peer around, trying to spot her eye-catching hair. I'm looking over my shoulder when she taps on the windscreen, and I flail in surprise. Thankful I didn't spring for a coffee which I would have dumped all over my lap, I lean over to pop her door.

Gloss in my shit car is as out of place as Gloss at my shit school. She gifts me with a gentle smile and starts to wind down her window. It obviously takes a lot more effort than she was expecting, and I start the car to cover my embarrassment.

I'm heading to school when she lays one finger on top of my hand on the gearstick. "Here, pull over. I need coffee."

My jaw unclenches. It's the first thing she's said to me, and her tone says she's not angry with me for being late, or weird, or having an ugly old car.

The parking spot is tight, but I manage not to embarrass myself. Gloss glides out and rests the generous curve of her hip against the door. She's wearing black today, top to toe like me, but it's elegant, not sloppy. I lean over to lock her door and do up her window before scrambling to follow her out of the car.

Gloss flicks her hair out of her luminous eyes, which are limned in shiny gold. Her dark lashes are thick and curling, brushing the delicate skin under her eyebrows. Her smile this time is wicked, showing pointed canines. "I'm a raging bitch before caffeine."

I liquefy with relief at the confirmation I haven't fucked everything up.

She's chosen a coffee shop with exposed wood and unmatched china. Nothing to-go. I wouldn't have even looked inside this place if I wasn't with her. Even though it's early, there's a crowd. They all look like young professionals. No kids or young people, like at Costas. Several people are on obvious conference calls. I'm so out of place there may as well be a sign above me inviting people to sneer at me.

Gloss slips her hand through my elbow and tugs me through the door, swanning up to the front counter. Everyone turns to look at me, their expressions disapproving. Or am I imagining it? Shaking my fringe into my eyes lets me avoid the issue. She orders for both of us—without asking what I want—and pays without blinking. My coffee costs as much as I spend on lunch in a week.

I follow in her footsteps, trying to relax, pretending I belong. Gloss leads me to a miraculously cleared table in prime window territory. Someone brings us our drinks like we're important, but nobody is paying me the attention I was afraid of. People are typing or speaking in low voices, snappy and staccato. It has the vibe of the angriest museum imaginable.

"We're not going to school today," Gloss declares as she

stirs her cappuccino, lifts the spoon out and licks the chocolate sprinkled foam off it. Her tongue is like a small, perfect raspberry. Dragging my eyes away, I bury my face in my enormous latte. It's too milky and sweet.

"Uh, we aren't?" The gulp I take burns all the way down.

"Yes. Do you need me to call in sick for you? I had my dad's assistant email the office for me." She watches me, appraising.

Mentally, I tab through my classes. Music is fine now I've given Mr. M what he wants, English I missed yesterday so what difference does another day make? And maths, well. I'm not exactly behind. Okay. Why not? I shake my head, deciding to see what the day holds. "No, that's okay." The school will phone home, but it doesn't matter. My mum won't pick up, and I can delete the answering machine message before my dad gets to it.

"Great." She sits back in her chair and switches her gaze to the window. I exhale into my drink. The taste is growing on me. It's more soothing than my usual, bitter black.

"What do you want to do?" I venture, eyeing her through my fringe. I can see from my window reflection that my hair is even wilder than usual, puffing up in every direction. Not in a good way. I never look like those artfully ruffled musicians I swear I have the exact same cut as.

She grins and leans over, tugs a lock of my hair between her fingers. She pulls hard enough I feel it in my teeth, but not hard enough to hurt, and the way she strokes my cheek with her knuckles when she pulls away makes me want to chase her hand with my mouth. "Fix this. And shopping. A lot of shopping."

I hate shopping with a fiery passion, but my traitor mouth says, "Sure," all bright and eager. Perfect. A day of trailing around after Gloss in absurdly expensive shops while she buys, I don't know, Fabergé eggs or something. Actually . . . that still sounds better than school. Seeing Danny every day is like pressing my hand against something hot to see if it will burn me. Surprise! It does.

After abandoning our cups on the table, we walk down to the high street. The town comes to life around us, buzzing with people on their way to work or school.

Gloss wafts through the pedestrians in a bubble. No one dares step inside it; everyone bends out of her way. I follow in her wake, tingling. She pulls into a Superdrug and leads me through the facial care department, dragging her fingers over little packets, bottles and sparkling jars. She makes selections, then passes them to me to put in a basket. I should feel like a servant, but instead, I feel important. Useful. Plus, it gives me something to do with my hands. I'm more comfortable with a task I can concentrate on.

We rack up a pile of goodies and head to the cashier. As Gloss unloads, she says, "These are for you. Let me know if you need help figuring any of it out."

For a frantic moment, I think she expects me to pay, but she pulls a gold credit card out of her tiny white handbag. The cashier zaps everything through, puts it in a bag and smiles at us. "Thank you, ladies, have a nice day!"

Her chirpy tone stabs me in the gut; I flinch.

Gloss pauses in swiping her credit card. "Excuse me?" The way she tilts her head reminds me of a Velociraptor sizing up its prey.

"Have . . . a nice day?" The cashier repeats, uncertainty staining her voice.

I concentrate hard on trying to melt into my own shoes.

"Even if you genuinely, fully believe that he's a girl, what about his presentation, style, clothing or fucking pronoun badge says to you that he'd like to be referred to as a 'lady'? What is wrong with you?"

"I . . . uh . . ." The cashier glances around, possibly looking for a manager. Her discomfort jangles in the air right through to my bones.

"It's okay, Gloss." I take her arm as carefully as if she was made of furious glass. I don't know how to explain to her that if I gave emotional energy to everyone who misgendered me, I'd be burned out in a week and never leave the house again. "It doesn't matter."

"It does matter," she hisses and then looks at me. There's a cold, dangerous light in her eyes, but it fades as we make eye contact. She gives me a sad smile. "Okay."

Gloss turns on her heel and stalks out of the shop, leaving me trailing behind to give the cashier an awkward, apologetic shrug. I hate that I need to comfort her when it's my identity in question. Gloss beelines down the high street, pink-striped paper bag swinging from its string handle over her shoulder. I scurry to catch her.

When she stops, it's under the huge, sky-slicing sign for a high-end hair salon. The interior is all stainless steel and glass, with tasteful trailing greenery and black leather. It looks like what I imagine Christian Grey's living space looks like based on Tumblr memes.

Oh no.

"On me, don't worry."

Great. Gloss thinks the stress on my face is because of the no doubt ludicrous price range of a place like this, as opposed to the fear that someone will tell me to leave.

"This isn't . . . I can't go in there." They'll think I'm a homeless charity project. Take a street kid for a haircut day. I take a step back and wobble as the edge of the pavement surprises my heel.

"Sure you can! You're wearing both a shirt *and* shoes," she chirps, taking my hand and tugging me forward. Inside.

Again, she's put me in a position where to free myself I'd have to really try, and I don't have that level of conviction in me. I don't know if it's calculated, if she reads me that well or if she's unable to hear the refusal. Either way, it works.

The room swallows me whole. I'm submerged in tinkling laughter and edgy-but-unobtrusive music. Drowning myself in screamo would help, but my headphones are on my desk. I ran out of the door without grabbing much beyond my keys and wallet.

Gloss squeezes my hand hard, anchoring me in my body, and tiptoes to whisper in my ear. "I'll take care of you, Max. Trust me? Besides, if we went somewhere where you were more comfortable than I was, you'd have to do the talking . . . I'll find you a rocker barber for the upkeep."

Gloss exchanges a flurry of words with the receptionist that I don't try to follow, hunching deeper into myself. Maybe if I try hard enough, I'll discover the superpower of sinking through the floor I've been trying to develop for years.

I have no idea why Gloss has taken any interest in me—let alone to the extent of following through on the haircut situation—but I need my hair. I hide behind it. Without it, I'm exposed. She might be protecting me now, but she could get bored of me any minute. Maybe Danny's set this up to make me shave my head for his final revenge. My body's tensed to bolt, but a part of me does wonder if there's something different I could do with my frustrating hair. And that part stops me from sprinting right out the door.

I'm guided over to an individual station. Somehow, I end up with a glass of fragrant cinnamon tea warming my icy fingers, which I squeeze while Gloss and a hairdresser talk over me. Gloss shows some pictures on her shiny pink phone, occasionally sifting her fingers through my hair. I want her to stop touching me. I want her to dig her nails into my scalp. There are sobs stuck in my throat, and I don't know where they're coming from or who they belong to.

They chat for a while like I'm not even there, as if I'm a mannequin. I pretend to be one. Gloss plays with my hair, and eventually, I relax into it, settle down in the chair and drink my tea. I remember how I looked yesterday in my bedroom mirror with that glow in my face and the ghost of Gloss's lipstick on my cheek. I want to trust her.

I close my eyes as the first snick of scissors echoes in my ear.

I HAVE MADE the same wish on every birthday cake, every shooting star, every four-leaf clover and every single 11:11 I've managed to catch in the last three years, since I realised who I wasn't.

Now, looking in the mirror, I see that my wish has clawed its way out of my chest and into the world. I look like the version of me I catch glimpses of in the corners of mirrors when I turn at the perfect angle. I look like a boy. No. What Gloss said the first day. A young man. My eyes sting, but I'm too mesmerised to look away.

The haircut isn't that different, but it's changed everything. The straight, harsh line below the tip of my ear gives the illusion of sideburns, the neatly trimmed sides make my jaw and cheekbones more pronounced and the fringe flops forward to give me intense, even brooding eyes. I'm . . . not ugly?

Gloss meets my eyes in the mirror. "Told you."

"Thank you." There's so much emotion in my voice that I flush, but Gloss laughs and tosses her hair before leaning down and pressing her mouth to my cheekbone.

"You deserve it," she whispers against my face, and the warmth of her breath and words tingles in my veins.

I believe her. I feel golden.

"Clothes now."

Gloss heads to the front desk, leaving me to gape at myself in pure, unadulterated joy. I'm so happy I might explode, confetti everywhere. There are a dozen songs waiting to be born out of this moment, the way I was born out of Gloss's direction. Maybe she really is my fairy godmother. I give myself a last look, stand and turn on my heel, walking after Gloss with a spring in my step, wondering where else following her might take me.

AFTER

3

THE POLICE OFFICER sits opposite me with the woman who I now know is a child support worker. My dad sits next to me without taking his arm away from my shoulders. I lean against his solidness, trying to stay anchored to the here and now, not slip away into confusing, whirling memories that make me scream inside.

Don't think about the balcony.

Don't think about the blood.

"Time is 7:09 A.M., Sunday, June 21st, 2023. For the record, this is Detective Inspector Gareth Rimmett of the Ridgepoint Police Department. With me are Max Fraser's father, Jack Fraser, Laura Ingleby, our social worker and Max Fraser himself, a person of interest in the death of Daniel Kensington."

Detective Inspector Gareth Rimmett has the washed-out, sunken look of a man who sleeps only if he can't avoid it. His eyes—fixed on me—are the only alert part of him, bright and brown and driving. I can't hold his stare. When I drop my gaze, I notice my butterfly tattoo has been bisected by the loop of bruising. I can't look at it. There's a stain on the wall behind the

DI. It's shaped like the Eiffel Tower. Gloss was going to take me. I stare at the shape until it blurs. My hands are shaking, making the chain rattle against the shackle, filling the room with a metallic susurrus.

Rimmett leans into my eyeline. "Could you state your name for the recording, please, Max?"

I open my mouth, but nothing comes out. My dad squeezes the nape of my neck. His hand is big and firm.

"Max, come on, kiddo," he urges me.

Slowly, I force the words out, each one tasting wrong in my mouth. "I'm Max. Max Fraser." Usually, saying my name, my legal name, makes me happy. Right now, it doesn't even crack the surface of the glacier inside me.

"Thank you." Rimmett nods encouragingly without taking his eyes off me. The weight of his gaze is physical, pressing my shoulders back into the hard metal frame of the chair. "We're here today to discuss the events of yesterday evening, Saturday, June twentieth, and early this morning, Sunday, June twenty-first. In your own words, Max, could you take me through it?"

"Gloss and I spent most of the day setting up for the party . . ."

My voice is slow and slurred. I trail off, and the detective clears his throat into the silence. "For the record, Gloss is Emily Devereux, is that correct?"

Emily Devereux. I'd forgotten her legal name. "Yeah. Emily."

My dad rubs my shoulder. "Okay, Max, you're doing great."

Starting earlier in the evening is easier. "There was stuff getting delivered, and we moved around furniture and shit . . . stuff. Sorry."

The social worker sways forward. "Don't worry about swearing, just tell us what you remember."

"People started arriving around nine-thirty." I remember a video screen, a pink cocktail in my hand, the doorbell ringing.

I'd just made a dirty joke. Gloss had asked, "What's gotten into you?" and I'd answered, "Watermelons."

"Do you remember who?"

"It was Michelle and Lina first. And then some of the guys. Grant and Mike, and then Devon."

"Do you remember what time Danny arrived at Ms. Devereux's?"

The cop is ready for any pause to try and lead me on and bring me to the part I can't think about, but it doesn't work this time. I search my mind—I can't remember him arriving, just seeing him sprawled against the wall in my bedroom.

Eventually, the social worker opens her mouth, probably to repeat the question, and I spit the words out so I don't have to hear his name again. "No. No, I don't remember."

Rimmett nods. I think he's Good Cop, but there doesn't seem to be a Bad Cop right now. Maybe they can't do that with people who are underage. I'm seventeen, though. Will they try me as an adult? Words dance in the back of my mind, the skeleton of a song I can't remember writing. *i never said thank you, or goodbye, but i hope you knew everything i never said.* But they aren't helpful, they don't explain anything.

"Okay, just tell me what you do remember."

I don't want to, I don't want to, but Danny's dead. I have to tell them what happened. Even if it's all snapshots, fits and starts.

A huge bottle of champagne, frothing over me.

Lina, organising body shots.

The skatepark, the dance party in the bowl.

Pink-soled shoes, swinging on the halfpipe.

Sprinting away from the police with Gloss on my back.

Spin the bottle, and Danny's lips on mine, his hand on my cheek.

His face, engorged with fury.

My razor, in his soft toffee neck.

BEFORE

3

WHEN I WAKE up, there's no text from Gloss.

I wonder if she'll be at school. After parking, I sit for a minute, tapping my hands on the wheel. My face looks strange and plasticky in the rearview mirror. The acne-killing hydrocolloid patches Gloss bought me are still stuck to my cheeks. They look like plasters. When I peel them off, I'm shocked to see they've worked. The bumpy red patches on my cheeks are less noticeable. I finger comb my new fringe, inspecting my appearance—usually something I avoid. My haircut is even better than I remember every time I look. Then I stall out. I'm thinking about *myself*, my hair, my face. Not Danny.

There's a spring in my step as I stroll towards the building.

"Hey, dude!" someone yells.

I spin to see Mike Jessup and Grant Okoye, two of Danny's buddies. Mike's on the footy team with Danny, and I know Grant from music, kind of. They're leaning against the low wall outside the school, vaping. Mike does a dramatic double take, not feigned, and it startles a grin out of me.

"Well, shit . . . Max?"

It's half a question, at least. He's wearing his classic uniform of Adidas stripes from top to toe, and his curly red hair is thick with the gel he uses to tame it. I don't think he's ever said my name before, this one or the dead one.

"'Sup, bro." I jerk my head at him. My buttery leather jacket cradles my shoulders like an embrace, like Gloss is standing behind me, holding my shoulders, reminding me to stand as if I deserve to exist, to take up space.

"Sorry, I thought you were . . . someone else," Mike ventures. "You look different."

"Yeah." My face might be splitting in half with the strength of my joy. I feel different today; It's not just the new look, it's the way I'm ignited inside.

"Party at my place on Saturday," Grant says, eyeing me.

My chest swells with a sharp inhale. That's an invite, right? He's inviting me? Grant is one of the popular lads—athletic, good-looking and moderately smart—but he's calmer, more aware of the world around him than the others. Mike has been the class jackass as long as I've known him, egged on by Danny and his other mates, but Grant has always tried to defuse things.

I'm tongue-tied for a moment. He's a decent guy, even if he is Danny's bro. I wonder what having a best friend would be like. What having *her* for a best friend . . . or more . . . would be like.

Grant breaks me out of my thoughts. "You should come. Bring the new girl."

Gloss. My ticket to a life I never thought I'd get. "Yeah, maybe. I'll see if we're busy." The "we" thrills me, dark and delicious. I watch to see how it hits and they act as if it's normal, as if I have a right to team us up.

"Cool." Grant pushes off the wall and strides over to me, nodding a goodbye in Mike's direction. He claps me on the shoulder, and we fall into step as we walk towards the double doors, which he shoves through ahead of me. The corridor feels different. Brighter.

"You're good at algebra, right?" Grant asks.

"Yeah, pretty good." I don't even sound uncomfortable. Who am I this morning?

"I have a project for tech, and the numbers part is really kicking my arse," Grant grumbles.

I miss a beat before I answer, but he doesn't rush me. "Maybe I can help you out."

"That'd be grand." Grant wheels off down towards the art block with a salute, and I float the rest of the way to maths.

Gloss is here today, but not in the back—she's right in the middle of the room. I dither in the doorway; Cool Max wants to sit where she is. Four girls are already gathered around the central rectangle table, vying for her attention. Danny's space is still empty. Ashdeep and Ritchie loiter by the windowsill, pretending they're not trying to be noticed. She has people oriented around her without even trying. Why would she want me?

As I slide towards my usual, unobtrusive seat, my heart pounds with the knowledge I basically implied to two of the coolest guys in school that Gloss and I are a thing. Together. A "we." And how could we be?

"Max!" Gloss grins at me, tilting her head. "I saved you a spot."

Relief washes through me. I stride towards her but falter, seeing there's no space for me at the table.

Gloss points at the seat next to her. Michelle is in it, and she gapes for a moment. "Thanks for keeping it warm for my guy, Shelly!" Gloss gives her a cool, even stare and Michelle gets flustered and nods, rushing out of the chair.

My. Guy. I have an out-of-body experience as the table rearranges to accommodate me. I give Michelle a sympathetic shrug even though it wasn't me who asked her to move. How will Danny take us sitting at the middle table? At the beginning of the year, he made it clear with pointed jokes and weighty silences that I wasn't to be near him.

A glance around confirms he's not here yet. He might only be late. It's a risk. Still, it's not like he'd pull me out of the chair in front of Ms. H. Probably.

Gloss rests her hand on my forearm, her knee nudging into mine, and heat blossoms in my veins, fast and wild. Who cares what Danny thinks?

"You know everyone, right? Willow, Lina, Helen and Shell." Gloss has given Michelle a new name, and she seems almost pleased about it. "Ladies, this is Max."

They all giggle and grin at me like they've never seen me before. Perhaps they haven't. I've never seen me before either.

"Morning." I sound normal, and the last twitch of discomfort vanishes. "How're you doing?"

"Lina's struggling with her trig, I said you'd help." Gloss grabs Lina's textbook and plops it in front of me. Lina hasn't said a single word to me in five years. Oh, I think she said "mm-hmm" once when we were partnered in foods in year nine.

"Uh, sure." I run my finger down the page. It's all easy, familiar. Is it cool to be good at maths now? Has Gloss somehow made educational achievement desirable?

Lina gives me a toothy smile. "Thank you soooo much, Max." The girls nod in agreement. I blush and grab my calculator.

Ms. H smiles at me a few times during class as I work with Lina on her trig, and I develop a new respect for her. Having a mixed-level maths class must be impossible to teach well. Lina doesn't know what a hypotenuse is, but she does want to show off her manicure. I help her as best I can and admire her nails. Admittedly, the tiny pieces of modern art are very cool.

She explains, in detail, how she got the little snakes to seem like they're moving with strategic glitter. I didn't know she was an artist.

Without anything pressing to do while Lina is working on a problem, I think about Grant's party, and my stomach swoops. A real, proper party. I don't know if I'm nauseous with excitement or nerves. What will it be like? No parents, obviously. No adults at all, or maybe older siblings? Will any of the queer kids from our year be there? It's not as if we're friends, but at least we have something in common. If they play music with a decent beat, I can dance. I'm not a terrible dancer.

Lina makes good strides forward with some prompting. Maybe she'd forgotten everything over break. Our last ever school holiday. Final term, the downhill slope to the rest of my life. The thing I've been waiting for, in stasis until I'm free of this shithole. I have no plans and no ideas beyond "get out of here," but I bet Lina doesn't either, and she's happy enough.

At the end of class, she gives me a glowing smile as she sweeps her books into her small, pink leather backpack. "Thanks, Max, you really know how to explain stuff."

The look she gives me from under her eyelashes is doe-eyed and flirty. I stall, with no idea how to respond.

The confidence that's been buoying me up pops. I duck my head and concentrate on packing up, mumbling a "You're welcome" into my backpack. Lina giggles—but it's kind, not teasing—as she moves to the door to congregate with the other students waiting for the bell. When I can't pretend to be packing anymore, I look for Gloss. She's leaning on the heater, gazing out of the window with a distant expression, like a statue.

"You do, you know," she says. "You see the heart of things."

What? I blink, surprised.

Ms. H joins us, her round face pink and pleased. "I agree.

It's good to see you working with other people. I should have had you tutoring all year."

Please don't make me. I mutter something incomprehensible and wish I wasn't blushing. Why am I blushing? Gloss's eyes flick to me, and she smiles as if she knows.

"How are things at home, Max?" Ms. H lowers her voice, and with the angle of her bountiful body, I think Gloss can't hear. Good. If she saw where I came from, she wouldn't understand. But she's watching from the corner of her eye—making sure I'm all right. Her invisible concern floats around my shoulders, a soft, weighted blanket.

"Home, Max?" Ms. H repeats. She strikes a good balance between waiting for me to get the words out and cueing me back to the topic when I space out.

"Okay, I guess."

Mrs. H knows things at home are very much not okay. At the end of last year, she was the first person I spoke to at school about changing my name, and she asked my parents to come in for a meeting. Only my dad obliged. He was pretty clear about my mother's reason for not being there—her belief that my being trans was the result of a mild concussion a few years ago, and that I'd get over it with time. Even though Ms. H isn't queer as far as I know, I felt safer coming to her than to the school Gay Straight Alliance. The Rainbow Society is not the place for me. I was exhausted for a week after one lunch session. The energy of some people! Fired up and wanting to change the world? I can barely change my socks. Where do they find the strength?

Instead, I came out to Mr. Murti and Ms. H, who helped me with the rest of the school stuff, name changes and bathroom access. This year, Ms. H has added a trans flag sticker next to the safe space sticker on the glass of her door. She's a good person, but there's nothing she can do about my home life. She can't make my mother understand me or even sober her up. No one can.

"You can always talk to me, Max. About anything," she adds in a low voice.

Danny pops into my head. If I told anyone Danny's excluding me, what are they going to do? Force people to be friends with me? Ms. H already tried that with Gloss. I guess I should be grateful, but I'm mostly just embarrassed.

The bell screams. Grateful for the release, I duck my head. Students tumble through the doorway, shoving and cackling—but not Gloss. Gloss turns from her position at the window, where she's been standing like a sovereign surveying her lands, and cocks an eyebrow at me, which either means "Are you coming?" or "Should I wait?" I get my zip caught as I try to yank it shut.

Both she and Ms. H are watching me with comparable, fond expressions when I manage to force the bag closed. Shielding myself behind my backpack feels safer than getting up, and part of me wants to lie down on it, hide my face until hopefully, they all go away and stop asking me questions I can't answer with expressions that make me feel clumsy and baby-ish. Except I don't want Gloss to leave without me. I want to hold her hand. With a sigh, I push my chair back.

"Things are getting better," I blurt in Ms. H's general direction. It's only half a lie. Things at home are the same, but things for me are getting better. Today's the first day in a while I didn't have to talk myself down from a panic attack before entering the building. Since Gloss arrived, everything is better, even my ability to walk away from my mother.

I meet Ms. H's gaze straight on. I've been on anxiety meds for over two years, and eye contact is often hard for me, but it's important that she believes me. I know how badly she wants me to be happy, how much she wishes there was more she could do for me. Her eyes are a faded denim blue, and the skin around them crinkles in pleasure, laugh lines creasing in the evidence of a life enjoyed. "I'm glad to hear that."

Gloss wanders around the table and takes my hand. Our fingers wind together as if they were meant to, and Ms. H's eyes flick between us. For a moment, she looks confused, unable to compute the idea of me holding hands with Gloss or possibly with anyone. Then she makes a visible effort to clear her face and smiles at us both with genuine warmth.

"My door's always open."

Before diving into the moving stream of humanity clogging the corridor, I pause to look back at her. "I know. Thanks."

Gloss puts her hand on my shoulder to guide me ahead of her. Without asking, I know it's so I can break through the waves of rowdy, oblivious idiots and make sure she doesn't get mussed. Usually, I'd slide along the walls, but not today. Today, I'm in the main flow. And people look at us, people say hi to us. To her and to me. They greet me by name. My chest swells, and I stride forward.

"HEY, MAX, WAIT up."

I pause half into my car and pull my leg back out. It's Michelle—Shell?—hurrying towards me in an awkward half jog. She's strong and athletic, she's on at least one school team, but she's not dressed for rugby practice. Her generous, pale chest is bursting out of her white shirt, her heels weren't made for moving fast and her brown hair is in her eyes instead of tied back. She clutches her phone with one hand. Diamanté flowers on the black-and-white case peek between her fingers.

Seeing Michelle makes me knot up with tension. She only talks to me when Danny's not around to see. I wonder if she wants to continue bonding about our shitty mothers, since I doubt she'll talk to me about Danny, who was our main topic of conversation. She's made it clear that no matter what happened between us, her allegiance is with him. I don't want to talk to her about anything else, but I can't quite shut the door in her face. I imagine what Gloss might do. Can't imagine her slamming a door. I try to make my voice firm and emotionless. "Yeah?"

She pushes her hair behind her ears with both hands and flashes her dimples at me. "Hi."

It would be better if she didn't clearly feel so guilty, giving me tragic sheep eyes when Danny's having a go at me. I know he told her to stay away from me, but couldn't she have told him to fuck off? She had a sly sense of humour I appreciated, and I thought she liked me. My impatience turns into a simmering boil of frustration.

"So what can I do for you?" I try to make it clear with my tone I'm not really interested in doing anything for her.

"Oh. I just wanted to say hi!" She's too eager, tucking her chin and looking up at me, smiling with all her teeth.

"Well. Hi." I get into my car but don't pull the door closed, even though the urge to do so is thick and hot in my fingers clenching on the handle. Ugh. Close the door, Max. Don't let her get to you.

"Are you going to Grant's party? He was talking to Gloss about it, and you guys are like, together, right? So you'll be there?" She peeks over the top of the open door, fingers curled over the metal.

"Maybe."

Despite my earlier excitement, faced with Michelle, I'm not sure I want to go to an entire house party full of people who, until this week, either hated me, acted like they hated me or completely overlooked my existence. Danny will be there, so I'll have to avoid him, and presumably Michelle will be stuck to his side. But maybe Grant and I can hang out, talk about music, I know he likes some good bands. And it could be cool to see people's faces with the new me, but what if Gloss doesn't want to come after all? Or she does and then ditches me to hang with other people and I end up by myself in a corner, panicking?

What if Danny sees me there, all alone, and sneers that even my body knows I don't belong?

"You should come. It'll be fun." Michelle sounds earnest, but I don't trust it. I still can't pinpoint if she liked me when we hung out last summer or if she put up with me for Danny's sake. Hard to know with how fast she dropped me.

"You've been having fun without me all year," I point out. Seven months with Danny acting as if I personally wronged him by telling him my truth. There's another trans guy on the footy team, and he doesn't get any shit. Just me for not blurting out my identity before he put his tongue in my mouth, I guess.

She scuffs her toe in the scant gravel so the rasping sounds underline her answer. "Well, I missed having you around."

"You missed me?" I scoff, finally letting go of my door handle, admitting I'll stay for the rest of this conversation. I prop my toes on the lip of the map pocket, and the sun soaks into my shoes.

She shrugs and cocks her head, taking time to respond while looking me over. "Danny was more fun last summer. Not as angry. He's angry all the time now. It's really boring. I'm the only person he can talk to about it 'cause . . . you know." A flutter of her hand encompasses all the things I know. "He won't shut up about you. Maybe if you were friends again, he'd get his shit together."

I didn't know *that*. It's not what I expected to hear, although a piece of me thrills to the thought of him talking about me. But Michelle hasn't said anything about missing me for me, only for Danny's sake. To stop myself from reacting, I shrug and turn my car on. The dulcet sounds of Thrice shrieking not to trust poisoned water shuts down the conversation. Apt.

"Like I said, maybe I'll see you at the party." I sound calm. "Later."

The door cuts off whatever she's about to say. Gotta bail before I ruin it. When I look in the mirror before pulling out, she's still standing next to my parking space, watching me drive away with unnerving steadiness.

I'M ANTSY ON the way home. Seeing Michelle puts a weird hat on a good day. I duck my mother and head straight out onto the roof, headphones clamped to my ears and notebook stuffed into my jeans. This time, I bring my blankets. I think I'm there to write, but I never pick up a pencil. I just lie on the roof and watch the clouds scud by.

When my phone buzzes in my pocket, I jump and, for a breathless moment, slide down the peaked roof, my feet skidding against the tile. I catch myself and laugh, startling a bird into flight.

It's Gloss. Excitement leaps in my chest, following the bird into the cornflower sky.

> Hey, sleepover at mine on Friday night

Michelle's question rings in my ears. "You guys are like, together, right?" We're not together, right? She just . . . takes me shopping and buys me stuff and tells me what to do. I giggle at myself for sounding like a toy boy, except aren't those gorgeous, muscular types? Not dorky emo kids. I'm not exactly winning her any cool points. The opposite, even. Although it doesn't seem to have slowed her roll as a talked-about person in Ridgepoint. Everyone wants to be around her, just like I do.

The girls opened to her like a flower, even the teachers. Ms. H wanted to please her in a way she wouldn't usually treat a student. I'm more convinced than ever that Grant invited me to his party in the hopes I'd bring Gloss. I'll take it, though. It's not like I'd consider going without her.

I haven't even asked her if she wants to go.

> sounds good. Should I bring anything?

I grimace as soon as I send it. Should I bring anything? Like I'm going to a garden party. What would I even bring? Scones?

> Your guitar

> ok

The idea of playing for her is both attractive and terrifying, and it mixes with my doubts about the party. My whole body vibrates with anxiety as I hunch over my phone and painstakingly type with shaking fingers, second-guessing every word, every spelling.

> there's a party on Sat, you wanna go?

> do you want to go?

Not really. Kind of. Maybe. Yes. No.

A weight floats off my chest when she makes the decision for me. A thought occurs.

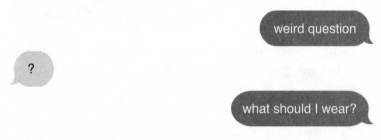

We text each other about clothes and music, school, and the town, about nothing and everything, until it's dark and I'm so hungry I have to leave the roof and forage for food. Thankfully, there's Pop-Tarts in the cupboard. Even more thankfully, my mum doesn't hear me tiptoeing around.

Falling asleep doesn't work, so I mess around on the guitar for a while, coming up with the rest of the melody that's been taunting me. It's pretty rough, but there's something there. Instead of my usual, heavy on the aching wail, this one borders on jaunty. Hopeful in a way I'm not used to feeling, let alone playing. I tool around until I'm so tired that I can't see, and even when I crawl into bed, I'm still turning the tune around and around in my head, clicking chords together, breaking them apart and slotting them into the right place.

AFTER

4

THE INTERVIEW BREAKS while I cry. Then there's more questions. Always more questions but no new information I can give.

No, I'm not sure how many people were at the party.

Yes, we went to the park. Oxwalk Crescent, not Churchill.

Yes, Danny was there, yes, I'm sure.

Who else? Loads of people, I don't know all their names. Michelle, Gloss, Grant, Mike, Lina, for sure.

Yes, we went back to Gloss's place after the police got called to the park. No, I don't know who came back and who bailed.

No, I don't know what happened after we got back. My dad tells them my meds don't mix well with alcohol. Probably not with whatever drugs I took either. Did the police take my blood? I can't remember that either.

I keep trying to see through the haze. I should *know*. I was there, after all. They pulled me off his body, he was in my arms, but everything before the balcony is vague and jumbled.

I remember that he broke my heart. That he treated me like

shit on his shoe for months. That he came to my end-of-year party and took my most precious possession.

People have killed for less.

Did I?

When I'm swaying with exhaustion, my dad and the social worker gang up on Rimmett until he suspends the interview. I'm drifting in and out as I'm led back through the concrete corridors. They put me in a cell on my own after taking my shoelaces. I'm too tired to do anything except curl up on the thin mattress with my face to the wall. I fight sleep as hard as I can, in the forlorn hope that when it takes me it'll be quick and hard and dreamless.

I'm losing the battle when a clatter startles me into rolling over. I bash my shin on the hard metal bedframe. It's dark—the thick metal door blocks most of the hallway lights, and the small window is dirty. Squinting at the door, a lance of light appears, and I watch it open. It must be time for round two. I'm nauseous and angry, and I'm going to throw up on the first person who says Danny's name.

"Hi, Max."

It's Laura, the childcare worker. Her beautiful face is marred by tiredness, and her braids are untidy. Rimmett is behind her, looking exactly the same as he did before. I obediently follow down the hallway without paying attention to what they're say-ing. I don't even notice we're not heading back to the interview room until I'm standing in the lobby. My dad barrels towards me and scoops me up in his arms. He smells like smoke and stale sweat, and I pull it to the bottom of my lungs. Or at least, I try to—his embrace is too tight to get a full breath.

"I knew you didn't do it. I knew it. Oh, Max, oh my Max."

He's crying a bit. It makes tears well up in my eyes too—and then what he's saying registers, sinking into my awareness like dye spreading in water.

I didn't do it?

But there's blood all over me.

"What do you mean?"

My dad mumbles into my hair with his arms tight around me, tethering me to this brutal world. "She confessed, son. I'm so sorry, but Gloss confessed. She killed Danny."

BEFORE

4

THE REST OF the week is as surreal as the beginning. People say hi to me in the corridors, and nobody accidentally-on-purpose jostles me. I catch Danny watching me a few times, but he steers clear, his face sullen and closed. Last summer, I studied every nuance of his expressions—traced his carefree smile with my tongue and his frown with my lips, learned how his dimples sat under my thumbs—but this is a new one. A mean part of me is pleased that he's hurting as well, but I don't know what his problem is. It's not like he's lost his friends or anything. Just because people aren't ignoring me now doesn't take anything away from him. He still has a crew, parading around the school like they own the place.

But Gloss is growing her own crew too now, and I'm part of it.

On Friday, I pack my bag in the morning for our sleepover. The last sleepover I packed for was with Danny on the beach. My hands go cold, and I have to do some deep breathing.

I don't have an iron, so I pick the least wrinkled of my two button-downs and a couple of T-shirts as well as jeans and some new cords the colour of wet slate. I dress in my new favourite outfit: tight black jeans with leather detailing on the belt loops and pockets, Dr. Martens and a plain, wine-red T-shirt that Gloss sent out to be tailored. The red sets off my pale skin and dark hair so I look vampiric, but it works. The tee hugs my shoulders without the fabric bunching over my binder and giving me the weird chest shelf that happens in T-shirts sometimes.

The difference a well-fitting shirt makes is a miracle. I stare at myself in the mirror. I turn, looking. The sleeves are clinging to my arms, but the tee isn't tight on my hips. I look kind of . . . good? Who knew fashion could be armour? I look . . . Not like a different person, but like the Max I want to be. I sling a button-down on over the top because I have to have something to tangle my hands in, but that sits well too.

Finally ready, I reach for my pronoun badge—always my finishing touch—and then freeze. Except for my mum, no one's misgendered me for days. Days. Smiling at my reflection, I tap the badge affectionately and leave it in its dish.

GLOSS MISSES MATHS, leaving me worrying she's changed her mind about the sleepover, even about being friends with me. But halfway through the block, I get a text that reassures me.

> things to do today, see you after school 💋

Despite the way I want to drift off into thoughts of what the night might hold, I don't have time for daydreaming. I'm swamped trying to catch up with English after skipping earlier in the week. Having a day without Gloss consuming my attention is for the best. With so much work to catch up on, I eat lunch in the music rooms, stuffing a Tesco sandwich into my mouth and trying not to drop crumbs directly inside my guitar.

When I burst out of school and into the sun at the end of the day, Gloss is waiting for me, leaning on my car. My whole skeleton thrums like a tuning fork when our eyes click together. She gives me a small, nose-crinkled smile as I walk over.

"Don't you look good."

A sun supernovas inside me. "I sure do," I joke, flinging my skateboard and schoolbag in the backseat. "Missed you in maths today."

Impressed with myself for not sounding needy or pathetic, I dash around and open the door for her. She looks me up and down, gifts me with a fond and affectionate smirk and then slips into the passenger seat. I'm nailing it.

"I was getting you a present."

I hop into the driver's seat and put us in gear, waiting for her to elaborate. She clicks her phone into the holder with a destination entered. Her house? A thrill of excitement runs through me at the idea of seeing where she lives. The place where she sleeps and showers. Concrete proof she doesn't turn into light waves and glitter when I'm not looking directly at her.

"Another present," she clarifies and then reaches over and tugs my earlobe with gentle fingers. "You don't mind me buying things for you, do you?"

It's phrased like a question, but it's a statement of fact. Her nails dig into my skin, the faintest hint of them. Goosebumps erupt. My breathing stutters. "Of course not." A bit of me does, but I have buried him under fancy skin-care products and clothes that fit.

"Good. I like it. My dad won't even notice." For a moment, she sounds wistful.

Gloss lets go of me with a last, affectionate stroke of my sensitive earlobe, and I stare at the car in front of us, hoping she doesn't see the tears that sting my eyes at the care in her touch. I'm sure she sees.

HER PLACE IS a condo, so new the scent of paint tinges the huge open lobby. A doorman greets her, calls me sir, and calls the lift.

The door facing us when we're disgorged on the penthouse level should have warned me—it is a good foot larger than any regular old house door and with stained glass set into a huge window in the centre—but even that didn't prepare me for what was inside. I trip over the doormat in the entrance, too busy gaping. I knew she was rich, but this is obscene.

"Pretentious, no?" Gloss rolls her eyes at me, depositing her handbag—she never carries a school bag—on a built-in bench. She sits to take off her heels. They're red today. Open-toed. Totally against school dress code, which doesn't apply to Gloss. Or maybe it does, and she just climbs out the window if anyone brings it up.

"It's . . ." Words fail me. Majestic? Overbearing? We're in an entranceway the size of my bedroom. There's a chandelier with a skylight above it. It's throwing light sparkles all over the place, and I have the hysterical urge to throw my hands up like it's an arena gig.

Past the entrance, the cream and gold tile gives way to a charcoal carpet. The lounge is furnished in steel, glass and white leather, shiny and so clean you couldn't merely eat off any surface you chose, you could lick it and taste the money. I do a slow circle, overwhelmed and not able or willing to pretend otherwise. "What . . . the fuck?"

"I'm pretty sure my dad buys whatever place is the newest

and most expensive wherever we move. Well, has his people buy it." Gloss offers me her hand. I take it, and she stands up in her bare feet. "You should have seen the place in Paris." Her toenails—apple red, matching her shoes—are more shocking against the floor. Don't stare at her feet, Max.

"Well, that'd do it." I wonder if he'd think he earned this place if he followed my dad around for a shift, if his job is important and hard enough that he deserves this absurdity. "What's he do for a living?"

"Business stuff. It's boring. Come on." She pulls me down the vast hallway, barely giving me time to glance through the many open doors. Natural light everywhere. No plants. Then we reach a closed door, and Gloss lets go of my hand to take the brass knob. "My room."

"Where is your dad?" Mostly I'm wondering if I need to prepare a speech of some kind. I thought it was an innocent question, but the way Gloss freezes halfway through the doorframe tells me it's loaded.

She looks at me with an unreadable expression. She's never looked at me like this before—the way she looks at people who displease her. I tense, holding back a shiver at the intensity of the blankness on her face.

"Sorry. I didn't . . . that was rude." Was it rude? Weren't we talking about her dad seconds ago?

The silence is about to crush my chest. Then she laughs, and the sensation evaporates, leaving me giddy with relief.

"Business trip, almost always. We're all alone."

Alone with her. Does that mean she wants to hook up? Do I want to hook up with her? The answer is a resounding yes regardless of how intimidating the prospect is. Best not to mention her parents being out of town when I text my dad to tell him I'm staying out tonight. Maybe he'll appreciate an evening that doesn't require him to referee between his wife and his kid. Hope it doesn't hurt his feelings too much, though his quiet sadness hurts more than my mother's anger.

Dad keeps me on a pretty loose leash. As long as I'm in contact, he doesn't bother me much. The third time I ran away, at fourteen years old, I made it to London and busked for change. Got picked up by the police on day four. Who knows if my mother even noticed I was gone, but my dad was out of his head with worry. I think he's so scared I'll leave forever that he tries not to hold on too tightly. It's endearing when it isn't exhausting.

I'll take a picture of the opulent living area, I decide, which should help placate any frustration at the short notice and the fact it's his first night back from duty and I've taken off without even saying hi. He'll understand why I wanted to come and check this nonsense out when he sees the display of gleaming gold coins mounted above the fireplace.

Gloss's room is dominated by a white four-poster bed with crisp cream sheets and matching pillows. It's surrounded by gauzy curtains. There's gold crown moulding around the ceiling. All the furniture is white and sharp cornered, and the carpet is thick and luxurious, the colour of the milky lattes she buys me. At the sight of its unmarred beige perfection, I panic. I never took my shoes off because I was raised in a barn by wolves. I hurry to peel them off in the doorway, bracing myself on the frame. Even the paint feels expensive, and I wipe imagined fingerprints off it with my cuff before edging into the room. Then I inspect my sleeves to make sure they aren't stained with Hungry-Man gravy from last night's microwave dinner.

Gloss shrugs her ivory suede jacket off and drapes it over the back of an egg-shaped thing that might be a chair. I tentatively step in, my still-hot shoes dangling from my fingertips. Everything is so clean. When did I last wash my clothes? Are my socks going to leave marks on the carpet?

Gloss curls up on one end of a window seat, so I pad over to join her. She smiles at me like I've done the right thing. My tummy gets warm, and my nerves drop away.

"You want your present?" She takes my shoes as I sit down, dropping them on the floor like it's no big deal.

"Sure?"

She gestures with one hand. On the tiny glass table within my arm's easy reach is a small, wrapped package. She's left it there like she planned this out—how I'd come in, how we'd sit together on the window seat. The paper is gold, with professionally crisp corners and a hot-pink velvet ribbon. It's about the size of a book, heavy in my hands when I pick it up.

The paper is silky, catching against my calluses and hangnails. I take my time, carefully unpeeling the tape to save the beautiful wrapping. Gloss watches, her eyes lambent with pleasure. Inside, there's a polished wooden box. I set the paper—folded—to one side and look up at her.

"Open it," she urges me, leaning forward to brush her finger down two small brass hinges on one side. Facing me is a small clasp.

It opens smoothly. Nestled inside rich, rust-red velvet are several odd items. A small silver bowl, a large brush—maybe for makeup—a black leather . . . pencil case? And a metal tub with a screw top.

Shaving cream. The tub says shaving cream in swooping cursive on the sticker. My hands are unsteady as I pick up the leather case. The tab pops open, the leather slick in my sweaty fingers. The straight razor slides out. The handle is black, and the razor is silvery. It's solid, a single piece of shining metal instead of a hinged clip to hold removable blades. On the blade in looping cursive is my name, *Max Fraser*.

My breath catches. I've been looking at straight razors online for months. It's perfect. It's beautiful. It's *mine*.

She's beaming at me. "Do you love it?"

She knows I love it. "How did you know?"

"You have about twenty different razor tabs open on your phone."

Entranced by the wonderful things in front of me, I nod. "Thank you!" She must have spent hundreds of pounds on me over the past week, but that's not what makes my throat tight. I wouldn't care if she hadn't spent a penny. She sees me. And she keeps telling me that she cares about what she sees. There must be something I can do for her in return.

"You're so welcome."

I investigate the shaving cream. It's thick and gloopy, and the faint scent reminds me of campfires, smoke and pine. I dab a little on my finger and rub it on the back of my hand. Gloss lifts the bowl out from the case.

"Here, use the scraper"—she points to a metal file looking thing with curved, glossy edges tucked into a notch in the case—"to put some cream in here, and then we lather it with the brush."

I lift a small glob of cream out with the scraper and deposit it at the base of the bowl. "How do you know how to do this?"

Her tinkling laugh bounces off the huge window. "I watched a lot of videos. Want to shave?"

"Yeah. Yeah, I do."

After grabbing some water in a bowl, Gloss gets me to sit in the egg thing. It turns out to be quite comfortable, even if it does look like something from a posh superhero's lair. It cradles my back with its soft curve while Gloss cradles my jaw in her soft hand.

I hold the lather bowl while she spreads foam across my lower face with the brush, moving it in circles. It tickles, and I have to try not to squirm. Looking at her face helps. She's concentrating on me, so I can look at her without being a weird creep. Her hair is tied back with a black velvet ribbon, which should be childish but on Gloss is sophisticated and perfect. This close, the gold specks in her eyes shine like little stars. Her delicate bone structure would make a great painting of an angel, but her eyes are too cold and harsh to be one of the gentle ones. An avenging angel, maybe, with a great big flaming sword.

Song lyrics unspool in my head. *i could watch you, and although i couldn't breathe, it was perfect, and you were beautiful, you were so beautiful, but i was an animal.*

"Stay still," she warns me and brings the blade to my throat. I swallow. My Adam's apple—harder since testosterone dropped my voice an octave—bumps against her thumb.

The music drifts away. I'll catch it later, because everything now is the scrape of the razor over my skin. My whole self tingles in my jawline, magnetised to the pressure of her fingers and the pull of the blade. She tilts my head this way and that, angling me how she wants me. I'll have to learn to do this myself, I guess—but maybe she'll do it for me again, I think dizzily. How often do I even have to shave? Aside from my trailer-trash moustache, I just have blondish fuzz you can see in the exact right lighting, at the exact right angle, but the sensation of shaving is more exciting than I imagined. Masculine and powerful, even though someone else is holding the blade. It drags over the creamy foam, sometimes smooth and clean, sometimes catching against my skin with a weird, vacuuming sensation, but she doesn't cut me. There's no pain at all, just care.

If this is why people go to the barber, I want to be a person who does that. Assuming Gloss doesn't want to be my own personal barber. Maybe she does.

"You're done," Gloss murmurs. I wonder if she senses the spell I'm under as well and doesn't want to break it.

The slick remnants of the cream slide under my fingertips. "How do I look?"

"Perfect." Her voice is light, but it takes me like a punch to the sternum.

"Thanks," I say, but it comes out faint, so I clear my throat. "Thanks." Better the second time.

Gloss puts two fingers under my chin and rubs her thumb over my lower lip. "Wanna do me to practise?"

"Uh . . ."

I am the most eloquent.

She laughs and takes her hand away. "My legs, Max. Do you wanna shave my legs?"

I have never wanted anything more in my entire life. I am a meteor of want. Hot lava swirls below my belly button. And I still don't know if she's attracted to me. I nod too many times.

"Wash your face first," she tells me.

When I'm done towelling off, she joins me in the bathroom, now in short silk shorts and a camisole top, and sits on the edge of the bath. The space feels small with two people in it, even though it's huge. As I watch, she lights a joint I didn't see her roll and points at the floor with it. "Probably easiest if you sit between my legs."

If I have a heart attack, then I won't get to replay every second of this later, I tell myself, doing surreptitious deep breathing while grabbing a towel from the heated rack to sit on.

I cross my legs and look at her knees. They have the smooth gleam of the inside of a nautilus shell. How can knees be so enticing? I didn't even know there was such a thing as a perfect knee, but now that I see Gloss's, there's no doubt. She could be a knee model. Unless I slice a huge wound in her perfect skin . . . I've never even shaved my own legs. It can't be that hard, right? People shave their legs all the time. I can't see any hair, so as long as I don't accidentally cut her foot off, we should be fine.

Taking pity on me, she seizes my hand and guides one finger up her shin bone. The faint rasp of invisible, golden hairs is so erotic my mouth floods with saliva. "For your face, you go with the grain, but for my legs, you'll go against it, slowly. Watch the angle of the blade."

With a deep breath, I reach for the razor, and she corrects me with a hum. Oh, cream. Yeah. Lather.

It only takes a moment to mix up a foamy bowl. I try to mimic how she applied it to my face, swirling circles up and down her leg. I've never been so grateful not to have a bio dick. Having an awkward boner would sully the experience. It's pure and beautiful. She trusts me. It's the most intimate moment of my life. More intimate than watching Danny—

I shake the thought away. Danny isn't welcome here.

Gloss smokes quietly, filling the room with hazy cirrostratus clouds. When it's down to the cardboard roach, she crushes it against the side of the bath, leaving a black mark on the porcelain. She doesn't offer me the joint, which is definitely for the best, because this is nerve-wracking enough with full control of my faculties.

Blade in hand, I go to work.

I MANAGE NOT to fuck up too badly, a tiny horizontal smudge of blood in one of the tender grooves of her knee the evidence of my sole transgression. She didn't even twitch.

"Nice. Now let's get fucked up, and you can serenade me."

Gloss unfurls from the side of the bath and does a little "I've been sitting really still" wriggle. It's so human it catches me off balance.

In the bedroom, she rummages in an inlaid wooden box and pulls out a new joint. "Why roll your own when you can provide employment to an enterprising local?" She smirks at me and flops down on the bed, joint curled in one hand. She lights it with her Zippo and then pats the pillow.

I join her, sitting cross-legged in my tight jeans. "What songs do you like?"

"I just wanna hear you play. Whatever you want." She takes a drag and offers it to me. I take it, between finger and thumb like she did. I smoked pot with Danny a few times last summer, so I know what to do. I wasn't sure at first. About the beers he brought or the weed. Seeing my mother's issues should put me off substance use for life, but it hasn't. I just have rules for myself. Never alone, for one. I'm not alone now. And weed makes things good inside me, makes the world a kinder place.

The smoke hits my lungs in a wave that wants to wash back up and close my throat. Somehow, the part I didn't inhale wafts into my eye, and I yelp, dropping the joint onto my thigh. Gloss giggles at me, not unkindly, while she recaptures the escapee. Her eyebrows curve when she smiles. I wonder if it's normal to want to put someone's eyebrow in your mouth. I want to look at her forever once my eye stops stinging.

"Play me something you wrote?" Gloss nudges me with her foot, and I start, wondering how long I've been contemplating. Could have been an hour. I chuckle and grab my guitar, running my hand over the curved wood. The sleek ambit could be the bend of a hip. Her hip.

"If you want." Nothing I wrote before her deserves to be here. It's all painful and hollow stuff full of torn-up pieces of my sad little life. I don't want to bring that into this clean, creamy room. Into this light. "I only wrote this last night, so it's a bit rough," I hedge, and then I start to play.

Stoned guitar is not as easy as I hoped, but not as horrible as I feared. The reduced anxiety offsets my slowed reactions, and I get used to the heightened sensations. My fingers dance.

I close my eyes before I start to sing. I don't have an amazing voice, but it's sort of fine, getting a gravelly edge that I don't hate. It's not done lowering, I don't think, but it's dropped over an octave, and I can listen to it without being uncomfortable now, which is a new and exciting turn of events. I thought I hated my voice because "everyone does," but as it turns out, voice dysphoria is a real and brutal thing.

Gloss wedges her toes under my knee, and the music rolls over us both, echoing in her minutely shifting muscles.

We smoke for hours. I play. Covers, mostly, but also messing around, making up lyrics about the town and each other. Our band name will be The Melancholy and the Serriform, and we will only play concerts wearing matching outfits in complementary colours. Night drops down over us, the huge windows showing the bruise and highlighter shades of a gorgeous sunset in high definition. When the horizon is a glowing line, Gloss clicks on the strings of lights that roof her bed. It's magical, a secret place surrounded by drapes and fairy globes that lock the world away from us, or us away from the world.

When my stomach rumbles, she orders Chinese food. We eat it on the bed. We are islands in among the takeaway boxes. Somehow, I manage not to spill sauce on her flawless sheets. I do get a bunch on my face, but that's to be expected.

Eventually, we're catching yawns off each other, and happy-dizzy, we get ready for bed. I change in the bathroom, then we brush our teeth side by side, making foamy faces at each other. When she falls into the bed in a graceless heap, I dawdle, digging my toes into the thick carpet pile.

"Where should I sleep?" There must be a spare room somewhere in this vast flat, but I don't want to leave her.

She pats the sheets beside her, and happiness fills me from head to toe. She reaches for something on the bedside table and then fixes me with a look that stills me midstep. She bares her teeth at me in a parody of a grin, and there's something different about them. "If you tell anyone I wear a retainer, I'll have to kill you," she tells me sweetly.

When I slide into the luxurious bedding, she reaches back for me with one leg and urges me close to her.

I never sleep in a binder. My dad made me swear a horrible oath after he did even more research than I had and bought me proper-fitting ones. No more than eight hours, ever. It can fuck you up, mess up your ribs, your posture. Even though my chest is unbound—I always sleep in a tight sports bra but it's not as good—I relax against her cottony warmth. I want to remember every millisecond, memorise this good, big feeling in my chest, but I'm falling asleep too fast. Pinching my thigh shocks me awake, so I dig a bruise there to make sure I savour every breath. The clock projection blinks to four before I capitulate to the warm, insistent fingers of sleep.

AFTER

5

"SHE CONFESSED, SON. I'm so sorry, but Gloss confessed. She killed Danny."

Everything blurs, and my leg bones turn to water. My dad growls and scoops me up, holds me against his chest like I'm a toddler. He carries me out of the police station, clutched in his arms while he barges through tangles of people. Their faces are smeared from my tears. They look like demons or dogs, slavering towards me. The empty black eyes of cameras surround me, flashing lightning. Hands pluck at my sleeve. If I close my eyes, the screaming sounds like the ocean. Danny will never see the ocean again.

Because Gloss killed him.

Bile rises in me, but I force it down.

Dad folds me into the front seat with hands so careful it makes a coil of something hot and hard boil in my chest. I want to yell and hit him, to smash the window and crawl out over the shards of broken glass and drag myself into the bushes to lick my wounds. Dad clips my belt in and starts the car. The town whirs past the windows. There's the coffee shop Gloss took me to. The road with the hair salon. The place where she pinched my butt so hard I leapt right into the street and she kept bursting out laughing all day long. None of it makes sense. How could she kill Danny when she knew what he'd been to me? How could she?

My dad keeps talking to me, not saying anything, just talking. About the station, about the guy who got stuck up a tree trying to get a cool selfie. I let the sound of him fill the car, my mind empty and blank. Don't think about her. Don't think about him. Don't think.

Our street is usually quiet with ample parking, but when we turn in, every spot is taken. There are news vans and cars, people milling around and a single policewoman trying to handle the pushing crowd. My dad takes one look at the mess and drives straight past.

I should have guessed where we'd end up. The station is dad's home more than the four walls he shares with my mother. He pulls in around the back.

"Wait here, bud. I'll be right back."

I'm not sure where he thinks I'd go. I watch the traffic lights change at the bridge. Red. Orange. Green. Red. Orange. Green.

When he comes back, Stefford is with him. Stefford is the biggest man I have ever seen, pushing seven foot tall and with shoulders like a fridge. I remember sitting on them as he galloped through a training course. I must have been about eight, and I whooped and yelled with excitement as he went down a ladder with me on his back faster than the other guys did unencumbered. Stefford takes up a power stance, blocking the turn in without looking at me.

I'm silent as my dad takes me through to the mess room. There's one engine in, one out, so half the crew is on a call and the rest are scattered around. Everyone stops talking when my dad brings me through the doors.

Surrounded by these strong, competent people, a scream builds in my throat. They walk into burning buildings for a living, and not one of them has any idea what to do or what to say. And if they don't, then nobody ever really does. I don't have anything to say to them, to my dad, to a world where this could have happened. I turn and walk into the dorm, heading for my dad's bed. At least when I have my eyes closed, I can't see the looks on people's faces.

BEFORE

5

SATURDAY MORNING, I wake to find Gloss curled in the window seat, watching the street. She has a ceramic mug clutched in both hands that's so big she looks like a child. She's wearing my ragged hoodie. I smile drowsily.

"Hey." My voice is husky with sleep.

"Hey yourself." She smiles at me over top of her coffee, sleeves covering her knuckles. There are pillow creases pressed into her cheek. Her face is glowing without makeup. She's so beautiful my soul aches. "You sleep okay?"

"Yeah, great." I did, thanks to the weed, the bed, the fullness of my belly or the closeness of her. Maybe all of the above.

"Are you a breakfast guy? I survive on coffee, but we probably have breakfast stuff. Or I can order in if you want."

"Coffee's good." I stretch, rolling over, and then suddenly become self-conscious. I'm sure my chest isn't hidden well enough. I can't believe I slept next to her like this. But Gloss . . .

Gloss has consistently treated me like a guy, hasn't slipped once. When she looks at me, I believe her belief in my identity. I don't know how I got so lucky as to have her waft into my life. I'm afraid that if I relax into it, she'll see what other people see—an anxious, useless mess.

"Be right back."

I watch her pad out of the room, too torn with mixed emotions about my sports bra's lack of compression to follow, then cover myself with the duvet.

Coffee in bed is good and cosy, with her leg hooked over mine. She's busy on her phone, but I'm content to watch her expressions change. Before I finish my cup, Gloss holds her hand out. For a split second, I think she wants to hold hands. Maybe we're dating? How would you know? Should I ask?

"Give me your phone."

Confused, I pass my phone over, and she takes it, then holds it out again, the screen facing me. The last reply from my dad is still up as a notification, unopened so I can see it when I check the time. Ok. I love you. The unasked-for affection warmed me when he sent it but embarrasses me now.

"Unlock it, silly." Gloss waggles the phone in the air, not handing it over.

Unable to think of a good way to say no, I obediently click my passcode in. All my lyrics are on there, my recordings of my music. Pictures of Danny and me I can't bear to delete. At least my lock screen isn't our shadows kissing anymore. What if she wants to look through my things? I promised him I'd never show anyone. Maybe that promise shouldn't mean anything anymore, but it does. I don't want to betray it. She'd probably think I'm pathetic for wanting to cling on to those sundrenched, incandescent days of falling, before I smashed to the ground and into pieces.

She presses a few buttons and then holds the phone up to her ear. Oh! She wanted to make a call. Not on her own phone, for some reason, but that's perfectly normal?

"Hi, Mr. Fraser!" Gloss chirps, and it takes me a moment

to catch up. My dad? Why does she want to talk to my dad? My mug slips in my hand, spilling the last mouthful of cooled coffee onto my shirt.

"Hello, yes, this is Gloss, Max's friend from school. Max stayed over with me last night. I was just calling to thank you for letting him, and to ask if there's any way you'd let me borrow him until Monday. He's been such a great friend to me, and I hate to ask, but my parents have to go out of town this evening and I'm a little nervous to stay in my house alone! . . . Yes, yes, I know it's silly . . . Of course . . . I could ask my father to call you, but he's rather busy with funeral arrangements . . . oh! Oh, thank you so much. I really appreciate it."

A small, cold dribble of suspicion runs down my spine. She lies so smoothly, so easily. What if she's lying to *me*?

"Oh, thank you so much. I really appreciate it." She's smug as she passes the phone back to me.

My face must show my discomfort, because she loses the grin and looks at me for a long second.

"I'm sorry, I should have asked." She leans over and puts her head on my shoulder. "We just had so much fun, and with the party tonight, I figured you'd want to stay with me after."

She bites the side of her lip and looks at me from under her lashes. She's right. Obviously I want to stay over this evening. She was saving me from having to tell my dad myself. My fears melt away in a burst of warmth. Grant's party and another night cuddled against Gloss? Even if this is temporary, as I'm afraid it will be, I'm leaning in. I want as much of her as she'll give me. I read somewhere that people are supposed to get five affectionate touches a day. I've had physical contact with three people in as many years. Touch-starved doesn't begin to describe how covetous I am.

"Yeah, sounds good."

WE SPEND A few low-key hours in her house, get brunch at a little boutique café down the road then spend the afternoon on the balcony, with Gloss teaching me how to paint her nails for her. We're drunk before we arrive at Grant's, cherry vodka filling my gut with red-tinged electricity. Gloss chose my outfit, and I like it; dark wash jeans and a new shirt. The button-down is silky with my usual black base but also has bright slices of red, yellow and green. It's weird to think that the lingering looks as we walk through town aren't people trying to figure out what's off about me. I'm so *confusing*, people often stare. Of course, the vast majority of the attention is on Gloss, but when eyes land on me, there's no bewilderment that we're together. I wonder what it would be like to have always lived that way. To always be seen right and approved of. How do people cope with the pleasure of it? I'll explode if this keeps up.

We hear the party from down the street. It's in the Crescent, near the skatepark—near Danny's place. I exhale sharply, déjà vu clenching a fist around my guts. I haven't been here since the end of summer, when I told Danny I was transitioning, that I'd be coming out at school when we went back. While I never went to his house or even up his street, I watched him walk away down this road so many times. He always turned back to blow me a kiss. He was such a fucking sap.

When we started hanging out, Danny and I were so separate from everything else it didn't seem real. Maybe the world didn't seem real. His friends away for the summer, my transition finally underway, even if no one except my dad and doctors had been told yet. The magic between us felt so strong I was so sure he already knew. How else could he look at me the way he did?

But he didn't. We were glass, not diamonds, destined to explode into vicious shards.

Gloss and I walk past the huge tree that looms over the park. Last time I saw it, I was staring at it, my ears ringing. Last time I saw it, I'd just told Danny the truth of me, and he looked at me like I'd slapped him. Like I'd betrayed him. Curled his lip and told me I'd better not tell anyone we'd been together. That was it. The end of us. We hadn't even really started.

I wonder what he'd do if he found out I told Gloss. I shouldn't wonder that—that's not a good thing to wonder when the bass from the party is slipping into my heartbeat. I need to be here and now instead of then. The vodka helps. Gloss helps. I take another swig from her flask.

Gloss takes my hand as we descend the concrete steps into Grant's sunken garden. Her fingers are dry, mine sweaty and hot. I want to stuff my hands in my pockets, but I've got to hang on to her, got to stay tethered. Now, not then.

People are scattered in clumps all over the place. There's a group clustered on the porch, sitting and smoking, and a few are lying down on the lawn as if they're sunbathing under the streetlights. There's a couple pressed against the fence making out with abandon, oblivious to their surroundings. I've never been to a secondary school party. Not this kind of party, any-way. Birthdays in year seven where the whole form was invited hardly seem to count.

Gloss's fingers laced through mine lend me courage, and I manage to nod a greeting at people who catch my eye on the way in. To my relief, no one seems pissed that I'm here. I recognise most of the faces, but none of them are unfriendly.

"Max!"

Danny looms out of the darkness of a doorway. He stumbles and grabs the wall for balance. His hand is big and dark on the white paint. It's the first time he's said my real name, and he says it like its slicing his mouth to shreds.

"Wow," he says.

He's glassy-eyed and rumpled, the high flush in his cheeks visible even in the dim hallway. I knew he'd be here, but I didn't know how it would feel. I still don't know. I'm suspended between emotions, and looking at him now, I might be sad for him. But that can't be right.

Suddenly, Gloss is angled between us, still gripping my hand. Even though she's looking up at him, she seems taller than he is.

"Walk away, Danny." Her voice is calm, but I hear the razor in it. Danny must not, because he keeps going.

"Glossy Gloss Gloss, the one with the goss," he warbles, slipping and then catching himself before he bounces off the wall. "You sure have a magic touch, hey. Look at what you've done to our boy here."

Cherry sweetness surges into my mouth. I drop Gloss's hand and bolt for what thankfully turns out to be a bathroom, slamming and locking the door behind me.

Our boy. I was never his boy. He thought I was his girl.

My knees crack when they hit the hard tiles. Vomit bites the delicate flesh of my throat, and the pain makes my eyes sting, but my stomach settles as soon as the vodka has forced its way back up. Doesn't even taste like puke, just alcohol and bitter fruit. Is Gloss outside the door, waiting for me? Or did she ditch me? Throwing up within five minutes of arriving at a party might be the saddest thing I've ever done.

I'd ditch me if I could.

I rinse my mouth out under the tap and help myself to toothpaste from the tiny cabinet. I wish I had a toothbrush, but I make do with a finger. Someone pounds on the door.

It takes me a few more minutes of inspecting myself in the mirror—pretending I'm trying to press my hair into its best self, not just killing time—before I can summon the courage to slip out.

Seana, from English, shoves past me, muttering, "Fucking hell, just about pissed myself," and slams the door behind her.

People pack the dark space, music throbs in the air and everything is laced with sweet vape smoke. There's Devon and the rest of the swimming team, and there's Anoush, the head boy, and the two guys he's always around with. But I can't see Danny or Gloss. Where is she? Why didn't she come after me? It's too loud and too much. The clothes don't fit. They're too tight, strangling me. I shouldn't have come. I don't belong here.

I bolt again, this time for the front door, darting through the mass of bodies. I knock someone's Solo cup out of their hand but don't stop to apologise. Fresh air greets me like a cool slap to the face, unlocking my lungs, and I gasp in relief. There are two empty chairs on the small porch space. I beeline for the closest, flop down and rub my face with my hands.

I want to leave, now, but Gloss is in there by herself. I can't leave her. Can I? She seems to have left me. I've known her for a week, and I'm already entirely reliant on her. Maybe she's gotten bored of me. What if I'm not the project she thought I was, too weak to bother with?

My sweaty fingers slide on the screen of my phone. The cracked glass slices into my thumb as I fire a quick text off to Gloss telling her I'm on the porch. She'll find me, or I'll stay here and scribble lyrics about how unfair it is for Danny to be so beautiful and so terrible at the same time. Hearing him call me his boy hurts more than any insult he's thrown at me. What I would have done to be his boy. What I'd still do. Classic Max. Same old bones underneath the remodel. Gloss won't want me now.

Behind me, someone coughs. I spin in surprise to see Michelle staring at me, lit orange by the glow of a distant streetlamp that spills a strip across her face. There are circles under her eyes, and her lip is shining wetly, almost bruised looking. She's sitting in a third chair, wedged in the darkest corner.

"Shell. Hi." I'm breathless.

"Hi."

She fidgets and pulls out a packet of tobacco. There's a few ready hand rolls tucked into the plastic. I notice her hands are shaking when she picks one out and tries to light it, but I don't ask. Snick. Snick. Snick. It finally catches. It's weird to see a young person smoking instead of vaping. She sees me watching. "It gives you something to do with your hands. 'Sides, it's easier to steal loose leaf. My mam always knows how many cigs she has left."

"Can I have one?" I don't smoke, but I need something. Something to take the edge off the anxiety clawing at my insides. She passes the one she's lit over without commenting and sparks up another for herself.

We smoke down to the spiralled cardboard in loaded silence. Words stack behind my teeth but don't make it past the bone gates. They're nothing words. Meaningless statements that could start a conversation but wouldn't discharge the pressure in the air. My phone doesn't buzz. Gloss hasn't come to find me. I should go back in. I'm steady now. I can handle seeing Danny; it just took me by surprise. I knew he'd be here, but I'm never ready for him. I don't know how to be. I have to do it, get on with it, exposure therapy. Eventually it'll stop being raw, right? Time heals, blah blah.

I should go back in, but I don't.

"You okay?" I stub my cigarette out on the wall and finally manage to ask because I'm the only one here and it doesn't seem like she is. Devoid of somewhere to hide my fidgeting hands, I settle for picking at the skin around my nails, hissing when I peel off a chunk.

After a moment, she murmurs, "I will be."

It startles a snort out of me. "Like, in the morning, or in some nebulous future where we're all okay?" I'm loose with anxiety and nicotine buzz on a post-puke stomach, forgetting we don't talk anymore. Ignoring the fact the only reason she said missed me in the parking lot the other day was because of him. Everything's always about him. Do I exist without another person, or am I only a shadow the bright ones cast?

Michelle grins, and passing headlights make a skull out of her cheekbones. "Both? We all just have to be okay, right? Some time. Even in this shitty town."

"That's the plan." I settle in my seat, propping my heels up on the edge of the pole stretching the baggy canvas. "Well, not in this shitty town."

"Bet you can't wait to get out of here." She leans towards me. I can smell her perfume, floral and pungent enough to sting.

"You got that right." I laugh, and it's too high-pitched. "As soon as I can. Right after exams." My dad promised, he promised me if I stayed and got my A levels, he'd help me move.

"Where do you want to go?" Michelle asks breathily, her knee rubbing against mine.

"London or Brighton." The answer is right there, falling off my tongue. The big, queer cities I can disappear in. Be a new man in. Maybe that Max will be talkative. I'm positively chatty right now. "I'm not applying to uni, not yet. Maybe not ever. I want to be my own man and make my own choices." If I can, I think. The future yaws beneath my feet, an impenetrable void of possible failures.

"I wonder what that would be like," she says, holding out another rollie. When I go to take it, she lifts it to my lips instead. Our faces are close together when she lights it for me, and I tense every muscle in my body against the cough that wants to come out. Coughing in a girl's face right after puking is one step too far. I refuse to be that gross. It hurts my chest, like I've swallowed a baseball, but I win. My body obeys.

"What?" I've lost the thread of things.

"Making my own choices. Would be nice." Michelle leans back into her seat, opening the space up between us, and it's easier to breathe again.

"So you . . . uh . . . have to stick around?" I try to prolong the conversation, not wanting her to leave me here, a lonely loser waiting for my only friend, too scared to go inside.

"I'm the eldest of six." Her inhale is huge, the exhale exhaustive, and she busies herself rolling before lighting up.

"That sucks," I offer.

She snorts. "A fucking bit. Yeah."

I don't know what else to say or do, and I'm in danger of burning my fingers if I keep smoking the stub of this cigarette. The spectre of Danny haunts our conversation, the thing we have in common. The thing we used to talk about.

"Danny got a scholarship. Did he tell you?"

Ah, there it is. It's almost a relief, in the way throwing up is a relief. "The Talented Athlete thing? Yeah. He did." At the end of the summer, when we whispered things in the dying rays of sunshine. He brought the letter, crumpled from his fingers folding and unfolding it. Like he couldn't believe it.

"Talented Athlete." She tilts her head back, inspecting the disintegrating underside of the small porch area. "So very, very talented. Everything's so easy for him."

I make a sound that isn't a laugh, feeling trapped and penned in all of a sudden. "It's not." If it was easy, he wouldn't be so cruel. The thought surprises me, but there it is. Happy people don't spend their time and energy making other people miserable; they're too busy enjoying their lives.

"It could be." She spits it, worrying at her lower lip with her teeth until I think I can smell blood on her in the smoke. "He's a big boy. He could choose to be happy."

If he chose me? No, it can't be that. I choke back a tingling burst of nervous energy. "It could be for all of us. It's just . . . not. Not here, and not now." I say out loud the words I usually keep to myself—I hold on to the "one day, one day, one day" idea of a future where I'm just a normal guy, going about my normal guy business. Maybe working in a skate shop or in music somewhere. And I never have to go home to my mother again. Then it could be okay. I have to believe that, or what else is there for me?

Michelle watches me with furrowed brows for a moment and then looks at her hands. "I thought I'd marry him when I was little."

My guts are squeezing. I feel sick again. She doesn't seem to mind my silence.

"What really fucks with me . . ." She lights another ciga-rette. Her hands aren't shaking anymore. "The worst thing is, I'd still go with him if he asked. I can't say no to him."

I laugh, frantic and thin. "Can anyone say no to him?"

She looks up at me, meets my eyes. "You did."

There's pressure in the air, thick and weighty, but I don't know what it means. I didn't say no to him. I said please, and he said no. I'm about ready to claw my own skin off to escape, so I nod—"Cool. Thanks for the smoke."—and get up. I have to get out of there.

Michelle reaches out and takes hold of my shirt, leaning into me. "Be careful with her, Max. You don't know anything about her, and you're already changing for her."

Yeah, changing into someone better.

Her hand's cold under mine when I cover it and gently peel it free. "Thanks for worrying about me, Shell."

Michelle doesn't respond, just turns away and stares out into the garden.

BACK INSIDE GRANT'S house, the party is still a lot, but I grit my teeth and push through the crowd. To my surprise, I catch a few fist bumps and nods on the way through. The sensation of acceptance soothes my nerves. Clearly, no one noticed my ignominious dash for the toilet. Or maybe throwing up is hardcore. Rock and roll. I prowl through the house, searching. Gloss isn't in the kitchen or in the living room, which has become a full-blown dance party. I'm about to head upstairs when someone slips their hand over my eyes.

Tension thaws out of me before I even turn. It's Gloss. I knew from the smell and the softness of her palm and the possession in her touch. She leans up to yell-whisper in my ear. "Hi. I missed you." Her eyes are big and blown.

A joint gets pressed into my hand from somewhere. Gloss brings it up to her mouth. She doesn't bother taking it out of my fingers, using me like a roach clip. I smile in relief, connected to her again. Danny didn't break the magic spell.

"Missed you too." I pause, my tongue pressing hard against the roof of my mouth, but the words won't stay in. "Where did you go?"

At least I didn't ask why she left me.

She slants her eyes at me. "I was giving Danny some instructions on how to be a better person."

I melt.

Pulling my hand back, I take my own drag and blow it to the ceiling. She grabs my free hand and leads me onto the dance floor.

There are flashing lights and pounding music and soft hands touching me, friendly faces and excited yells when the track changes, and I'm part of it, I'm in the belly of the music along with them. I know this, I know how to be here from count-less gigs. I pulse and move to the roll of the crowd against me, never losing hold of Gloss. Holding hands, pressed together, spinning out, hands again. Her face in my neck, whispering words I can't hear. I never want it to end.

Beer after beer is pressed into my hand, cold cans with the rings unpulled. I'm high, and drunk, and wild on the smiles and nods of people who looked right past me before Gloss moved to town.

It's my bladder that insists I leave the dance floor. The downstairs bathroom is occupied. I wait for a bit and then hammer on it like Seana did earlier. That's allowed—see, if people take too long at parties, you can tell them you really gotta pee too.

After a while of me slapping a two-handed beat on it, the door opens, and it's Danny. Of course it is. It's Danny, holding his open jeans up with one hand. His face is bloated and red with rage. He yells, "Fuck off," right in my face before slam-ming the door again. I saw, though. I saw over his shoulder. There was a girl in there, splayed out over the sink, gasping, her pink-soled shoes swinging.

The stairs are tricky to navigate, but the wall helps if you slide along it. Reminds you where the floor is. Finding Danny with a girl shouldn't hurt, not after a night spent wrapped in Gloss, smelling her vanilla and sandalwood hair, but it does. It hurts so much. There's a noise in the air, and it's coming from me. I collapse on the landing, curled into my own knees. It hurts because he never took me to a party, even when things were really good. Like he knew there was something waiting to break us. He knew there was something wrong with me.

I'm the worst at parties.

Voices roll in and out around me. Maybe they're talking to

me, maybe not. And then there's a hand in my hair, pulling me out of my own lap.

"You don't get to do that."

Danny.

He's too big, too loud. His mouth is so red. I want to kiss him. I want to throw up on his shoes. He pushes me against the wall and holds me there with one splayed hand, his body close. He looks so sad and angry it makes me scream on the inside.

"You don't get to fucking look at me like that." He mumbles it into my hair like it's a secret.

"Get off, get off me," I say, but I'm so quiet I can't even hear myself. Panic buzzes in my chest, under his hand.

"Don't fucking act like you didn't do this. You liar!"

I wish he'd stop yelling. My head hurts, and I have a crying headache even though my cheeks are dry.

"I'm not!" I have to protest, because even though the words don't make sense, I know what he thinks. He thinks I was lying to him, that I never should have kissed him back without telling him this, but he doesn't know. He doesn't know what it's like for everyone to see you wrong. It's not my fault his eyes don't work.

"I hate you," he screams in my face, and then he kisses me, and I fall into him like it's the first time all over again.

The loud hallway drains away, and even though a small part of me knows this is terrible, I can't pull away. He tastes like cider and weed and the ocean—he always tastes faintly of the ocean. His hair tangles in my hands when I curl around him, and he holds me against the wall with his body, but gently now, as if I'm precious.

Then just as fast as it happened, he's gone, backing away from me with horror in his eyes and blood on his lip. I can taste the metal of it on my tongue, my lip bruised and split from the force of his kissing. I get one last glance at his desperate expression before he ducks away and dives down the hall, disappearing into the gloom of bodies.

"Woah, dude."

It's Mike, pulling a face like he can't decide if it's hilarious or not. I sag against the wall, my shoulder blades cracking against the plaster.

I want to go home.

My hands are shaking, shaking. I drop my phone twice before I manage to text Gloss.

> I have to go

My phone buzzes against my overheated thigh as I trudge up the concrete stairs to the road. My body weighs a thousand pounds. Gravity has never been so powerful.

> wait for me

> what happened

I sit on the steps, in the way of anyone who wants to leave or arrive. It's 3 A.M., and the moon is a swollen wound in the sky. There's still people making out pressed against the fence, though it's a different couple than before. My phone's in my hands, and without really meaning to, I flick to the folder where I saved the DMs Danny and I sent to each other. The day I gave him my handle, he asked why it was "butterfly-BOY," and I had to tell him it was from my lyrics. He asked to read them, but I never let him.

Gloss is immaculate as she picks her way through the scattered people and over broken bottles. I burst into tears as soon as she touches me, keep crying as she weaves her hand into my hair in the same spot Danny did. Her hand is so small and gentle, and his was so large and rough, but they both wreck me.

I'm wreckage.

Gloss climbs into my lap. I'm not sure how she's so light and so vast at the same time. The moonlight shines only on her now; everything else is darkness.

"What happened?"

"He kissed me." I choke it into her neck, hot shame filling my belly. I let him. I wanted him too. I always want him to.

She stiffens in my arms, scratches my scalp once, twice, and then pulls herself free of my embrace. She's cold, her face still. She looks like an angel again, like vengeance. She twists on her heel without saying a word, and this time, people get out of her way as she walks back towards the path. I dash after her, stumbling and bouncing in her wake.

"Gloss, Gloss." She doesn't pause, I can't catch her.

She finds him in the kitchen. He's sloppy drunk and half-way down a bottle of Jack. She shoves the whisky out of the way. She shouldn't be strong enough to move him, but he's weak-wasted and staggers backwards.

"I told you to stay away from him."

It's not a yell, but it fills the kitchen. Silence falls over everything, a blanket so heavy I stop breathing. I'm trapped in the doorway, my feet cemented to the liminal space between the bright kitchen, lit by them both, and the dark hallway. The energy between them sparks and tingles. I can almost see it in the room as something tangible. Something that's been cryst-allising since that first day, when Danny tried to draw her away from me and she refused to let him. Because she wants me? Or because he tried to tell her what to do?

"Make me," Danny slurs, half falling, throwing his arm wide and sloshing booze onto the floor. The sharp scent fills my nostrils. I can't move. The world is falling away from me, ashen and roaring. Not a panic attack, not now.

Gloss has something in her hand. Metal glints in the harsh fluorescents. She flips it around her fingers. A stainless-steel straw shouldn't be terrifying, but it is.

"If I have to make you, you won't like it." She leans in, says something I can't hear, my ears full of blood, and then she turns to me smiling a shark's smile. Has she always had that many teeth?

"Let's go, Max."

I follow her out, again. Like I'm tied to her.

On the street, she turns me, under the light, and looks at my face. Hers crumples. "Oh, Max."

I don't want that. I don't want sadness and pity and oh, poor Max, what a disaster, but it's written all over her face until she steps closer. She presses herself against me and runs her hands up and down my spine. I start to pull away automatically—being touched when I'm trying to fend off a full collapse usually makes things worse—but the pressure of her body helps. The slow rise and fall of her ribs leads, and mine follow suit, settling into real breaths instead of gasping, desperate pants. The boulder crushing my chest lifts slowly, fades and leaves my limbs weak and trembly. Gloss holds me, her hands hot through my shirt, until I'm crying instead of dying, and then she slides her hand down to mine and weaves our fingers together, and we walk home, hand in hand.

AFTER

6

APPARENTLY, I DO fall asleep because I open my eyes to a humpbacked giant looming over me. I shriek and flail away from the monster, and then my eyes make sense of what I'm seeing. Grant.

Grant is in the fire station, in my dad's cubicle, carrying my guitar case in one hand. He has a backpack slung over his shoulder and a duffle under his arm.

"Heard you could use a place to crash for a few days. Your dad gave me your keys, and I swung by and grabbed your car and some of your stuff." His eyes are puffy and swollen like he's been crying. He sees me looking and shrugs.

"The press isn't at your place?" My voice is desolate.

He shakes his head, then leans my guitar against the bed and transfers the duffle to his other arm. "I didn't get arrested for murder. You're such an attention whore these days."

The joke is leaden and tired, and I can't even push a ghost of a smile onto my face. Can't engage with it at all, or I'll shred into jagged little pieces that used to be a boy.

"Are you sure you don't mind me crashing?" Pushing my

hair out of my eyes, I grind my palms into my face, trying to shake off the dead weight of exhaustion.

"Nah." Grant moves from foot to foot, glancing out the window. I've never seen him fidget before. "It'd be good. To be with someone."

Grant was Danny's best friend for over a decade. What could he possibly be going through right now? What right do I have to be this unravelled? Gloss has been here for four months. Danny and I had six weeks of perfection a year ago. How can I be so ruined by such brevity? What's wrong with me that I keep sewing my entire self to people who don't truly care about me?

Grant's waiting for a reply. What was the question? Oh, his house.

"Uh. Okay then. Thanks." The idea of going back to my mother right now is bad. Gloss's is impossible. The last time I was at Grant's place was the cherry vodka and panic attack party. It was Gloss, threatening Danny in the kitchen. Now, Gloss is in prison for cutting Danny's throat. My hand spasms and my stomach cramps, but there's nothing in me to throw up. I don't have anywhere else to go or anyone else to be with.

I grab my guitar and gesture for him to lead the way.

Dead air, thick with ghosts, hangs between us as we walk to my car. Grant climbs in the driver's seat, although he's not in much better shape than I am. I get stuck with my fingers wrapped around the door handle. The passenger seat is where Gloss sits . . . sat. Where Danny sat.

I wait for it to hurt, to twist in my guts, but all I am is empty.

BEFORE

6

BRIGHT LIGHT DRAGS me awake. I'm facedown, pillow in my open, drooling mouth. My head hurts. I inch the duvet over my head, hoping that dulling the light will soothe the pain.

It doesn't. Gentle hands slip into my thick hair. She rubs my head with strong, sure fingers, easing the edges of my headache back. Her knee presses against my shoulder blade. Her skin is cool, or mine is hot. Awareness trickles through me. I'm shirtless, braless, binderless. The cotton sheet is bunched around my hips. I don't remember getting back to Gloss's house.

But I remember Danny's face when he screamed that he hated me. His lovely, splotchy red face, bloodshot eyes. The tears in them. The pain in them.

I want to go home, but not to my home, my parents' place. A different home. One I've never had. I want to go to a place that's safe. My eyes flood. I sob into the humid crease of my elbow. Gloss shushes me like a baby, lets me get snot and tears all over her crisp sheets.

The light's changed by the time I've cried myself out, Gloss stretched out beside me like a cat. Ants itch under my skin, the need to pull away from her and hide, the need to roll over and press myself against her. I'm at war with my own body.

"It's okay, it's okay, Max."

There's no doubt in her words. She's saying she's iron; she'll make it so.

I remember her and Danny in the kitchen, the metal flashing in her hand. I've never seen someone furious on my behalf. My dad doesn't really get angry, just sad, like me. It was both horrifying and wonderful.

"What did you say to him?" I huff it, laden with tears.

"I don't remember." Her breath ruffles my hair.

But she's lying, I know it. She doesn't want to tell me. She's protecting me again.

"Do you want to have a bath?"

It seems like such a weird thing to do, but yeah. As it transpires, I do want to have a bath. While she runs it for me, I struggle out of the sheets, tripping more than once in the tangle of sweaty fabric. My backpack is strewn open on the floor from choosing my outfit last night. I yank a T-shirt over my head, relaxing instantly once I'm covered. I want to put a binder on, but I don't have the energy to look for a clean one. Last night's is clammy and smells bad.

When I pad into the big ensuite, Gloss is leaning over the bubble-filled bath, her hair a bloody scarf around her pale neck. Like a slit throat, I think, and shudder. She smiles at me.

"It's ready. I'm going to order us some food and pick some movies, okay?"

"Okay." Takeaway and movies sounds good, sounds like no pressure to do anything except exist in the same place. I don't want to talk about what happened last night. I don't want to think about it.

She straightens up from the bath and turns the taps off.

"You want to skip school and take shrooms and be in the forest tomorrow?"

It takes me a moment to process the question—she says it with no weight. I've skipped more since Gloss moved to town than I have in all the preceding years packed together, even last September, during the height of Danny's cruelty, when things were the worst.

But not facing him tomorrow sounds perfect. Not facing anyone, even better. Mike was there, wasn't he? When Danny kissed me. Everyone has to know. There's a sharp, mean part of me that wants everyone to know.

Even though most of me hates him, the rest of me can't stop replaying his devastated expression and wondering how to fix it.

"Yeah." I nod, decisive for once. "That sounds good."

When she leaves me alone to strip down, I take my meds— sure as shit not going to skip a day after my first panic attack in weeks—and get my testosterone supplies out from my sponge bag. I wonder if part of me knew I'd still be here on Sunday when I'm due for my biweekly injection. I prep myself quickly: antiseptic wipe to the thigh and the lid on the vial of hormones, waterproof Band-Aid opened and ready to be peeled and applied. Shaky, I draw the clear liquid up into the needle. I'm usually good at this, quick and efficient, but today, I take my time, not trusting my hands. I find the right spot on my leg and fuss with the hair there for a moment before pushing the needle in. I hiss out a little breath, as I always do. Pull back the plunger, no blood swirling, clear to continue. Depress, remove the needle. Antiseptic wipe over the spot of welling blood. Plaster on. Done.

The bath is still piping hot when I slide in. The bubbles close around me, hiding my body. I slide down until my chin touches the white foam, then duck under completely. The quiet water envelopes me, hot to the point of pain, dark under the bubbles. Safe. Alone, remembering, despite my best efforts, the scrape of his stubble over my philtrum. Danny kissed me. Danny wanted me.

I open my mouth and scream into the bitter water.

I THOUGHT GLOSS would make me talk about what happened with Danny, but all we do is lounge around, eat and watch terrible movies. We're like the kind of friends I've seen on television. That night, we fall asleep with her head on my chest, arm and leg flung over me. There's no sex in it, though, and my body's not even confused. We're just close.

"We're gonna have the best day," Gloss mumbles sleepily into my armpit the following day—shroom day. She rolls over, wriggles out of her sheets and yawns, stretching onto her tiptoes, like a little kid. The silky fabric of her pyjamas drapes so close over her skin I have to look away.

"We need to pack for our adventure."

"I've never done mushrooms before," I tell her, suddenly feeling like maybe it's not a great idea. "Will I, you know, have a bad trip because I'm sad?"

She eyes me, sucking her lower lip, and shrugs a shoulder. "I don't think so, but maybe. Or maybe it'll be awesome. Either way, you'll be with me." She gives me a demure grin. "I'll take care of you."

As much as I'm intimidated by the idea of taking psychedelics, I also really, really want to. I want to be the guy who takes mushrooms in the forest with a beautiful girl. I want to be a Max who has done mushrooms in the forest with the most wonderful girl in the world. My last term of school and I'm finally starting to ask normal questions like "Should I take shrooms with my brand-new best friend (possibly girlfriend)?" instead of "Is getting out of bed worth the effort?"

"As long as you don't leave me alone, no matter what." There's need thick in my voice. Embarrassed, I turn away, digging in my backpack for clean boxers. I hate how clear it is that I don't only mean today.

"No matter what," she repeats.

WE FIND A quiet clearing far from any roads, a mossy hollow at the base of a tree perfect for our blanket. It reminds me of the day we lay on the grass at school. I've only known her for a week. Surely, I've known her forever? Or maybe I was waiting for her for so long that time has stretched and looped. Who even was I before her? I can barely remember.

We drink mushroom tea out of a metal thermos, Gloss first, then me. It tastes bad—honey and lemon smooth a bitter, astringent taste but don't erase it. I scrape my tongue with my teeth, trying to clear the flavour off. Gloss laughs and passes me a can of orange juice. It's sugar sweet and still cold. I take my skate shoes off and stuff the can inside one's padded grip.

Lying down on the blanket, I cradle my head in my laced fingers. The sky is warm blue today. I could float right off into it. Gloss pillows her head on my stomach without asking, and I bring one hand down to hold hers. My mind wants to land on Danny, tries to trick me with thoughts that start innocent and bend towards him, but I pull myself back again and again. Back to here, and to her.

Clouds scud past. My body starts to feel weird, and everything gets bright, lit from within. I squint at the world and press myself down into the blanket so I don't fall up and away.

"I used to live in Paris." Gloss squeezes my hand. "This feels like Paris."

Paris? I giggle because the sprawling forest is all oak and beech. It seems like a very British forest to me. But how would I know? I've never been anywhere. "Sure, you can see the Eiffel

Tower if you look at that cloud just right." I point at a triangular tree to emphasise my statement. She used to live in Paris. Of course she did. Why would I know that about her? I don't know anything, only that she's kind to me.

"I'll take you," she says, and it sounds like she means it.

We lapse into silence, comfortable, and there are horses running past us, pounding their hooves into the green, thick moss. It takes me a while to puzzle out that it's our heartbeats. I'm getting higher and higher, thinking loopier and loopier thoughts, catching lights and sparks in the air out of the edges of my vision. Gloss pins me to the floor with her body weight, stops me from inflating and untethering from the earth. I am a balloon boy, a butterfly boy, a boy of sound and reverberations. A boy who can be whole and hale and loved, because I'm full of love and surely, that's all that really matters? Isn't that all anyone really wants? To love and be loved?

"Are you a witch?" someone asks. The slow voice belongs to me.

Gloss snickers, brings my hand up to her mouth and bites the inside of my wrist, not hard enough to leave a bruise. Just right. "Sometimes I wonder."

She chuckles, and I catch it. Our laughter weaves together in a bright orange ribbon, winds up through the branching shelter of trees. A mouse moves under my leg. No, it's just my phone vibrating in my pocket. My bones buzz. It's good. Buzz, buzz, fuzz.

"If you're a witch, you're a good witch," I decide. And then another thought hits me, my brain switching tracks midthought. "Would you still like me if I wasn't trans?"

It's born of insecurity, and I immediately wish I hadn't asked. The words hang between us, heavy lead weighing down our wafting bodies.

She licks my wrist over the spot she dug her teeth in and then returns our hands to rest on her stomach. Her ribs rise and fall. Precious air, inflating and deflating meat. We are such simple things, muscle and sinew and blood. All the same and all so unbearably different.

"Oh, Max." She looks up at me, spring-green eyes so bright I fall inside them. "I don't care why your heart is broken."

It's not a good answer. I don't really understand what she means, but I don't have it in me to ask again.

Heartbroken. Am I that? In general, not even because of Danny? I should stop wearing my heart on my sleeve—but my sleeves are covered in hearts, small and wet and messy, ready to tumble out and stain my white palms crimson. A sad, broken boy is all I've ever been.

"You won't ever leave me, will you, Max?"

Gloss's eyes are hard and piercing. She's a falcon eyeing my pounding mouse heart. I swallow. My pulse thrums in my wrists. It's the question I asked her, but she means it differently.

"No," I tell her, biting back the words that want to follow: *I don't think I could.*

"Good."

She settles back against me. Her eyes are kind again. It's so good to be needed. Wanted. I've spent my whole life waiting for someone to want me.

Both Danny and Gloss, the two most vibrant people I've ever met, have wanted me. To be with me like this, the two of us, somewhere private. Secret. Maybe I'm too awful to be seen with in public?

But Gloss is with me all the time in public, unlike Danny. She's only real like this when there's no one else around. It's true as soon as I think it: she's realer in the dark, pressed against me in soft cotton, than she is in her armour at school. She's so hard to solve—her puzzle pieces won't align, and I'm not sure what the picture is supposed to be, anyway. I make a jigsaw out of the sky, that's easy, because I know what it looks like. Like blue eyes and sea spray and empty spaces torn by the wind.

The sadness in my chest is vast, too big for my ribs. It's not a black hole, but it sucks at me like one. You can't escape something that's a part of you. It'll eat me eventually. I'll swallow myself alive.

Gloss kisses my knuckles, and the beast in my chest shuts its mouth, rolls over and purrs. "Tell me about when you got your first guitar," she says.

I tell her how Mr. Murti let me use the school equipment even when I was a brand-new student of his, eleven years old, skinny as a fretboard and not nearly as well put together. How he taught me a few chords and lent me a beat-up old guitar the school didn't use anymore. I took that guitar home and played until my fingers bled just like the song. Then I played some more, and the skin hardened. I saved up for two summers of lawn mowing and odd jobs before I bought my own second-hand guitar. It's my favourite thing, the warm orange wood, the chips and dents that are part of her body the same as mine are part of me. I tell Gloss other stories, some true and some rambles made of mushrooms and sunshine. I spill all the words inside me about Danny, about how knowing him changed how I know myself. I talk about my cruel, useless mother, and my gentle, useless father. I sing to her. I ask her questions. She won't tell me about her tattoo, which I now know is a small, bold semicolon on the inside of her wrist, but she promises to tell me another day. I make her pinkie swear.

Much later, I climb a tree and graze my hands, smearing them with moss that smells of the forest and fresh earth. She braids a plait into the top of my hair and tells me I look like a Viking. I run my fingers through her mane and tell her she looks like a princess, no, a queen. She kisses me hundreds of times on my forehead and cheeks and tells me I'm good and deserving.

When we walk home, holding hands in the lengthening shadows, I am washed clean.

AFTER

7

GRANT'S HOUSE IS different in the daylight. The worn concrete steps are riddled with cracks that catch on my soles, and the lawn is balding, dirt patches illustrating hours of footy practice. Even though the whole place has the same grimy vibe as the rest of the rows, bright cloth shimmies in the window frames, and the door is a clean and welcoming yellow. Neither of us looks across the road and three doors down where Danny's bedroom window is sucking all the air out of the street.

We were silent the whole ride over, taking turns to draw breath and then release it, like surfers missing a wave.

Grant stands with his keys in his hand for a moment, then his face twists between grief and rage. "Did you know? Did you know she did it and cover for her?"

I crumple. "Of course not. I didn't . . . I was there. But . . . I didn't see? I don't know what happened. I didn't know it was her." I shiver. "You think I'd take the fall for her? You think prison is a place I'd survive?"

Grant shakes his head, hard, like he's trying to get the

thoughts out. "No. Sorry. I don't. I don't think that, not really. I..."

He shrugs helplessly. Tears well in my eyes, splitting his face into fragments.

I wouldn't take the fall for Gloss—I'm not brave enough, or decisive enough, or anything else. Even if she killed him because of me, it's not my fault. I have to believe that it wasn't my fault, or I'll sit down and never get up again. Then the worst thought of all hits me, and my knees buckle.

Gloss is brave enough, decisive enough, and everything else. What if... What if she's covering for me? What if I did do it and I just don't remember?

Grant doesn't seem to notice my sudden lack of stability. He pulls out his phone on the way through the door.

In a static panic I blurt, "What's the time?"

"Four-twenty, blaze it," Grant replies, the addition obviously automatic. His face wavers, and tears spring into his dark eyes. I don't even think about it—I grab him. He flings his arms around me like a drowning man, and we clutch each other too hard, fingers digging dents into muscle and bone. His back is shaking, and mine is too, and something rips loose inside me. We cry like men cry, not like boys. In deep, broken breaths and gasping, raw sobs. A misery too deep for wailing.

The grief passes through us, leaving us weak and leaning on each other, but lighter. Like draining a wound. I lean my forehead on his shoulder for another moment and then straighten up, rubbing my hand over my face, looking for something to say, something to do. "I would definitely blaze it."

Grant's mouth twitches. "I'll text Mike."

BEFORE

7

TURNS OUT THE buzzing in my pocket was my dad. Seven missed calls and twelve texts. The school called him, I'd better have a good explanation for this, etc., etc. I'm still high enough to stare at my phone like the answer to what I should do will jump out at me. Call him, text him? I should tell him I haven't run away. I wonder how long it will take for him to call the police this time. I can't decide how to answer, so I do nothing. I want to stay away from my real life for a little longer. Away from my broken heart.

The last fingers of sunset are curling over the horizon when we get back to Gloss's flat. She pads off to her bedroom while I flop down on the couch and watch the sky change into velvet darkness. I rest my phone on my thigh so that the slightly tacky case grips the fabric of my black jeans and balances there. The crack I can't afford to fix catches the light from the hallway.

Another notification pops up.

> Just tell me you're okay.

That seems like a totally reasonable request.

I'm okay, I just don't want to talk

Where are you?

Gloss'ssssss

Are you safe?

I type "is anyone ever safe" and then erase it.

Yes, and I've eaten, and I'm going to school tomorrow

I'm back on shift tonight.

I know

Come by the station after school tomorrow. That's not negotiable.

Fine.

You can bring the girl if you want.

Hard pass but thanks

:-) I'm glad you're making friends

A HUMMING NOISE fills the air, and slowly, I come to the conclusion that it's being made by the shower. My mind shivers over thoughts of Gloss, wet and soapy, and then I feel like a perv, so I get off the sofa to find something to do. The fridge yields snacks. I chop up a melon and put the wet slices in a pink bowl.

My juice-slicked fingers slip on the pictures on the fridge door when I put the unused melon away. I didn't really look at them before. I don't want Gloss to think I'm snooping. I imagine her asking me to leave, sending me back to my lifeless, unpleasant and dirty house. Now I've gotten melon stickiness on them. Shit.

I grab a neatly folded cloth from the huge white sink and wipe the fingerprints off the fridge and then run the cloth over the photos, slow and careful, daring to look. The first is a portrait: a couple that must be Gloss's parents stare piously at the camera. They look like a magazine advert for watches, maybe perfume. Gloss has her father's hair—his is short and cropped, but the same rich, red waves. Her eyes, green and arresting, are her mother's.

There's a shot of Gloss as a kid, head back and laughing. She's halfway up a climbing frame. Another kid lurks at the corner of the shot. And then another picture, which I think is of Gloss, until I look at it more closely. The eyes aren't quite right, too wide set. The chin is a touch less pointed. The bridge of the nose has a slightly different cast to it. A smudged reflection.

"My sister."

Gloss's voice makes me jump. I drop the cloth, and it lands with a meaty splat on the pristine tiles.

She leans in the doorway, head cocked. Her hair is up, dry, in a messy bun, and tendrils escape to wrap around her neck, like blood rivulets on marble.

"I didn't know you had a sister!" This seems like exciting news, a chance for a real insight into her life. I always wanted a sibling. Someone to see the world through the same experiences I did. To know me.

Gloss gives me the faintest trace of a smile. There's a stretched-out moment, and then she moves, steps past me, to the wine fridge. She bends down and runs her fingers over the labels. "She's dead."

She says the words so airily it takes me a moment to register the meaning. She's dead. My stomach clenches. I want to ask how, when, apologise for asking, but my lips refuse.

I autopilot, taking a step towards her. The dropped cloth squelches under my bare foot. I slip, my feet shooting out from under me. I flail backwards and manage to grab the edge of the counter to avoid falling to my doom.

Gloss giggles at me, laughter lighting her face. "You wanna watch a movie?"

The way she says it lets me know that the subject of her sister isn't up for discussion. I want to push, but my nerve fails me when I catch her simmering jade glare.

Later, I lie awake, thinking about how she laughed a breath after telling me her sister was dead. Tears start in my eyes in a prickle of imagined pain. No wonder her walls are so high and resistant. I'm just glad she's starting to open up. I try to believe that the awful look was from grief, not anger that I invaded her privacy. Why shouldn't I look at her photos? They're on display in the kitchen. Was her sister older or younger? When did it happen? She keeps all her secrets behind locked doors but demands mine. And I acquiesce, again.

THE NEXT DAY at school whooshes by. I have so much to catch up on. I bury myself in work in my free block and during lunch and slink into class right at the bell so no one has time to come over and ask me about the party.

Danny's not even at school as far as I can tell. Or maybe he just skips maths now. He was never any good at it.

After school, I can't avoid the trip to the fire station or my dad. He's gonna be pissed, and that's fair. Explaining that I missed school yesterday because I was on drugs in the forest wouldn't help. I have to find words to make him understand that important things are happening to me, things that make sitting in a classroom a waste of time. Drawing out the minutes until I have to face my dad's disappointment, I grab my board from the back seat of my car and leave the Jetta in the parking lot. Classic insecure housing kid—I keep a lot in my car where I can get it without braving home. My car may be old and messy, but it's given me freedom, a place to sleep that has a lock on the door. If I could afford to fill my tank, I'd drive and drive along the coast as far as I could.

The weather's perfect for skating—not too hot, a crisp breeze. The wind speeds past my face, making the buzzed sides of my head prickle in the rushing air. I ollie off the kerb and get creamed by a car coming the wrong way out of the school entrance. I'm catapulted forward, off my board. Jack shit I can do about it apart from brace for impact. Gravel rips my hands, elbows, my leg, my face. The car pulls in. Grant leans out the window. His bright pink shirt contrasts delightfully with his skin. Music blares out of the open window.

"Bro!" He's half laughing in shock. "I coulda killed you."

"Fuck." I roll onto my side and take stock of the situation. Skinned palms, graze on my jaw that stings, right arm's ripped up. My jeans are threatening to fall apart, but the fabric saved most of my skin. I try to force the huge fabric flap closed, like I can will it back together, until I remember that Gloss has provided me with multiple pairs of jeans.

Grant hops out of the car. Someone lays on the horn as they squeeze past, and he waves his middle finger in their general direction. "You okay?"

The adrenaline has left me shaky and smiling. "It's a one-way system, dickhead."

"Yeah, yeah, my bad." He does sound sorry, and he helps me up, brushes my shoulder off and picks up my backpack. "You need a ride?"

My hands are bleeding, but there are baby wipes in the car. I mop myself up in the front seat.

"At least your board's okay." Grant turns the music down, starts the car and pulls onto the main road. "Where to?"

"Fire station," I say, inspecting the bloody gouge down my jawbone in the mirror.

"Dropping out? With your grades, who can blame ya?" Grant jokes.

"Yeah, figured a big, strong guy like me's a born firefighter." I give up on my face and resign myself to dad assuming I've been beaten up and am lying about it. Wouldn't be the first time.

"Already mastered the three-hundred-pound deadlift?"

"No, but I practise carrying the weight of everyone staring at me all the time," I say, but it's too bitter for the joke we were sharing, and I regret it as soon as it's out of my mouth.

Grant stays quiet for a moment and then nods. "That must suck." It's a measured, thoughtful answer.

"It's not my favourite."

We fall silent. I'm kicking myself for making it weird when I finally recognise the music piping out of the speakers as Sheer Mag. Funny, I wouldn't have pegged Grant for a punk. The song changes to "Nobody's Baby," and Grant turns the music up.

"What a fuckin' banger!" he yells out the window as if the

nearby pedestrians care, but it makes me laugh. He's always been pretty quiet—or maybe it's hard to be loud in Danny's shadow—but now, he's boisterous. He sings along in his London accent and taps his strong athlete's hands on the steering wheel. I flex my own hands, self-conscious of their slender bones, and wince as I tug at the new road rash.

Grant sings and I stare out the window, watching things roll by. Chippie, pub, tattoo parlour, chippie. Closed-down pub, pharmacy, church, Chinese restaurant, kebab shop, flats, more flats and the craggy shadow of the old castle wall far in the distance.

Grant shoots me a side glance. "How long have you been skating?"

"Like eight years."

"Used to see you at the skatepark in the Crescent." He flashes me a grin. "I'd have worried more when I hit you if I hadn't seen you take a dozen headers before."

I laugh, surprised. "Yeah, well, I wear a helmet at the ramps."

He snorts and nods. "Aren't you supposed to wear one when you're on the roads?"

"Don't wanna ruin my hair."

"Your girlfriend might not like it." He nods sagely and then shoots me a cheeky look. "Or boyfriend. Man, you're a player."

I freeze, bracing for the follow-up. The wounding insult.

But nothing happens. There was nothing mean in his tone—he sounds amused, genuinely friendly, even. But he's also Danny's buddy and could be messing with me. I don't know how to respond, so I don't say anything, and after a minute, Grant punches me on the shoulder. It's a bro's punch, though.

"Dude, you gotta relax."

"Easier said than done," I snark, but loosen up a little.

"I guess being trans and bi or pan is a lot to have rattling around in your head."

He shifts gears. I can see the station at the end of the road. Is this a lead in to asking me about the party? Suddenly, I'm desperate to escape the confines of the vehicle, even though a horrible conversation with my dad is on the horizon. But Grant doesn't make me respond. "Not everybody cares, dude. You act like everyone does, like we automatically hate you 'cause of who you are. Some of us know what it's like to be prejudged." He gestures at his face with a "duh" expression.

Grant's one of maybe six Black kids in our whole school. That can't be easy, knowing the people around here. I hunch down, chastened, and he laughs. "I'm tryna bond with you here, not tell you off for being insensitive to my tragic plight as one of the only people in this place that gets asked why I'm buying sunscreen."

It's impossible not to smile at his dancing eyes, and when I do, he winks at me in such a ridiculous, overstated way my lips twitch into a grin without my permission.

We pull up at the station. I yank the door open and slither out. My hands have left bloodstains on the naked wood between stickers on the underside of my board. I pause. "Thanks, man."

He jerks his head at me and offers me a fist. I bump it and slam the door behind me.

MY DAD IS out of the huge door before I make it across the concrete driveway. The big red engines squatting behind him are menacing, not like when I was little and he used to let me climb up in the cab.

"What happened to your face?" He grabs my jaw in his big hand and tips it gently so he can see the blossoming bruise and gravel streaks.

"Came off my board." I hold up my free hand to show him the palm, which is still oozing lymph and dark blood. His face freezes for a moment, like he's trying to choose what expression to wear, and then he slings his arm around my shoulder and steers me towards the station.

"Let's get you cleaned up." He looks over his shoulder as Grant pulls out onto the road, in the correct direction this time. "I thought she'd be prettier." He gives me a dad grin, all pleased with himself for the stupid joke, and I roll my eyes.

"That's Grant. We have music together. And he's actually very pretty."

I've never come right out and told my dad I'm not straight, but I'm sure he knows. I had to come out as trans. I couldn't face another year of the name I used to carry shredding me every time someone addressed me. At least this way I'm giving people a chance to know me. But I'm asking them to question, to think and grow and change their language, and people resent it, resent me for making them feel old-fashioned or uncool, as if being trans isn't something that has existed throughout for all of recorded history, despite numerous attempts to wipe us out. I'm seventeen years old and want to piss in the right bathrooms and go through the right puberty instead of letting oestrogen fuck my body up in ways I'll never recover from. What is it to do with anyone except me and my doctors?

Dad hustles me past the guys—and two women—sitting around the table. They all acknowledge me with varying degrees of interest. There's a few who've been around since I was small, and I see the double take in Donnelley's face as she puts together the disparate pieces of information that make me my dad's kid, who used to be known as his daughter. I don't blame my dad for not throwing a gender reveal party at the station or anything, but it makes my tummy squirm to see people trying to make sense of me.

My dad sits me down on his bunk before ducking out of the room for the first aid kit. I shift on the navy blankets in the little cubby, uncomfortable. There's a picture of the three of us, a few years old, tucked into the frame of the plexi window that separates the cubicle from the next bed. My mind jumps back to the photo at Gloss's. In this picture, dad's got his arm around my shoulders, and we both look happy enough. My mum is looking at something out of shot, her eyes distant. I can't tell if she's drunk or not. I trace my finger down the edge of the picture.

He returns with a first aid kit and cleans my grazes out, sprays stick-on-skin over the weeping injuries and covers the one on my face with a trimmed gauze bandage.

"There, now you look tough."

He ruffles my hair. I would love to look tough. I'm more sort of emo scarecrow than anything threatening.

"So now you talk," he says. "Where've you been, what've you been doing? Why are you missing school?"

I exhale, closing my eyes for a long second, and then start to tell him about Gloss. I leave out the parts where we took mushrooms in the forest yesterday instead of going to school, and gloss over—pun intended—the less-than-savoury moments. I talk instead about how she stuck up for me in school, and people are treating me better, and she helped me pick a haircut that looks good. In classic dad fashion, he doesn't seem to notice that my outfit is new, the upscale version of the worn-out skate punk look I used to live in. The party balances on the tip of my tongue. But there's no way I wouldn't let on that it hurt me, and he'd see. He'd know something bad happened, and he'd be sad. I hate making him sad.

He lets me talk for a long time, leaning against the wall behind the bed. Turns out I missed him while I was at Gloss's. He's away so much of the time I forget that we can be comfortable together, especially if my mum's not around to wedge her claws into everything. When I was a kid, I used to wish they'd split up. That my mum would go back to her family in the States and I'd get to be with my dad. But I grew up and learned that wouldn't happen with his job. I'd have to live with mum either there or here, and that would be worse. I'll be eighteen next year, though. Then I can leave, even without my dad's help. The thought of it makes my palms itch, knowing how many choices are coming for me, whether or not I'm ready to make them.

Our conversation meanders easily, reconnecting, and I relax into it. There's a moment—when did I last go to the beach?—when Danny's name is heavy in my mouth. Could I even find the words? While I'm frozen, the air bursts with sirens and my dad leaps up and into action. He yells "Love you" on the way out of the door. I see his friends teasing him for it as they pull their gear on.

I stay out of the way until the engine's siren is out of earshot and then scribble my dad a note. *See you at home. Max.* I don't add *stay safe* or *be careful* or any of that stuff, even though they beat inside me like a drum when I know he's on a call.

AFTER SPENDING DAYS in a space where I wasn't under constant surveillance and judgment, the idea of going home sucks, and the thought of seeing my mum makes me drag my feet all the way back to school to pick up my car. It's a long walk, but I'm too sore to skate. I take as long as possible, but it's not even six when I climb the front steps to my door. It used to be bright red. My mum painted it every couple of summers back when she still did things. Out of nowhere, I remember her helping my too-small hands balance a brush and streak vivid, fresh scarlet over the old, sanded-down coat. I pause in the doorway, running my hand over the faded panel. It's been at least six years since she last "freshened it up." Six years since she gave up on therapy and started self-medicating.

There's an open, half-empty wine bottle on the table by the

door. I spin to check the hooks. Keys—still there. She hasn't taken dad's car.

"Is that you?" she calls, adding my deadname to echo off the walls and slap my skin.

Who else would it be, mother, Santa Claus? He hasn't been around for a long time.

"It's Max," I yell back, kicking my shoes off with jerky, awkward motions. Home five seconds and I'm so angry my stomach is roiling; it's been so long since she even tried to care about me.

"Did you bring groceries?" The Americanism grates. She never lost her accent, and sometimes I notice the patterns in my own speech. I hate that I have anything from her. I hear a thump, and then another—she's making her way to the door. For some reason, I quash the urge to race up the stairs before she makes it. The memory of her hands over mine, maybe.

"No, I didn't. I'll run out and get some." There's no point in asking what she needs because she won't even think about food. She'll ask me to pick up a bottle of wine with some risotto rice, which will never get cooked. I'm hungry, though, and she probably hasn't eaten in a while. "Do you fancy burgers? Or chicken kiev?" That's what I want and what I can cook. At least I'm trying.

She looks at me, a sly expression on her wine-blotched face. "Burgers. There's a good girl."

It takes everything in me not to grab the wine bottle off the table and chuck it at her, but someone has to be the adult here. "Boy. I'm a good boy, mum. Be right back." My voice is so emotionless I sound dead.

BEFORE

8

ALL WEEK AT school, I brace for the confrontation I'm sure is going to happen. Danny's primed to explode. He kissed me in front of people, and Gloss shredded him for it. There's no way to avoid a showdown.

Except apparently, there is, because I don't see Danny all week. The tension in my neck ratchets tighter every day he avoids being in the same room as me. Meanwhile, staying with Gloss has drawn into sharp focus how stressful being around my mother is, and while I'm at home, I can't stop thinking about getting out of there. My dad gets home on Thursday, and things ease up again, but then he's back on shift on Sunday and I start to suffocate. I text Gloss Sunday evening.

> Can I come over

Always

I glow inside when I read the message, and reread it, and reread it again. Then I screenshot it for posterity. It takes me five minutes to stuff clothes in a bag, grab my school stuff and head for the car.

It gets harder to go home, even when my dad is around. Gloss clears out a drawer for me and empties some wardrobe space in her room. Her parents are never there. Every now and again, I'll hear a door opening when we're both lying in bed or see a pair of shoes somewhere it didn't used to be, but the people may as well be ghosts. I always sleep in her bed. We don't talk about it. We fall asleep tangled around each other, my face in her hair. We wake up and sip coffee in the window seat with our bare toes touching. We might be best friends or in love. I can't tell, and I don't think she can either.

There isn't anyone else for either of us, whatever we are. I know because when we're curled up together, her eyebrows relax. I know because when it's only us, her smile is kind and warm, not sharp. I know because I feel it in every bit of me— that we have chosen to take care of each other.

One day, we're sprawled in the living room doing home-work when my eyes land on her tattoo, small but vivid against her bone-white skin. She catches me looking. Her jaw muscle ticks for a moment. Then she takes a deep breath and pushes her highlighter-striped textbook aside.

"My sister. Camilla. Millie . . . She died. She wasn't ever strong, and then she got pneumonia, and then she died." She rubs her thumb over the black dots on her wrist. "After . . . well. I thought about it. Going with her. But she'd have hated that."

Gloss trails off. I should say something, but there's no words inside me. Only pain. The photo on the fridge. Gloss's blurred reflection. Someone she knew her whole life. The bridge of my nose goes tight and tingles inside.

She fills the silence that was space for me to comfort her. "The semicolon is a suicide survival thing. When the author could have chosen to end their sentence, but they didn't, you know?"

"I'm sorry." The sentence drops into the ether, inadequate and useless, like everything I say.

"Yeah. Me too." She gives me a pale imitation of her usual smile. Meeting my eyes head on, she sniffs, then swallows hard. "She was two years older than me. My parents named me Emily, even though everyone except them called her Millie. She called me Em until I was eleven."

This is the slowest Gloss has ever spoken, the most unsure she's ever sounded of her words. I'm frozen, the books on my lap threatening to slide clear if I shift an inch. There are words in the world that would help, that would prove sharing with me is the right choice, assure her that I'm here for her, that I want to know her. I sift desperately for those brilliant phrases that could unlock her, but as always, without a pen in my hand, there's nothing but static and longing.

Gloss studies my face. The whites of her eyes are so clear they're almost blue, like snow. She reaches for my hand. "She got this tube of fancy lip gloss for her birthday, her thirteenth. Well, I was angry with her for some reason, no one could remember why after. I decided to wear her new favourite makeup to her party. When I went to open the tube, I squeezed too hard and it shot out all over my face, right when Millie and her friends walked into her room. Hence . . . Gloss."

My heart thuds in my throat, but then an image of eleven-year-old Gloss covered in expensive lip gloss assails me, and my lips twitch. Before I have to figure out what to say next, we're interrupted by her phone. It lights up and dances on the wide oak coffee table. She stares at it for a moment, then her eyes shoot to the large clock above the mantelpiece. It's five after six. She hurries to pick up the phone and accept the incoming video chat.

"Good evening, daddy." Her tone is modulated to a polite, refined pattern I've never heard before.

"Hello, Emily. You're late." The voice is English, posh English. All I can make out from this angle is the vague impression of a white man in a dark suit, at a desk, with a sheaf of papers spread out on the wood and what looks like a glass and decanter set behind him.

"Sorry, daddy. I was revising." Her muscles are marble stiff, but her face is smooth, and her voice is still unrecognizable.

"What are you working on?"

"A paper for Social Studies on the ways that sexism impacted the spread of the Black Plague." She swallows, a delicate bob of her throat.

Her father sniffs. "I'm sure. Send it to my secretary this evening."

"It's not due until next week." Her cheeks are going pink in the way that usually precedes someone getting torn a new asshole. I hope her dad chokes on his little crystal glass of whisky when she yells at him.

"Tonight, Emily. In case you need to redo it." He gestures at someone off-screen and then exchanges some papers and a flurry of words. Gloss's cheeks aren't pink anymore. They're glacial white.

"Yes, sir."

It's the dead tone I use with my mother when I can't give her anymore of myself. My hand darts out like a snake, clutching Gloss's leg convulsively. She starts and then leans into my touch.

"Good girl. How is everything? Are you meeting all your commitments?" He doesn't give her a moment to answer. "I'm glad to see I was correct in thinking it would be harder for you to get into trouble outside of London, but I have noted your credit card expenditure increasing." Gloss takes a breath to respond, but he's still talking. "See that you behave more responsibly, or I will have you itemise your receipts. I'll let you know when to expect my next call."

"Yes, daddy."

The call disconnects from the other end. She drops the phone on the sofa like it burned her.

I've never seen her curl in on herself like she does now. Suddenly, I understand what she means when she tells me to relax, what Grant meant in his car. I ball up like that all the time. I sit up straighter.

"Do you like hot chocolate?" I don't know why I said that over anything else. Mostly, I want to tell her that her dad is a *dick*, but it's what comes out.

She narrows cat eyes at me. "What kind of a monster doesn't like hot chocolate?"

I squeeze her knee and head for the kitchen to give her a moment to collect herself.

The kitchen is stocked for any occasion. Squirty cream— the kind in a can that is somehow real anyway—chocolate flakes, the works. I'm considering plopping some chocolate ice cream in for a temperature experiment when Gloss slides her hands around my hips and, leaving one flat on my belly, seizes the spoon. "I'm not cleaning up your puke."

I look down at her over my shoulder. "You totally would."

"I'd fish you out of it and call Stephanie, and you know it," she says lightly, snagging a spoonful of ice cream and stepping back from me to eat it. I grin, leaning on the countertop with one chocolate-smeared hand.

"The mysterious Stephanie. I've never even seen her." I've never seen her parents either, and they don't seem to have noticed that a random boy has moved in with them. Even my mother would notice if I had a new roommate. I start to tidy up the mess I've made while the hot chocolate—no ice cream—steams.

"Maybe there is no Stephanie and I get up in the night and put my marigolds on."

The thought of Gloss in marigold washing-up gloves is too funny, and I belly laugh into the freezer as I close it, putting the ice cream away.

"What if you messed up your manicure?" I tease, grabbing our full mugs before heading back to the lounge, beyond relieved that the sadness in Gloss's face has washed away, buoyed up on having handled this in a way that didn't make things worse.

"Then thank goodness I have geography first block tomorrow, because Mr. Hanez is scared enough of me to mark me present even if I am very, very late due to emergency nail care needs."

I get a whipped cream moustache on my first sip. I lick it clean with great relish before responding. "Everyone's scared of you."

"Except you."

"I'm terrified of you!" I poke a pillow into place between us like a barricade. I think I'm joking when I say it, but after the words slide out, I know I am. Terrified she'll leave me, terrified she'll hurt me, terrified that this intense connection we've forged will suck me in until there's nothing left of me without her.

AFTER

8

WE WAIT FOR Mike silently, lost in our own thoughts, sprawled on uncomfortable metal chairs in what passes for a back garden: a square of concrete over broken ground. The tall fences on either side make me uncomfortable with their huge, inescapable shadows. I keep shifting, trying to stay in the small patch of sunlight passing overhead.

Mike slams his way through the gate. His face is puffy from crying, and he looks like he's slept in his clothes, or maybe not at all. His hair is stuck up everywhere. The knuckles on his right hand are red and grazed. Behind him, Michelle daintily steps through and closes the latch behind her, locking the four of us in. It's obvious that she's tried to hide dark smears under her eyes, but it hasn't quite worked.

Grant holds out his hand and twitches his fingers in elegant request, and Mike digs in his pocket before throwing a baggie at him. Michelle looks around the space, surveying the lack of chairs and convenient sitting spots, and then her eyes land on me. She steps closer, and I turn, ready for a hug. We could all use more hugs, I think. Then, to my complete surprise, she slides her arm over my shoulder and perches herself on my knee.

I narrowly avoid dropping her, which would be embarrassing if there was anything left inside me to bother with such unimportant emotions. I end up with my arm around her waist, and she snuggles into my chest. The comfort of her body is nice. I'm so fucking lonely. She's so soft and warm and alive. Tears spring into my eyes, and she seems to sense them because she starts carding the hair at the back of my neck.

I lean my head on her shoulder and hold my hand out for the joint in silence. The bruise on my wrist from the cuffs is spreading like ink under my skin.

"Do you remember when he got us kicked out of the Swan for breaking the window with a pool ball?" Grant asks, propping his feet on a terra-cotta flowerpot that's seen better days.

Us. My throat aches with wanting things to be different. Then and now. All my stories with an "us" are ruined. There's no one left but me.

Mike makes a sound like he's been punched. "Fuck, yeah. No one would believe he was aiming for the pocket."

"Lifetime. Ban," Grant enunciates, waving the dead joint in his hand.

Mike's already rolling a replacement. "What about when he punched that squaddie and we got fuckin' chased by the whole army?"

There's a military base south of town on the river, and the army boys roll into town every now and again. I imagine Danny punching a big man with a buzz cut, goading him on. I can picture it all too clearly.

Michelle twirls a piece of my hair around her finger. When I look up at her, her eyes are kind and understanding, like she knows what I'm thinking. "What about when he put that ladder up between our bedroom windows and crawled across it and got stuck halfway?" she chimes in, still playing with my hair. It's a more wholesome image. I'm grateful for it.

"How old was he?" The boys don't hear me, but Michelle does.

"Twelve, I guess? He was grounded. We could talk across the window gap." Michelle gestures, encompassing the narrow paths from the front to the back of the house. "You know we were neighbours, right?"

I didn't. I'm seized with the aching need to see Danny's space. I was never invited there, never allowed. It was too dangerous. His dad might catch us. Well. Not much worse can happen now, can it, Danny? "I want to go to his house." The idea shoots through me and out of my mouth. I sit up straighter, dislodging Michelle so she squeaks and grabs on to the back of my neck for balance.

Mike and Grant pause their conversation and turn to me in unison.

"No you don't, mate." Mike shakes his head. "Nobody wants to go to Danny's house."

"I'll come with you." Michelle traces a finger down the side of my neck, on the tendon, making me shiver.

"I won't." Grant glowers at the ground. "His dad's a weeping sore on the pestilent face of humanity."

"How long have you been saving that one up?" Mike knocks Grant's knee with his foot, but Grant doesn't answer.

My initial burst of bravery is draining away, so I have to press on before it's lost entirely. "You know we were . . . a thing. But he always kept so many parts of himself away from me. I never saw his room or anything. I . . . wanna be close to him again for a minute."

I want to mourn Danny before I mourn Gloss, before I think about her, the tatters of my life she's left behind her— and what it might mean if she's lying.

BEFORE

9

IT'S BEEN FIVE months since I last set foot in the skatepark. At first, I kept going back, every day after that awful one, hoping he'd talk to me again, hoping we could fix it. He didn't come for me on the ramps, although sometimes I thought I saw his curtain twitching. In school, he ignored me unless he was making shitty comments for me to overhear, shoving past me in the corridor, or drawing attention away from me. Then, one cold Friday evening, swollen with beer and rage, he found me on the halfpipe.

He told me none of it was ever real if I'd been lying all along.

But this morning, when Gloss suggested that we go—on a gorgeous, summer's-coming Saturday, after a blissful week together—I knew it was time to reclaim one of my sanctuaries.

She packs us a picnic—no mushroom tea this time—while I shower, and we amble the ten-minute walk to the bus station instead of driving. I used to think Gloss wouldn't be seen dead on a bus because she has that moneyed, snobby vibe, but the more I get to know her the more I realise most of that's a front.

She prefers things to be nice and easy, but if they're not, she takes it on the chin and doesn't complain about it or guilt-trip me. Oh, sure, Stephanie comes in and cleans her house twice a week, takes her laundry and brings her shopping. She's spoiled rotten, but it hasn't spoiled her. Not entirely, anyway. For all the skipping, she works hard at school. Before she lost Millie, maybe she was as shallow as she seemed if you weren't looking for the hidden depths.

We hop off at the railway bridge and stumble-run down the grassy verge. I catch her at the bottom as though we'd planned it, my arm hooping her waist and spinning her around so she ends up laughing into my neck.

The park's bumping, which is expected on a Saturday afternoon, but Gloss manages to stake out a patch of grass close enough that she can watch me from her blanket. She grins at me from over top of the dense philosophy book she may or may not be reading. Her bookmarks always move, but I never see her eyes on the pages. I walk backwards to the ramp, pulling my black, bestickered helmet on over my messy hair and poke my tongue out at her before turning around and making my way across the grass.

I hear Danny before I see him.

I'd know that crowing laugh anywhere. As much as I try not to, I look over. There's a little pack of them, sprawled in the shadow of the biggest tree in the park. The best spot. Mike is up the tree, feet swinging, with a tall can in his hand. Some other kids from school are sitting in a cluster. Danny lobs something up at Mike, and girls shriek as he misses the catch and whatever it is plunges into the middle of their group. They scatter, pinwheeling—and Danny looks right at me. The corner of his mouth tilts in a half smile for a moment before he turns away, face shuttering, leaving me with the memories stamped all over the park. But I'm happier now, I remind myself. There's more in me to push back against the creeping curdling of my joy. I'm doing all right in school, people say hi to me, I have a place to sleep that I don't have to grit my teeth before entering.

So what if Danny laughed and pushed me on that swing, his head thrown back with joy while the moon silvered his hair and painted him as white as I am? So what if the skateboard in my hand is the same one I dropped when he stepped into me, hooked his fingers around my jaw and kissed me that first time? The clatter it made skidding down the ramp was music with his mouth on mine.

So what if . . .

I jump onto my board as soon as my feet hit the concrete. Pick up speed past some little kids practising their very first ollies, nipping through their disorderly group. Then I'm onto the empty kinked rail. Most of the serious skaters won't come out until later, so there's not many people to avoid. I thunder down the metal rail, board skidding, on the edge of control. Feet up, and my board leaps into my hand for a second. I curl my fingers around the smooth wood to hold it, grip tape scraping my calluses, then down and landed. Shaky, but upright. Adrenaline flushes away the echo of Danny swinging his legs from the top of the ramp. I don't know if he's watching. I don't care.

One of the little kids whoops at me as I shunt my board past, over to the bowl.

I'm sweating through my black T-shirt by the time Gloss wanders over to lean on the rail, an ice lolly dripping in each hand. She takes a long, slow swipe at her frozen treat with her pink tongue. I miss my landing, stack it and roll down the ramp, banging my elbows and knees.

Gloss waits until I'm standing up to laugh at me. I scowl at her without much heat as I traipse over, limping only a little— it'll wear off in a second, skater life—and grab my ice lolly. It's sticky sweet and sweating rainbow droplets down its stick. I flick my wet hair out of my eyes before starting in on the lolly proper. Gloss drapes her arm around my neck, then snatches it back, disgusted by the slide of my wet skin.

"Ew."

"You're welcome." I laugh at the unhappy look on her face.

"You're gross," she says, eating her ice lolly in dainty little nips, white teeth closing on the colourful ice.

"What, now you don't wanna get sweaty with me?" I tease.

She shoots me a side-eyed, smouldering look and bites the top of her treat right off.

"Do you want to go to London tonight? One of my old friends is throwing a party." Is she asking me on a date? I sneak a glance at her face, but she catches me. "I promise not to abandon you."

Reddening, I mumble, "Yeah, sure. Assuming you're gonna be my sugar momma." She pays for everything, always, but whatever, it's not as if she earns it.

"You know it, toy boy. There's nothing I'd rather spend my father's disgusting money on than you."

She pinches my cheek with tacky fingers, and I grimace, pulling my shirt up to scrub at my face. When I drop it, I catch her looking at my stomach. I raise an eyebrow at her. I'm quite proud of my stomach; I do a lot of sit-ups. My snail trail has been coming in over the last couple of months, and now there's enough to see. Convincingly manly if I don't lift my shirt higher than the rib line. She's never weird about seeing me in my binder, but I am, all awkward and fumbling and hiding. I wish I'd had top surgery, could be contented topless in this wet heat like the boys running around the park with shirts trailing from their back pockets or flung on the ground at the base of the ramps.

Gloss brings her eyes up to mine and blinks, slow and vacuous. "Have you been working out?"

The banter comes easily with her now. "If you want to watch, you only have to ask."

Back at the blanket, I upend a bottle of icy water over my head and sticky hands. We chill for a while, lounging in the dappled sunlight streaming through the trees. Gloss puts her book on my stomach, and if she's not reading it, she's at least turning the pages.

My eyes are closed, and my head is resting on my skateboard, when a darker shadow falls over me.

Danny.

I know before I open my eyes. He's a tightness behind my belly button. Even his shadow has a taste.

Gloss sits up immediately, book in her hands, and hovers over me. "What do you want?"

I pull myself up with my stomach muscles, prop one hand on my knee and one hand on Gloss's lower back, silently telling her to chill. It's too gorgeous today to let Danny ruin it.

"I, uh." He's framed by the sun, blond hair glinting. He has polarised sunglasses on— I can't see his eyes—but he sounds like my Danny, unsure and vulnerable. "I wanna talk to Max."

He fidgets with his phone, and the mirrored silver case casts glares of reflected sunlight across his chin and cheeks. My stomach flips. He used to mess with me when I was catnapping on him in the sun, bugging me with light flickering against my closed eyelids until I woke up and wrestled him for it.

"Anything you have to say to him, you can say in front of me." Gloss narrows her eyes at him. "Go ahead."

Danny takes his glasses off and hooks them on his necklace, the same worn-smooth wooden surfboard he's been wearing the whole time I've known him. "Please, Max." The pleading is naked on his face, and I waver.

Ugh. He knows I can't say no to that. "Fine. Gloss. Can

you give us a minute?" I grit my teeth, waiting for her to rip him a new one, but she stares at me for a moment and then stands up.

"You have as long as it takes for me to get drinks," she tells him. "Call me if you need me, love." She demands eye contact and waits until I give it to her and nod. Twisting her lip to the side in disapproval, she scoops up her handbag and stalks away.

The shop is a few minutes away, so she's giving us maybe fifteen. Generous.

Danny and I watch her go. After a few minutes of nothing, he sits down next to me—on the grass, not the blanket—with an arm's length between us. I want to know if it's because he doesn't want to invade my space or doesn't want to be close to me. I don't know which is worse.

"What do you want?" I echo Gloss's question. It's dislocating, being here in this place with him in the sun. Feels like old times. My fingers twitch with the ghost of his strong hand spreading my narrow bones out to fit his. I imagine his friends' eyes on us, pricking me like needles.

"I want to apologise." He takes a deep breath. "I'm sorry for how I've been. For everything."

My gaze darts to his face. My stomach does a full, slow somersault. His earnest expression makes him look like a little kid—he always does when he's serious. All big, hopeful eyes and pouty mouth. Waiting for me to say something. A quote from the counsellor's wall pops into my head. *The best apology is changed behaviour.* I have to fight to keep from laughing.

"Okay, you've apologised. What do you *want*?" Old Max wouldn't recognise me between the haircut and the clothes and the no-nonsense question.

"I . . . don't know." He sighs, sounding heartbroken. "I'm not gay."

I don't reply, just raise an eyebrow.

"But I thought . . . maybe. We could not hate each other."

I breathe in deeply and inspect the scuffs on the side of my Vans. Danny waits for me—he was always good at that. Made space for my words as though he wanted to hear them, as if they were precious. Like old times, I find them for him.

"I never hated you, Danny. You're the one who left. You're the one who screamed, remember? I'm never the one who makes any choices about how things are going to be. But I made the choice not to hate you a long time ago. It was too hard." My skin is oversensitised, tingling.

"I'm sorry," he says again, his voice breaking.

I want to reach out to him, pull him into the crook of my neck and let him cry there the way he did after his dad gave him a black eye for stealing his beer. I don't, even though my hands ache with want. Why do I still want to stop him hurting? I'm so weak.

"Why now?" I can't believe how steady I sound, how little my seething heart affects my words.

He tugs intently at a tuft of grass. There's a scrape on his knuckles, like he's been fighting. "Grant, uh, may have had some words with me."

Grant? Woah. Maybe we are friends.

"Time's up."

I jump. Gloss has appeared out of thin air, offering me an open bottle of beer with condensation rolling down it.

Danny gets to his feet, stares at me, works his mouth like he's about to say something else and then nods and turns. I watch him walk back to his group, back to Michelle taking his hand and pulling him down to the grass. I catch Grant's eyes, and he tilts his head, a clear question even over the space between us. One short jerk of my chin is all I can manage for him before I have to look away from the whole lot of them for wishing I was part of it.

"You okay?" Gloss plops down next to me and hooks her ankle under my bare calf possessively, glaring at Danny's back.

I nod, breathing in the scent of grass and Gloss and her aggressive care. "Yeah. I'm okay."

AFTER

9

FLOWERS ARE PILED up on the wall in front of Danny's house. They're lurid against the worn stones. The house itself is plastered brick, cracking away at wooden window frames that needed painting a decade ago. I inhale, hold it, exhale. Five times, concentrating on how my body moves as the air comes in and out. It helps. A bit.

My knock is inappropriately loud for the quiet pall hanging over the street. The door jerks inward, surprising me, and I teeter on the top step, my heel sliding off so I have to pinwheel my arms.

The large bald man in the doorway curls his lip at my gymnastics. The hair he's missing on his head shades his jaw blue as steel. He has the look of someone who's muscular under the beer belly, a rugby player gone to seed who could still lift me up in one hand. "Whaddya want?"

I have a split second of regret for telling Michelle she didn't have to come here with me—Grant and Mike didn't even offer—because this guy is an entire fucking unit, and she's definitely tougher than I am.

"Uh . . . Kenny?" Grant made it clear that I should never, ever call this man anything other than Kenny. "Mr. Kensington" is a surefire way to get a slap, apparently. Come on, Max, use your words. "My name's Max, I'm . . . I was a friend of Danny's."

He looks me over, and I try to stand square, be someone he can't dismiss. "I ain't never seen you before."

Guess they didn't release my picture with the story about my arrest.

"Yeah, I, uh, don't live around here. I'm sorry to disturb you at home, but I was really hoping I would be able to, uh, have something of Danny's to remember him by." Is that why I wanted to come? "Just like, a little thing. Please," I finish, praying my eyes aren't glistening.

The man turns, leaving the door open behind him. "His room's upstairs. Take what you want, I'm getting rid of it anyway."

Kenny leaves me in the narrow hallway. The stairs are right in front of me, clad in worn khaki carpet that might once have had some pile. There are three men in the living room, right off the front hall. I can't hear what they're saying, only their angry, buzzing tones vibrating through the wall, competing with the rugby game on the television.

"Your son died yesterday," I say to a fist-sized hole in the wall.

The stairs are a mountain. It takes all my oxygen and willpower to get to the top. I'm drenched in sweat when I get there, nauseated with anticipation. The hallway sways, and I put my hand against the wall to steady myself. It's not the weed we smoked at Grant's, it's the intimacy. I've thought about what Danny's bedroom would look like a thousand times. About showing him around mine. I've never had anyone over to my room. Not even Gloss. Only my parents have ever been inside, and I haven't let them in in years.

His door, covered with peeling white paint, says DANNY'S. KEEP OUT in childish block letters.

"I hope you don't mean me, Danny," I mutter, pushing the door open.

BEFORE

10

LONDON. MY FIRST time coming to the city with a plan instead of trying to escape. I'm clean, smelling faintly of the sandalwood shaving cream Gloss bought me, and dressed in my best party-ready outfit—shit-kicking boots, tight black jeans that cling to my calves, a white T-shirt thick enough my binder doesn't show through and a black denim jacket. Right now, it's slung over my shoulder because the early evening is too hot. I had it tied around my waist until Gloss reminded me with a raised eyebrow that it doesn't go there without dramatically emphasising my hips.

Gloss is still wearing what she was in the park earlier, and somehow, it's transitioned from day- to nightwear with a change of makeup and hairstyle. She's artfully dishevelled, her hair mussed up enough to look like she's recently rolled out of her swanky bed. Her makeup is immaculate. As we walk down the London streets towards the mysterious friend's, I spin around and pop my hip, turning back to her and grinning in triumph at her happy face.

"Here." She passes me something small and hard. It's a ring, chunky and black, shockingly weighty. It fits on my thumb like it was made for me. Maybe it was. "Mmm." She beams at me. "You look very cute."

"Thanks," I say, and I mean it. It turns out that believing people when they say nice things is amazing, and happiness is a good look on everyone who wears it.

Gloss's hand slots into mine, our fingers lacing with the comfort of familiarity. Her fingers are small and delicate. I am strong and brave.

"I'm hungry," she announces as we approach a fish and chip shop filling the air with the thick scent of salt and vinegar. We both take a big sniff at the same time, then collapse into giggles, shuffling into the queue. All I've eaten today is an ice lolly! The whisky we shared on the train sloshes hot in my belly, and music blares from a nearby club, making me bounce my feet to the rhythm. Gloss pulls me into a dance with her, whirling around me with flicking hips and flashing eyes. She could be a siren, I think, and I catch her hand as she slips under my arm. A siren who calls people towards her, beautiful and terrible. It doesn't seem hard to imagine her eating someone, and not in a fun way. Her teeth always look so sharp, like they could pull the meat off your bones without even trying. If I were a mythical creature, I'd probably be something pathetic like a gnome or a bog goblin. Gloss drags my hand over her stomach, and the thought flees.

A few men try to insinuate themselves into Gloss's space while we're waiting, but she brushes past them, holding my hand. I see the questions in their eyes, the same ones people have at school. Why does she want me? But I don't care why, only that she does.

LIAM LOOKS ABOUT twenty. He's a short, stocky guy with rich amber skin and curling dark hair. He lifts Gloss up onto her tiptoes in a hug as soon as he's opened the door, and when he sets her down, they're both laughing. "Baby girl, it has been too long." She rolls her eyes at him, pushing his chest so he backs up and she can get in the door.

"Yeah, yeah. This is Max. Max, this is Liam." She stands on one leg to unzip her boots and leave them in the pile at the front entrance. It's weird to see her with no shoes on in someone else's house, her stockinged feet all too human and vulnerable.

"Nice to meet you, man." Liam greets me with an enthusiastic handshake. I smile at him, less nervous about coming to a party where I don't know anyone now that Liam's proven friendly. He's wearing gold eyeshadow, which helps.

"You too," I reply, trying to inject confidence into my voice.

Gloss is already on the way upstairs—so much for her promise not to leave me—but she turns around as I think it. "Come on, boys, you can compare tales about me upstairs."

"Ooh, tales." Liam sounds delighted. "Has she told you about her fifteenth birthday party?"

"Not that tale," Gloss throws back down the stairs as I traipse after her.

Upstairs, the lights are low, and music is weaving around tangled threads of conversation. It's a chill vibe: people lounge in chairs and on the carpet, pressing their backs against furniture or their friend's knees, some lying on the floor itself, watching mirror balls dance above them. Gloss plops herself down in an armchair that is somehow empty, like it appeared out of thin air to ensure her comfort. Liam sits on the arm of a long, black leather sofa, close enough to Gloss to talk. Excluded already, I'm about to find a quiet spot to hide in when Gloss glances at me, rolls her eyes and holds out her hand. Grateful, I scamper over, and she tugs me onto the arm of her own seat.

"This guy!" she exclaims to Liam, but it's affectionate, and she leans her head against me.

"He's sweet!" Liam responds, offering me a screw top bottle of cider. I grab it and hide my embarrassment by downing half the cool, tingly drink.

I relax against the edge of the chair, scanning the room while listening to them talk—Liam telling Gloss about his first year as a photography student, and Gloss describing our small town in acerbic, cutting and accurate terms. She's right on the money, as always.

"Eight churches, eleven pubs, six chip shops and not a single acupuncturist. There's a place called Puke Alley, Liam." She shudders genteelly, giving me a little side smile to show that I'm not included in her dismissive tone. "The pharmacist lectured me when I picked up my birth control. There are Brexit stickers everywhere." A dramatic sigh. "The only good thing that place has produced is Max." I sparkle.

The room is full of pungent smoke, which wreaths bodies into misty apparitions. The lighting's muted with bright, woven scarves tacked over the lampshades. Warm reds and oranges gleam on excited faces. I catch friendly gestures aimed at me from all over the room, people noticing a new face and greeting me. I smile back, nursing my cider, my free hand toying with Gloss's hair.

There are definitely queer people around. I catch a "what's up, friend" nod from a masc-presenting person with a trans flag tattooed on their wrist. I see other queer signifiers—androgynous outfits, makeup meshed with facial hair, telltale signs of binders under shirts. For the first time, maybe ever, I'm not too quiet, too queer or too anxious. A soothing kindness permeates the air like nothing I've ever known. I fit into this space. This space fits into me. I'm safe here. I've never been somewhere that felt so much like everyone cares about each other and wants to make sure everyone is okay and happy.

Gloss turns to me, dabs a pill onto her tongue, arches a cheeky eyebrow in question and then tugs me down to her mouth. I go like I'm melting. We've never kissed before, and it's a warm, slow firework spiralling around and around in my belly. I haven't kissed anyone since Danny—or ever, except for Danny. It's nice, to kiss someone for fun at a party. Not to wonder where it's going and what it means and if she'll love me in the morning. I know she will.

Gloss nips my lip and leaves me with the bitter taste of the pill she pushed into my mouth.

It comes in waves, washing me from head to toe with pleasure, and everything is fantastic. Gloss's mermaid hair on my knuckles is fantastic, seaweed pulling me under. I slip half behind her, lying across the chair so my stomach is her resting place, like the first time. The smooth beads of her spine press against my ribs. She laughs at me and leans back to ruffle my hair. I can't concentrate on what she's saying to Liam anymore, but my body feels so good, so good.

It's my first time taking pills. I didn't even think about saying no. It was the right thing to do. I'm embraced by the connectivity in the room, and I want to dive into it.

A six-foot-something queen in a gold minidress touches my cheek on her way past, fingers dragging over my skin, leaving fireworks in her wake.

There's dancing now, people whirling and winding across the thick, plush carpet. It hums through my socks, brushing the floor. I want bare feet. It takes me so long to try and peel my socks off with my toes—without dislodging Gloss, who squirms plaintively as I wriggle—that some kind soul takes pity on me and pulls them off, balls them up and passes them up to me. I stuff them into my pocket and then chuckle at the bulge I've created. I could compete for Mr. Big Packer. At some point, we move onto the sofa with Liam, and Gloss pushes me into a pillow and settles against me. Her shoulder blade is bruising me but I like it, the hard point of bone jammed into the dent between my ribs. I wish it was a tattoo, a sunburst. I remember Gloss's tattoo, I remember her sister, and reach out for her hand. We weave fingers on her tummy, and Liam covers our hands with his bigger one.

"I wish Millie was here," he tells Gloss. The words drag my attention back to the world with a snap that clacks my jaw together.

Gloss prods him with her bare foot, toenails sparking gold and glitter. "Me too."

I'm frozen midbreath. Millie—Gloss's sister. So Liam knew her. Millie, the shadow in Gloss's eyes.

"She'd hate this party," Liam says, buckteeth pushing at his upper lip. It's endearing. It makes me want to chew on his mouth. A fun side effect of starting testosterone is being attracted to basically everyone all the time. I guess that's general teenage boy life, though. Not only me. There's not really a more inappropriate time to be noticing someone's mouth than during this conversation, but here I am, being gross. Shrinking away, I try to extricate myself from their sharing. I don't deserve to be part of it. Gloss tugs me back, making a headrest of me, and I can do that. I can hold her. Breathing is easier when I hold her.

"Too loud," Gloss agrees. "She and Max could be quiet together."

"Do you remember when she turned the hose on you all?" Liam tips his head back, gazing at the ceiling. He sounds amused, but hollow.

"God, yeah. I was so pissed." Gloss snickers, kneading at his leg like a cat with her feet. His hand is warm over my hand.

"Your face! With your pink top staining that white skirt, oh man."

Liam blows a smoke ring. The joint comes to me and I hold it cupped in one hand, the orange heat throbbing at my palm until I flip it over to take a drag. The urge to press the heat into my skin and let it sizzle fades.

"That was hand-dyed! She could be such a wild bitch," Gloss says, but she makes it sound more like Millie was a hero.

"Yeah." Liam turns his wrist over and rubs a matching semicolon tattoo. "I can't believe it's been a year."

A year. The earth has fully orbited the sun with Millie dead, leaving Gloss alone. Not all alone, no, but by herself in that mausoleum or another, interchangeable one. The way I'm alone is not the same, but perhaps it's what pulls us so close together. This is the realest, deepest relationship I've ever had, no matter how fast it's grown. I know there's something true between us. A need in me that recognises a need in her and vice versa.

"A year. I can." Gloss takes the joint out of my unresisting hand. The glow lights her face from below and makes her eyelashes spark. "It's been forever."

"She's supposed to be here." Liam's voice crumples, and so does his face. Gloss wriggles out of my chest to move to him. They hold each other and cry, and it's private and naked. I can't look at them, so I stare at the bulging socks in my pocket. Hot tears sting my eyes, but I don't know why. Because Liam is crying, maybe? Or because Gloss looks so tender? Words stick in my throat like stones.

I stay on the couch, curled into the side, overaware of their heat and closeness next to me. Gloss presses her foot back, and I take it in my hand, nesting my thumb into the delicate arch.

The crying is brief, and when Gloss pulls back to kiss Liam's face, it's a benediction. He looks up at her like he's a sunflower, lighting up. I'm overtaken by their beautiful love, and I wriggle forward to hold them both. My arms slot around them perfectly, and Liam fists his hand in my shirt, between my shoulder blades, holding me there. This is everything, here in their arms, in their care. This is what living is *for*. The air tastes like salt and heat. Gloss's mouth is on my throat, breathing my skin. We cuddle until the music changes, and Gloss pulls us both up, demanding we dance with her. We spin around her in an orbit I hope never decays.

BEFORE

11

AWARENESS SPOOLS THROUGH me limb by limb. I'm cradled in arms and feather-puffed bedding. There's a hand tucked around my hipbone. My face is against skin that smells like maple syrup. I fade into the room, into my body and the nest of lazy limbs and cool cotton. I blink my eyes open. Expanse of soft, brown, hairy chest. Nipple hardening against my jaw. Liam's tangled black hair in messy peaks, and his sleepy brown eyes, warm and gentle.

"Shhh," he murmurs, scooping us both closer. Gloss pushes my leg over his thigh and climbs half on top of me. Pinned down, I drift back out to sleep.

The next time I wake, it's more permanent. The sun has stolen through the blinds, and I click into wakefulness like changing gears. The side of the bed that used to hold Liam is empty, but Gloss has rolled over and taken me with her.

I try to lie still with her for a while, but I can't. My bladder has demands. My wriggling out of bed makes her grumble, but she stays quiescent. I pause on the carpet for a moment to look at her. Her hair is spread out over the pillows, her porcelain skin lustrous in its contrast to the rich navy sheets.

Liam's room features tapestries, esoteric trinkets and books galore and smells like Nag Champa. Photos are arranged in artsy groupings all over the walls. I didn't see much of it last night; I hardly remember getting to bed. I have vague memories of brushing my teeth on the toilet while Gloss washed her face and Liam waxed poetic in the doorway about an artist I'd never heard of. The photos reel me in. I lean on the wooden bed frame to get a closer look at one of a girl's rain-misted window reflection. I think it's Millie because I can't imagine Gloss has ever looked that insubstantial. The girl in the image has one hand up, covering half her face.

The first door I open in the corridor is a linen cupboard. I stare into it for a moment. There's a cupboard next to my bedroom at my parents' place. Inside, there's a broken Hoover, a pile of Argos catalogues and a lot of spiders. Here, there are clean sheets and towels, and everything's folded. It sets a flare in my gut that Gloss's home never did. Everything she has is so far out of reach for me to be ludicrous, a holiday from real life. But this? Folded clean sheets waiting to be needed. That seems attainable. I find the bathroom on the second try. There's a basket of unopened toothbrushes set in a basket labelled HELP YOURSELF. Tiles chill my feet as I rinse my face and brush my teeth.

People clutter the flat. Three bodies have managed to share a camping mattress, two more are curled up on the sofa, one in the armchair. There's a group sipping steaming mugs by the window. A few bottles and cups are on tables, but there's none of the debris I saw at Grant's. No broken glass or spilled ashtrays, no slowly spreading stains. I find Liam in the kitchen, doing dishes while the radio buzzes a quiet, summery tune. The sun drowns him. He's got silvery aviators on, but I see the crinkles around his eyes when he catches sight of me in my reflection in the narrow window over the sink. Grateful for the warmth in his face that indicates I'm welcome here, I beam.

"Coffee's on the side," he gestures with a cocked hip. The machine is bubbling, and the smell teases me. While it brews, I rustle around the kitchen, gathering empties and sorting them for him to rinse.

"Did you have fun last night?" Liam looks at me over the top of his glasses, boyish grin giving him dimples deep enough to lose a skittle in.

"It was . . . really beautiful." I tried to think of a different word, something that makes me seem less intense, but that's the only one that fits.

"We promised, you know. At Millie's funeral. That we'd get together every year to remember her. All of us. She was ours."

"Who was she to you?" I think I know, but I have to ask, the questions that were lodged behind my tonsils last night still riding with me.

"She was my girlfriend. Since we were twelve. Seven years. Six countries. Until she died."

His whole face is shadowed now. A bruised purple cloud outside the window mirrors the pain in his voice.

"I'm sorry." My heart hurts for him, my thoughts fluttering to what it would be like to lose Gloss. And I've only had her for months. Not years. Not yet. I try to picture a world without her, and it stings so much I have to catch my breath.

He doesn't answer, just sighs and turns the water back on, flushing out the sink. The coffee maker beeps, and I hurry to it, finding clean mugs right next to it with sugar at the ready. So organised. I want to tease him, lighten the room, but I don't know how to walk back from the ghost of Millie hovering in the corners.

The coffee is good, nutty and sweet. I sit on the counter

with my legs dangling, sipping while I watch Liam clean. He's methodical, dishes first and then clearing surfaces of the things I didn't move, section by section. He doesn't seem stressed; in fact, it seems to settle him. He arranges the clean dishes so the blue lines on their edges match up. The glass-fronted cabinet is smudged with fingerprints, and he buffs those off as well. When I finish my coffee, the last sip is cold and bitter.

Voices murmur next door, and Liam sets his shoulders back. "Take Gloss some coffee, would you?" He pulls his sunglasses off, folds the arms and sets them on the table, then slips out of the kitchen into the lounge.

Sleep-rumpled and tousled, Gloss rolls over blinking when I enter the bedroom. I love her in the morning before she puts her polish on. I love that I get to see her creased and pouty, indignant line in between her arching eyebrows.

"Hey, baby," she says when she sees me. The pet name nestles behind my sternum.

"Morning." I want to respond in kind—babe, or gorgeous, or something—but I'm not quick enough on the draw, and then the moment passes.

She squirms upright, pulling the duvet around herself. A queen in ermine, but her eager hands held out for a bowl-sized mug of coffee are all greedy little kid. I slide in beside her and pass the coffee over. She snuggles into my armpit, pushing my body into the shape she wants it. I let her mould me, affectionate grin tugging at the corner of my mouth.

"Stop thinking I'm cute," she grumbles into her caffeine.

"You are cute," I tease, tugging a strand of her hair, remember the whisper of it between my fingers last night when I was spinning and flying.

"No, I'm gorgeous." She's playing at a sulky voice.

"That too," I agree, amiable with her curled up against my chest. I don't know where my binder is, but that's the first I've thought of it all morning. She makes me feel so safe. Apparently, Liam does too. He didn't even glance.

"Glorious," she continues.

"A glorious bitch." Liam is in the doorway, tousled and leonine.

"Exactly!" Gloss pats the bed demandingly with her foot. "I should get that tattooed on my butt."

Liam obediently wanders over, letting her pull him into the space under her knees. Clearly, he also does as he's told. Maybe Millie was like Gloss that way too.

"We should get tattoos today." Liam sprawls one long leg down the bed, the other tucked under Gloss. I'm jealous of his strong brown legs. His knee presses against my thigh. Gloss rubs her thumb over her wrist again, and Liam catches her hand and holds it. "New ones. We survived the year."

"Okay." It's me that said it, surprisingly, but it's right. "I didn't know Millie, but I survived too. I'm still here."

I didn't survive the way they did, but I'm fighting my own war.

Gloss leans up to kiss my cheekbone, "And I'm keeping you here, beautiful boy."

Liam leans over and kisses me on the cheek as well. I wonder if he was always so gentle. If he had never known her, never lost her, would he be so sweet?

LIAM FLINCHES—A TIGHTENING around his sparkling brown eyes—as the needle touches against the back of his arm. He chose a flower, a tulip, bright orange and red with a green stem.

His piece takes a few hours, and I volunteer to go next. The closest I've ever been to a tattoo is poking myself with a compass and rubbing fineliner into it during boring classes, so I don't really know what to expect, sensation-wise. Judging on Liam's response, it hurts at least a bit.

The artist shaves the inside of my wrist—unnecessary even after eight months on hormones—wipes me down and lays a stencil of the image I chose. The bright blue lines look good against my creamy skin. The butterfly is perfectly positioned in the centre, about an inch down from my palm. Pleasure floods me. The ink isn't even in me yet, but the sense of ownership spilling through me, the act of making my body look how I choose—I can tell this is far from the only tattoo I'll end up with.

"Ready?" She's businesslike, looks at me with professional eyes until I nod and exhale.

"Ready."

The leather padding wrapped in cling film is hot under my forearm as she starts the machine running. She lowers it to my skin, and I promise myself I won't flinch away. The needle touches, drags; it's like the scab of road rash pulling against fabric but sharper. She steadily fills in the stencil, her hand barely moving, eyes focused to the point of not even seeing me. I'm canvas. I'll take the buzzing pain with me when I leave, the echo in my bone marrow to stay.

I love it.

Gloss lays her hand on my knee, hot over a rip in my jeans.

It's over pretty quickly, a mere hour and a half of the buzzing sting before thick black lines are ensconced in my skin forever. She puts a dressing over it. Entranced, I run my fingers over the covered skin. I only listen with half an ear to her care instructions, too in love with the mark I've chosen for myself.

Gloss pouts and hisses her way through her tattoo—a teeny, tiny, delicate heart, not stylised but anatomical in miniature, snug behind her ear. With her hair down, it's invisible, a secret.

When we tumble out of the tattoo parlour, Gloss having paid for everyone's ink, we're arm in arm and giggling. The delicious, faint throb of my wrist reminds me what I did. My dad's going to be shocked, but he has enough tattoos of his own that he can't really disapprove.

The day floats by, on ciders and sausages with mashed potato, shared puddings and terrible games of pool, in which I am by far the worst. Everything is golden and magical and I never want to leave. I want Gloss and I to stay with Liam forever. When Liam drops us off at the railway station, he crushes me to his chest. His whispered words urging me to look after Gloss—"Be careful with her, bro, she can take things too far."—spiral through my veins all the way back to Ridgepoint. Of course I'll be careful with her. She's my best friend.

I have to go home because my dad's off duty, so I prepare to say goodbye. As we get closer to Gloss's condo, my body starts to sensitise. Is she going to kiss me again? Am I going to kiss her? There's a sadness in her eyes when we pause at her door. I waver for a moment, torn—if she needs me, I should stay. The world tilts under my feet at the idea I could be needed.

I step towards her. She tilts her chin up, and I dip to press my mouth to hers. Her palm is hot on my neck, fingers curling as if to anchor herself. They're gentle and slide away as our lips part. It was a friendly kiss, but it still makes me grin like a doof as I stumble down the corridor to the stairs. I don't hear her door close, but when I glance back, the hallway's empty.

AFTER

10

DANNY'S ROOM ISN'T like I imagined. I assumed it'd be full of him. Surfing posters and clothes all over the floor. Instead, although it's small—smaller than my old room by a lot, like maybe the space was intended to be a large cupboard—it's neat and tidy. He wasn't really a neat and tidy guy, but here, everything is out of sight. There's one poster on the wall. It's a motorcycle pinup girl, and a painful laugh catches in my throat. The only part of the room that's Danny is the smell.

I have to sit down. The bed catches me, and the thin mattress compresses under my butt with a plasticky crinkle. With my head between my knees, I do some more deep breathing until I'm back in the room.

Kenny splays a ham fist on the doorframe. "Just checkin' you didn't help yourself to his computer or somethin' like that."

It's clearly a warning, and it's unnecessary. I've seen Danny's laptop. No one would want to help themselves to it. "Of course not, I'd never do that. I was thinking about taking his naked lady poster." It's a completely wild statement, born from the fact that there's nothing else personal in the room and my brain is full of bees. "Uh, is it okay if I stay for a minute?"

"What, are you a homo like him? You his little boyfriend?" He sneers at me.

I am a towering mountain of rage dressed as a boy. Oh, Danny. I'm so sorry.

Apparently, being frozen in anger is enough of a denial to appease him. "You've got until halftime." He stomps back down the stairs.

Well. If I don't take the poster now, he'll be suspicious. And it should cement my disguise as a Very Normal Cis Het Boy as opposed to illicit trans boyfriend. But first, I run my fingers through his shirt drawer. I take his Sunset Boulevard sleeveless T-shirt, knotting my fingers around it like it'll keep me in the world, like I did when he first kissed me.

BEFORE

12

"SO EVERYTHING'S GOING okay . . . at school?"

My dad pushes his mashed potatoes around his plate to hide the fact he's not eating. They're gluey and lumpy. I force the paste down anyway, trying to cheer him up. He always overboils them. Mum is busy slopping vodka on the counter. Her feet are bare on the worn linoleum of the kitchen floor. They look like mine.

"Everything's good!" Too bright, too upbeat. I've never sounded that happy in my life, and the hollow note is unmistakable, even though I'm telling the truth. I might tell him about London, but not in front of my mum. She'd find a way to shit all over it.

"Living with your friend . . ." He trails off, glancing at mum with wary eyes.

I plunge in, not waiting for the question. "Part-time. And it's great. We have lots of time to revise, and her house is really quiet so I can concentrate."

Mum's movements are jerky as she comes back to the table. "We're not good enough for you anymore, is that right?"

Anger rushes me, swift and hot, muting me. When I'm furious, the words swirl around in my head and bounce off my skull instead of making it into the world. *You were never good enough for me. You never even tried to be good at all, let alone enough. Gloss is the only person who's ever made me feel like enough.* Then my traitor brain reminds me that for one glorious summer, I was enough for a boy with sun-kissed hair and salt-sea eyes.

Mum stares at me, challenge in her eyes, until I look away. There's no point in fighting with her, even if I could make myself say the things I want to say. She'll have forgotten this whole conversation by the morning. I'll reenact it in my head for weeks. I lose either way, so I may as well not try.

"Leave him alone, Moira."

My dad chimes in too late; there's too much pressure in the air. The moment teeters and totters—will she sigh and down her drink, or will she explode?

In a few seconds, I find out.

"Why are you always on her side! Why do you never stand up for *me*?"

Mum shoves back from the table, chair legs screeching. She's half out of her seat when dad replies, "Because you're the one being a raging bitch," in a low, dull voice.

Still, I don't expect what happens next. Mum picks up her glass and hurls it against the wall. The crash makes me jump, and I almost fall out of my chair in shock. Looking at the shards, I think of Liam, carefully tidying his beautiful glassware away. Dad stays hunched over in miserable silence. I slide out of my seat, trudge up the stairs, grab my bag, guitar and keys and am out the door before the tears start to fall.

I DRIVE RECKLESSLY, but it's not far. My body is pent-up and aggressive. My limbs belong to someone else, jerking the gearstick until it crunches, slamming the brakes. I've never seen my dad so defeated and flat. I park at an awkward angle, away from the kerb, but I'm too shaken up to redo it. All the way up the stairs, I pick at the edges of the bandage covering the tattoo on my wrist. It's less than eight hours old, but it belongs like I've had it forever. I dig my thumb into the tender skin, the pain crystallising into a solid and pure sting that lets me breathe again.

All I want is to collapse into the downy bed and have Gloss wrap herself around me, warm and loved and safe.

But when I knock on the door, there's no answer. The key she gave me digs into my palm—I'm still not completely comfortable coming and going without Gloss knowing, and I didn't have the wit to message her. I rap again in case she's listening to music or something, but no footsteps click towards me on the other side of the door. I dither for a minute, then let myself in. I catch a glimpse of myself in the hall mirror as I toe my shoes off, waiting for Gloss to burst out of one of the doors and see my face. I'm wan and worn, with a stripped ache in my eyes I can barely look at. I leave a palm print smudge on the silver glass when I drag my hand over it as though I can wipe it all away.

I don't even know why I'm so sad. It's not as though my mum hasn't been half in a bottle for most of my life. I wonder what it's been like between them while I've been away at Gloss's.

Gloss isn't in her bedroom or the bathroom. I check the other rooms in the house, calling her name at first before giving up and pushing open doors without expectation. It's even vaster, a mausoleum, without Gloss's wild energy cracking through the place.

Thumbing out a text, I shuck my clothes and climb into the cosy pyjamas that showed up on top of my clothes in the cleaned-out dresser two days after I moved in.

I'm at urs. Mum kicked off

Twenty minutes later, she still hasn't responded, no matter how many times I check my phone. A tingle of worry wriggles down my spine. Gloss parties hard, and no one else around here will have her back. There could be squaddies out from the local army base, definitely the general pond scum that stumble between pubs every evening in towns with nothing else to do besides drink. Where is she? She's probably out getting dinner or a drink, I tell myself firmly.

Three shows about home renovation—less fun without Gloss along to heckle the terrible decor decisions—and a joint later, the urge to call her wins a wrestling match with my pride. The phone rings. And rings. And rings. Images of Gloss crushed at a zebra crossing or assaulted on the street assail me. I force myself out of bed. It's okay, it's okay. Nothing has happened, she's just out, she's just not here. But I need her here.

I don't cry into the pillows, but I do curl up on the side of the bed that smells like her and inhale deeply, in for four and out for eight, with my mouth pursed into a little straw, like I read somewhere that the samurai do, back when I was obsessed with all things noble and pure, before I realised the world was a garbage fire full of idiots afraid of anything they don't understand and furious with anything they're afraid of.

It's gone midnight, sleep evading me like a particularly talented thief, when I think to check her social media. Gloss uses Instagram like a celebrity, endorsing brands and products, posting perfect, stylised shoots and only the most beautiful selfies—not that I've ever seen her take a bad picture, wasted or not. She's always receiving little boxes in the post of makeup and nail polish and jewellery.

Her latest update was three hours ago. In it, she's laughing, head tossed back against a phenomenal sunset, balanced on the rail we left ice cream fingerprints on yesterday. The park by Danny's house. In the corner of the image, behind the rails, there's the blur of other people's faces. I see the sparkle of a lighter, a flick of blond hair and ocean eyes.

It takes a moment for him to come into focus because it doesn't make sense for him to be there. His mouth is wide open, laughing as much as Gloss in the picture.

I'm instantly nauseous. The dislocation of Gloss, there, with him instead of here with me boils acidic in my stomach. Half of me wants to storm down there and demand an explanation. Gloss not answering her phone takes on new light. He apologised! He said sorry, but he didn't mean it, he only wanted to get close to her. It was all a lie.

My heartbeat thuds through my head, an angry rhythm inciting me to grab my board and head down there. But I can imagine it all too well: the disdainful curve of Gloss's lip as she asks me why I think I can dictate where she goes, Danny's smirk as he wins another person away from me. I don't want to believe it—here in Gloss's bed with her scent thick in my lungs—but my brain is convinced.

Everybody leaves. Everybody chooses someone or something else over me. Either booze, or a job, or Danny tells them no, like he did with Michelle. No one has ever chosen me. Nobody loves me.

Eventually, I fade into a grudging, uneasy sleep. Nightmares claw at me, and I jerk awake over and over, hoping this time Gloss will be there to explain why she was with him, and why she was on Insta but not answering my texts. I check my phone for the fourth or fifth time, and I have twelve notifications. Four missed calls, all from Gloss. The rest are text messages. The first few are nonsense, garbled words I can't make sense of. The last two stop my heart in my chest. Fifteen minutes ago.

Max it's Danny. I found Gloss's phone but idk where she is. She was pretty wasted man.

Someone said she went to Mike's I'm omw!

BEFORE

13

DANNY PICKS UP on the first ring, and his voice is rough and fuzzy with drink. "I'm not there yet."

"I'll pick you up, where are you?" I slam the car door behind me, wedging my phone against my shoulder and starting the engine. I was supposed to take care of her, but I wasn't there when she needed me. If only I'd answered the phone. It doesn't even cross my mind that I'm inviting Danny into my car, where I will also be, until he answers.

"By the bridge."

I hang up without replying because I can't get my throat unstuck. It's a forty-minute walk from the park to Mike's, but Danny's over halfway there. He must have been running. What's he afraid of? He knows Mike better than I do. Nausea twists in my belly, and I swallow hard, peering through the fogged-up window, the streetlights halo my vision until it's hard to see the road. Trusting headlights will warn me of any incoming cars, even on these twisty country roads, I speed up. There's no thinking about Danny and me now, not if Gloss is in trouble.

Danny's well past the bridge when I get to him. I pull over into the bus lane, and he turns with his hand thrown up over his eyes, shielding himself from the glare. After a squinting second, he yanks the car door open and slides in. Since I started hanging out with Gloss, I've been keeping it a lot nicer in here, and I see it in his eyes as he scans the dash. Coffee cups and scraps of lyrics scribbled down in the parking lot before school no longer clog the footwell. I'm embarrassed, suddenly, like he's seen me naked, and it's marginally better than the fear that's been swirling in my belly since I saw his messages. I'm scared because he's scared. But I'm also incredibly aware of his physical closeness, how his splayed open legs leave his knee inches away from my knuckles on the gearstick. How he smells like sweat and beer and it's delicious. All my insides and my emotions are in a jumble, a mess of jangling nerves. I can't make sense of any of my thoughts, and I'm worried about having a panic attack, so I focus everything I have on driving perfectly.

We don't talk except for Danny giving me directions. Mike's house is out of town enough that there's no lights, looming trees shielding the narrow road. The turnoff happens so swiftly I almost miss it, but Danny grabs my elbow and points. I wheel the car over, gravel crunching like sugar crystals under my tires. The house has a porch light that jumps on when we get out of the car and illuminates neat hedgerows and a garage. Fancy.

It's Monday, in that odd time between late and early, and the windows are dark and unwelcoming. Danny knocks when I hesitate. If Gloss isn't here, I don't know where we would look next. If Mike's parents answer the door, what will we say? But Danny's confident and determined, like it's his responsibility to take care of this. I wonder if it is. Did he get Gloss wasted?

Mike pulls the door open on the third knock. His cautious

expression fades to confusion when he registers who's standing outside his door. "Dude, what're you doing here?" He yawns at the end of the question, not bothering to cover his mouth. He's shirtless, and his boxers are slung low enough to be indecent. He has a nice, sturdy body, notes the part of me that's an incessant pervert.

"Where's Gloss?" I demand, my words thick and hot with emotion.

Mike looks at me like he didn't even realise I was there. His short, curly red hair is flattened on one side by a recent pillow. He shifts his weight, like he's considering shutting the door in our faces. "She's sleeping. She lost her keys."

"And phone," Danny says, leaning a hand against the frame. His hand is strong and broad pink scar on the back of the knuckles from a nasty stack when I was teaching him to kickflip.

Mike narrows his eyes, and there's something in his face that sends a cold finger across the back of my neck. I push past Danny and duck under Mike's arm before he has a chance to stop me. I don't know where I'm going, but there's only one light on inside, and I follow it up the stairs and into a room that must be Mike's. He's right behind me, hissing urgent words about his mum and dad and how late it is, but Danny's right behind him, and Mike doesn't try to grab me.

Gloss is curled up in the bed, facing away from the door. Her dress—I recognise it from the picture—is in a heap on the black floorboards, and her shoulders tell me she's not wearing a bra or a shirt. Furious, I whirl around, ready to rip Mike's face off for the implication of what happened here, but he doesn't look guilty, just annoyed.

"Oh, I see. Jesus. Really? Rude, man. Go check the sofa where I've been curled in a ball 'cause she took my bed."

Reality readjusts. She's not hooking up with him, but she's here in his bed instead of home with me.

"You really think anyone could make her do something she didn't want them to? I couldn't even make her wear a fuckin' shirt, so she's getting her titties all over my Man U sheets. She's fine."

He shoulders past me into the room and brushes his fingers gently across Gloss's shoulder blade. "Hey, your white knight is here, and he's clearly not going to leave until you tell him to."

Gloss wriggles over. The sheet falls away and she is shirt-less, shirtless and achingly beautiful. Mike pulls the covers up and pins them there with one hand, covering her. He raises an eyebrow at me like, "See?" Gloss blinks, slow and heavy with sleep. There's eyeliner smudged on her face, and she's got her earrings in, even though she hates that. Behind me, Danny moves closer, his body heat radiating through my shirt. I want to collapse back into it.

"'M fine. I can take care of myself. For fuck's sake, Max, you're not my boyfriend." Gloss's voice topples me, but Danny arrests my stumble.

She's groggy and grouchy but sounds normal, not like she's been drugged and assaulted. The fear of that falls away and leaves me rejected and alone.

I leave her there, in his bed. Better Mike than Danny, anyway.

Danny stumbles after me out into the night. I start the car with a shaky hand, and he climbs in just in time to avoid me leaving him there.

I WANT TO be angry. Hot flames of rage would be better than the icy coldness, the rock in my stomach. But no matter how I prod myself—she left you; she doesn't want you; she didn't even check to see if you were okay, back at home with your folks—the fire sputters out before it catches.

Next to me, Danny keeps opening his mouth like he's going to say something. I'm braced for whatever cruelty he pulls out. Probably he'll point out how no one wants me. I don't know why he bothered to call. The rolling lights turn him ash and orange in turns, speeding over his face as fast as my heart bounces between anger and sorrow so thick I can taste the tears in the back of my throat.

Finally, he runs his hands through his hair and asks, "Want to go to the beach?"

It catches me off guard, and the shock is enough to pull me out of the slide of see-nobody-wants-you-no-one-will-ever-want-you churning my belly. "Sure."

We sit in silence until I pull onto the motorway, and then Danny clicks the radio on. He huffs disapproval at the blast of rock and roll and changes the station to something mellower. Despite myself, my lips twitch as I sneak a finger out to change the station back. We used to do this a lot. Drive out to the beach for a bit of privacy, a space where no one could see us, and wouldn't know us even if they did. Sometimes Danny would bring his board—strapped to the roof with a range of unsafe, non–roof rack solutions—and I'd sit on the shore and watch him fly in.

Danny lets me win the radio war. My hands start to tap the steering wheel along with the beat, and out of the corner of my eye I see him smiling too.

I park in my usual spot. Barely a lay-by on the side of the gravel track to the main parking lot for the larger beach.

"Do you have your tent?"

"Yeah, always." I jerk my head at the boot of the car. Being a firefighter, my dad has a bit of a passion for emergency preparedness. I have a bulging emergency car kit, packed with blankets, water, food, a tent and a variety of other useful bits and pieces neatly organised in the boot. You know, in case the apocalypse busts out while I happen to be in my car. Came in handy for the nights when I can't bear it at home. Before I had Gloss and somewhere else to go.

Danny digs around in the map pocket of his passenger seat. Confused, I raise an eyebrow in question. After a moment, he pulls his hand out with a dramatic "Score!" and waves what he's found at me. Ziplock baggie with weed and some rolling papers. "I see you didn't completely clean your car out, or you'd have found my stash!"

"When did you even put that there?" I ask, laughing.

"Uh, I think I left it in here the weekend Michelle made us watch that horrendous romance trilogy." He waggles his eyebrows unabashedly. I remember that weekend well. Michelle and Danny "on a date" in her room, covering for us to hang out because the weather was brutal, a high summer storm. Danny and I pressed together under her duvet, holding hands where she couldn't see even though she knew about us. Sheltering that tiny illusion of privacy, savouring the brush of his thumb against the back of my hand, and the tingles it would send through me.

"And you didn't offer me any?" I gasp, mock offended, stepping back into our easy banter without meaning to.

"Are you kidding? I didn't know how many films there were. What if I'd run out and had to suffer through sober?"

Danny pops the car door and jumps out, stretching his long body out and reaching for the stars. The sliver of flesh between his jumper and his dark jeans glints at me, moon pale.

"Mmm, I see your point, but I still feel betrayed. You're sharing tonight."

"Well, yeah, or you'd be able to drive home, and we wouldn't get to camp." He winks at me.

I head around to open the boot with the key. Danny, on autopilot, grabs the tent, the emergency kit and the blanket.

I snag the folding chair—remembering my plans to find an extra for Danny with a lurch in my stomach—the food and water and my beanie. It's chilly enough that we'll have to share the sleeping bag if we want to sleep. It was Danny who asked about the tent. What is he expecting?

I refuse to investigate that line of thought any further because that would only lead to asking him if he's changed his mind about hating me. If this is leading to something more than friends. It'll hurt too much when the answer's no. I balance my load and lock the car.

We pick our way down the uneven, rocks-and-sand "cliff" until we reach the cove. With the familiarity of practice, we fall into our jobs. I set up the tent while Danny makes a fire. When we first started coming out here, he had no real idea how. He would light a bit of paper and confusedly watch it burn out without lighting any of the wood he'd stacked around it. Now, he's humming to himself as he lays a fire starter from the emergency kit against some of the wood from the back of the cove. It seems no one else has been by since Danny and I frequented this place. I remember that humpback-shaped log. It took both of us to pull it in. This whole place is thick with good memories. It's easy to pretend things are fine between us, even if they're not the way they used to be.

Tent pitched, I blow up the slim thermotech mat, cover it with a silver survival blanket and throw my sleeping bag, unzipped and messy, over top. I back out of the tent feetfirst— it's a one-man, and when Danny and I are inside it together, we spoon or lay one on top of the other. Danny's sitting on a rock next to the camp chair, joint in hand, waiting for me to join him. He's placed a pot of seawater next to the fire to heat. I drop the boil-in-a-bag meals in and then sit down.

My phone buzzes and buzzes again. I pull it out to turn it off, but the WhatsApp notification catches my eye.

Urgh seriously this town needs
to get on a ridesharing service

Really, Gloss? It's a let's-pretend-none-of-this-ever-happened message.

"Is that her?" Danny is staring into the fire. I switch my phone to silent and shove it back into my pocket.

"Not really any of your business." I sound firm, but reasonable. Fair.

He respects the boundary, and something between us shifts again. For a while, we pass the joint back and forth, watching the water heat, bubble and finally start to roll. The weed settles me, loosening my chest up, making me quiet and still. Not empty like only a few hours before, staring at Gloss in Mike's bed. The heat from Danny's leg increases, more and more as if he's leaning closer.

If he knocks his knee against mine like we're two bros chilling, I'll scream. He starts to close the final gap, and suddenly, I can't bear it and leap up, a stupid, startled animal. "The food!" I shout. The words hang, thick and fat over the sound of waves breaking.

"Yeah, I'm starving." Danny sits back so there's more space between the chair and him. I wonder if he's letting me take the out. Does he feel the same as I do? A mess of wanting and impossibility? What could it be like to be straight, to be so sure you're straight and yet be into me? How does my existence make him question his own understanding of himself and the world? I wonder what he's thinking, what he wants, what he's ever wanted. I fish the bags out with shaking hands, dumping them on the sand to cool.

The brief respite lets me get my head back together, and by the time we're digging into our food, I'm recovered enough so I can open my mouth without saying something tragic or absurd. But my earlier questions resurge with a vengeance.

"Why did you want to come here?" I don't look at him, intent on excavating chunks of probably-meat from sticky brown sauce.

He stills, his mouth full of food. I shouldn't find it cute, but I do. I love the boyish enthusiasm he has when he's genuine.

I push the affection away, reminding myself what he did. How he hurt me when he should have held me and told me that he loved me and was grateful for my trust and truth. Seven months of cruelty and silence. Seven months of hating me for not coming out before he kissed me the first time. As if I knew that was what the way he looked at me meant. As if I knew anything except how good it felt to be near him and how awful it was to be thrown away. Anger turns into thorned words, lashing at him. "Did you think we'd come here and fuck? What, do you think I'll be a girl for you? That I'd be your dirty little secret?" My eyes are stinging, and there's a treacherous burn in the bridge of my nose. Am I going to cry in front of him? I've never hated myself more. I juggle the packet of food so I can scrabble around in the sand for the whisky. The sear of the liquor explains the tears.

"No, of course not." He sounds hurt, startled. He takes a huge breath and puffs it out. I force another swallow of whisky down. "That's not . . . Max. I never meant . . . I know you're not a girl . . ." He trails off, helpless.

"And you keep hurting me." The thickness of tears tightens my throat. He knows I'm a boy, does he? Finally, he knows.

"If I could take it back, I would. I'd take it all back." He sounds like he might be crying too, but that can't be right. Danny doesn't cry. I'm the weeper in this nothingship. "Except if I took it all back, I'd never have known you at all."

I lapse into silence, unable to sort through words to make

them come out in the right way. He could have known me without hurting me.

"I thought . . . I thought if I pushed you away enough, you'd stop looking at me like I was special." His voice trembles, each word spaced out and separate, careful. "The way you'd look at me, God. I couldn't . . . I couldn't bear it."

I'm angry, again, flushed with it. I burst out of my chair, scattering food and the whisky bottle—closed, thankfully, 'cause I'm going to need that later—onto the sand. Jittery energy burns in my stomach, and I pace around the fire, digging my frustration into the sand with my stomping feet. "Everyone looks at you like you're special."

"People look at me to see what they can get from me. You looked at me like . . ." He trails off again, and I can't stop myself from looking at him. He's got his head thrown back, both hands dug and clenched into cold sand. "You looked at me like I was special to *you*. Like I was precious. You looked at me like you loved me."

"I did."

He looks at me with wide, raw eyes.

"I do." The words bubble out. I knew that I loved him, of course I did, but saying it out loud strips me of my last defences. My insides do an odd contortion that settles into want, pure and simple want. I still want him. I wish I didn't.

"Yeah." He laughs the coldest, saddest laugh I've ever heard. "Me too. You, I mean. I loved you. Love you. If I didn't love you, it wouldn't hurt so much."

I sit down too close to the fire, and it hisses and licks at my knees until I have to shift backwards. We look at each other, look and look. He's a study in precious metals, limned in silver, gilded by gold. There's an aching sadness in his eyes. I wonder what I look like to him, dark-eyed and pale as death.

And all the time we sit and look, I want him. I want to know what we could be like.

The fire dies down to embers. I struggle to my feet, legs cold and stiff from sitting too long on the cold ground. Danny watches me, his face miserable. I hold out my hand to him and he unfurls—so graceful I want to hate him again—and strides to me without a moment's hesitation. Our fingers lace together. His hands are a little bigger than mine, but we've always fit together so well. The magnet that pulled us into our first kiss, and every other kiss afterward, is pulsing between us again. I don't know how I can still want him, after all this, but I do. I want to hold him and drown in the divot of his collarbones. I want to have him go pliant and malleable for me, letting my hands guide him, undress him.

Wordless, I lead him to the tent.

We used to be rushed and desperate. Fumbling with each other's clothes. Danny always, always let me decide what was staying on and what was coming off. A perfect gentleman. Even though he didn't know why, he knew I was uncomfortable with my body. He'd follow my lead, wherever I took him. He'd look down at me with wonder in his eyes, move under me like he couldn't believe I wanted to touch him like that. His hands would tug my hair so gently I couldn't stand it, would make him tug harder. I'd make him dig his hands into my shoulders. With encouragement, he'd leave bruises I'd press my fingers into the next day.

This time, it's different.

It's different because I have a dick in my boxers and a binder tight around the chest I'd never let him touch. It's different because we love-hate each other. I crawl into the tent ahead of him, pull him on top of me.

He settles against me, his eyes wide and lip trembling. We kiss like we're learning how. Studying each other all over again.

But it's gentle and slow and sweet and everything I never dared to hope my first time could be. I guide his hand down my body and press it against the hardness between my legs because I won't have him pretending I'm someone I'm not. A dick doesn't make a man, but it can help, upon occasion. He shudders and lets out a soft, animal moan, then muffles his mouth with my neck. There'll be a bruise there in the morning. I wonder, for a fleeting instant, if I'll be pleased to see it.

There's no space. It's crowded and cramped, and our elbows bang material and each other. Danny's jeans end up kicked out the door in a fit of giggles and leg-flailing teamwork. I keep my binder on but let him touch me, let him trace his fingers over my collarbones and stomach. Let him kiss his way down my hipbones. He asks me, with his voice, with his face, with his body, "Is this okay? Can I? Let me?" and I say yes, yes, yes. I want him, and I take him, and he wants me, and he takes me, and after, the tightness between us has transmuted into something softer. Like we've said our goodbyes to this impossible thing.

But when I wake up in the morning, I'm alone.

AFTER

11

ONCE I'M SURE Kenny's gone, I hop onto the bed with my shoes still on—sorry, Danny—and grab the nudey poster by the top corners.

As I pull down, something drops from behind the paper and bounces off my shoe.

A dirty envelope. The outside is blank, but the flap is tucked inside.

I grab it off the mattress, curved under the pressure of my feet. The paper is crumpled, creased where it's been handled a lot. My whole body is poised for the sound of Kenny coming back up. I have definitely outstayed my welcome, and whatever it is Danny had hidden, he can't have wanted Kenny to know about it.

The envelope doesn't show when it's slipped inside my pocket. I roll the poster up on my way down the stairs, walking out the front door without saying another word.

I wanted to find Danny in there, but there's more of him in the wind on my face than in that cold house. I roll down the street on my board, hyperaware of the paper sticking from my pocket, poster under my arm.

Going back to Grant's would be the right choice. He's there, and Mike and Michelle too, waiting for me to get back. They could be with me when I opened the envelope. There's probably nothing inside. Or something stupid, like a receipt. Maybe Grant would recognise whatever it is and bring meaning to it. But I'm a loner by nature, and I've been around people nonstop since I was arrested. Phantom handcuffs squeeze my wrists, and I make fists and box the wind to shake them off. The whirring of wheels soothes me, and I press back on my right foot, lifting the rear of my board and creasing a sharp turn, hitting the hill that heads down to the school.

The speed bumps are fun to cruise over. They're so wide and smooth it doesn't take much adjustment. I breeze past the entrance to the school, where Grant once took me off my board with his car. The person who got into Grant's car doesn't exist anymore, although getting in was one of the first brave things I did. It's amazing how brave becoming yourself can make you if you can find the strength to start.

I grind to a halt at the riverbank. The water is muddy brown with the clay from the wide banks, and a single seal bobs in one of the eddies behind the bridge support. The air smells of salt and mud, but when I hold the envelope to my face and inhale, Danny's all over it. I imagine his wide, strong hands worrying at the packet. My belly clenches at the stray thought it might be connected to his violent death. It's too thin to be a wodge of bank notes, but it could easily be money. If it is, I'll ask Grant what to do with it.

I can pretend I haven't looked yet if it's something I wish I hadn't seen.

My justifications are weak, but I'm selfish and sad, and the possibility of a piece of Danny, hidden away, for me to find, is too attractive. The paper wrinkles under my eager fingers, and

I force myself to slow down, untuck the triangle and fold it back with care.

There are two things inside.

A strip of photos from a photobooth, and a single sheet of folded notepaper.

BEFORE

14

IT'S UNINTENTIONAL THIS time, but I fall back asleep when I realise Danny left me there. Sleep is great for avoiding things. I don't wake up until lunch—I've missed maths, which is great because the idea of seeing him makes my whole body hurt, but I've missed music too.

I get away with promising to stay after school so Mr. Murti can check in on my album progress. I've recorded two tracks now. I spend the day turning and walking in the other direction whenever I catch a glimpse of Gloss, which I know is stupid and unfair. She's allowed to spend the night wherever she likes, of course. But I can't walk up to her with the image of her saying "you're not my boyfriend" playing on repeat in my head.

She didn't think for a second about leaving with me that night. She didn't even look happy to see me. What if in the morning she decided she wanted something else from him when he was such a gentleman? Did she kiss him to thank him? What if she's with him? What if they're holding hands and giggling, and she doesn't have time for me anymore? The fear that she's going to ditch me for someone less needy seems unfounded based on the messages she's sending. None of them address me galloping across town to save her only to be sent away with a cruel edge she's never really turned on me before.

But her phone—battery dead now—is an uncomfortable weight in my pocket. I need to give it back. I need to speak to her. I need to decide if I'm going to hers or to my parent's place, or the beach tonight. My stomach churns miserably.

"Hey, Max." Grant's voice—recognisable immediately even though I'm distracted—breaks through my cyclical thoughts.

"Hey." I nod at him, relaxing a little despite myself.

He falls into step with me. "How's it going?"

I almost laugh in response. At the idea of trying to explain my useless, tangled emotions. Oh, fine, really . . . Dashed across town like an idiot, got dumped by someone I wasn't even dating and then fucked your best friend and woke up alone. How about you, dude?

Can't say any of that, so I dig Gloss's phone out of my pocket and proffer it to Grant. He takes it, confused.

"Can you give that back to Gloss?"

"Hey, Gloss, I have your phone," Grant declares, and his smirk is all aimed over my shoulder. I flinch before Gloss slides her hand into my hair and tugs gently. I lean back and meet her eyes. Grant fumbles Gloss's phone and hands it over. She takes it with her free hand, the other still tangled in my hair. I don't pull away.

"Thanks." She dismisses Grant, moving between us in a practised motion that leaves him on the outside. He raises an eyebrow at me over her shoulder, but I shrug, and he peels off down the stairs to the gym.

The air is full of crackling pressure, but I can't tell if it's coming from her or from me. I press my fingers into the healing tattoo on my wrist, making the scabs crackle. Gloss takes my hand, pulls it free and threads our fingers.

"Don't pick at it."

She's going to carry on pretending that nothing happened, that I didn't show up in the middle of the night looking for her and then sprint into the darkness like an alien who doesn't know how to human good. I could be grateful. I could slink back into the safety of being hers, but I want more than to be her pampered lapdog. I want to be better than that. Have some self-respect, maybe?

"Don't tell me what to do." I want to sound determined and confident, but it comes out close to whiny.

Gloss looks at me for a long second, her pale jade eyes sparkling in the white stripes of sunshine painting the room. She's wearing a mask made of sunlight, and she doesn't even squint. "It'll scar."

"It already has." And I'm not talking about the tattoo anymore. I'm talking about the hole in our relationship, whatever it is, that ripped open when she looked at me with contempt in her eyes last night.

About half of me can't believe I'm taking the risk of alienating my one friend, the person who brought me into classroom society and into myself. Even after everything that's happened in the last two months—crying at the party, being kissed by Danny in front of everyone, and turning up at Mike's—school is different, friendlier than it was before. Fewer sharks, or maybe they never had as many teeth as I believed they did.

The other half of me wants to be someone's first choice for fucking once.

"Are you coming home after school?"

Home, she says, like that word means nothing, has no weight. Like I belong with her.

The words that want to come out are an accusation. *You weren't there*, I want to spit at her. She should have been there when I needed her, but instead, she was off getting trashed, and then she was pissed off at me for being worried. But I wasn't there for her either when she was texting me. So maybe we're both shit friends. I shake my head, a jerky, angry motion, and shoulder past her.

"Max," she calls after me, her voice high and thready, like she can't believe I'm walking away from her. *How dare you?* spins in the world around my ears, as clear as if she'd shouted it.

I duck into the men's washroom, where I hope she won't follow. It used to thrill me to come in here, but now all I see is cracked tiles and smudged mirrors, graffiti marring every surface. Soap drips on the floor, pink and gooey. I splash some water on my face, which is blotched and peaky. I'm pale from lack of sleep and inner turmoil. Was I always such a mess? Or is this a new thing? I'm angry and my body is violent. I want to throw my skateboard down on the concrete and catapult myself into making kinetic energy. But I have to go to English, and I've missed enough school. Gloss has encouraged me to miss enough school. I remember Liam's flat, those clean linens in the cupboard. If my grades plunge, the only future I could look forward to is a shitty job in a shop or cafe after graduation, making some extra scratch busking like I already do. If I want more than that, I'm going to have to work for it. Which was my plan before summer.

And Danny.

And Gloss.

I'm late for English, but I give an earnest speech to Mr. Beamish about how sorry I am and work my arse off for the rest of the block, contributing to every discussion—even though I absolutely hate speaking in public—and making copious notes. I need to go back to the original plan, keep my head down and get out of here in one piece.

Everything else can wait.

BEFORE

15

IT'S A SOLID plan. It should work. Except it turns out that without Gloss, school is dull and grey. I'm glazed over, bored of everything, and desperate for a bit of excitement to break up the monotony of classes and homework and my drunk mother. When dad's back on shift, I walk on eggshells—landmines, even—at home, and at school, I try my best to stay out of Gloss's way. She's letting me, I have no doubt about that. Danny barely comes to school, and when he does, he avoids looking in my direction. Ms. H kicks him out of maths, and after that, I spend the days pretending I'm not trying to catch glimpses of him in the halls.

My head is full, everything inside jumbled. I'm angry, like Gloss cheated on me—which she hasn't—and I'm sad, like she's abandoned me—which she hasn't. I'm jealous, and I'm worried she didn't tell me about the party at the skatepark because she wanted time away from me. I'm freaked out about Danny because he's not okay, but he's acting like I don't exist again and I don't know what to do about it. It's been a week of walking around as if I didn't lose my virginity to him, and I'm annoyed with myself because if I just got over all this dumb shit, I could tell my best friend about it. But she didn't even care that I was worried or that something terrible could easily have happened. If your friend sends you incoherent messages and doesn't answer the phone, you're supposed to go and look for them. But she made me feel like an idiot for caring, and in front of Danny and Mike as well.

It's a nothing Wednesday lunch break on my phone when I see that the Wild Claims are playing in the next town over that evening. I bite my lip. I'm pretty broke, but there's a lot inside me that I could do with dancing out. Mind made up, I DM Mandy—the bartender who likes me—and she texts back immediately, confirming she can let me in. I have an idea and start walking.

Grant greets me from his position sprawled out on the stone steps, Michelle leaning on the wall next to him with her feet up next to his thigh.

"Sup." Grant leans over with his fist out, and I tap it.

"Sup. Hey, Michelle." For some reason, including her in a "what's up" greeting makes no sense. She gives me a grateful smile, shuffling to get her tits at the best angle. My eyes drop on autopilot, and when I flick them back up, she's smug that she's caught me.

"Hey, Max." It's draped in sugar, and she leans her shoulder against Grant, touching her fingers to her collar lightly.

Embarrassed, I remember what I came over for. "You hear that the Wild Claims are playing at the Roxy tonight?" Please like the Wild Claims.

Grant moves his feet down a stair, which has the effect of dislodging Michelle without him actually having to move away from her. She doesn't seem fazed, leaning back and pulling a bottle of nail polish out of her backpack.

"No shit, that's awesome. How did I miss that?" He grabs

his phone and sighs. "Sold out, of course. Shit. Bitter Ruin are opening too. Brutal." I must have a look on my face, because he squints at me. "You got a spare ticket or something?"

"Nah." His face falls. And then, I say, "I can get us in though."

He beams, leaning backwards. "No way!"

"Yes way." I cross my fingers that Mandy won't mind me bringing a friend.

The lunch bell rings in the distance.

Michelle blows on her nails and gets to her feet. "Have fun on your date, boys."

I grimace at the words, which remind me of Danny in jarring double waves. "Who would want to date you?" he'd said. But what else was the night on the beach if not a date?

Grant breaks me out of my churning thoughts by laughing at her. "Oh, we will, Michelle."

He holds his hand out to me, and I grab it, hauling him up. He's heavy, and I have to work for it, but I don't show it as far as I can tell.

"Text me," he tells me before snagging his bag and sauntering off.

Michelle blows me a kiss before following him. I look at her retreating back, wondering if she feels left out. Opening my mouth to call after her and invite her with us, I pause. She ditched me. If she wants to be friends, she can try harder.

GRANT'S WAITING IN front of the ratty wall covered in posters, surrounded by a cloud of vape smoke, when I find him later that night. He smells like the forest. He jerks his chin at me in greeting. "Nice outfit."

The best part is, I think he means it. We're pretty close to matching, but not in a ridiculous way. I'm wearing ripped black jeans, not the expensive ones Gloss bought for me—since I moved back in with my parents, it's too weird to wear the stuff she paid for. I hid it in a box under my bed. Maybe my mother will find it and sell it, sparing me the need to decide whether to keep it or send it back to her.

So I'm wearing my old stuff, but I've learned my fashion lessons well. My jeans are rolled up around the top of my brutalised Dr. Martens, thirdhand when I got them for that authentic grunge vibe. Sitting in the best spot to slim my hips, my belt is plain with a thick silver buckle. My tight black shirt is unadorned with logos or slogans but fits well. I have a hot split second of wondering if he'd say "nice outfit" to a cis guy, if Danny was here instead of me, and then I imagine Danny in grunge chic and I choose to smile instead. I spiked his hair up once, and he looked about seven.

"Ta." I take the compliment at face value.

Hope Mandy lets him in! Earlier, she replied fast enough I think she might have missed me. The thought buoys me.

We only have to wait a few minutes before she opens the door. I greet her and kiss her smooth brown cheek when she proffers it. She's that kind of person, likes to be loved. I wouldn't know anything about that. Warm pleasure fills my belly at Grant's appraising look. "This is Grant."

"How's it," Grant drawls, in a gravelly voice I've never heard out of him before. I'm pretty sure he blushes as soon as he says it.

"It's a midweek gig for a popular band," Mandy replies with a cheeky grin. "By which I mean busy as fuck and understaffed. Get inside, will you?"

We will.

It's dark and smokey, glowing vape lights in the crowd and a sweet burn in the air that hovers, lit up by flashing lights, in front of NO SMOKING signs. Grant pushes my elbow to urge me towards the bar, and I thread us a path through the roiling crowd. With the music pounding around me, I fit in. I know the beat and the beat knows me and the crowd knows that. I can do this without Danny, without Gloss. I'm seamless here. People can't see my frayed edges, just my ripped jeans.

I shoulder my way to the water-stained wood and prop one foot on the brass bar that gives me an extra inch of height and adds to my "bar presence." I order us two pints, and Grant leans towards me while Mandy's getting glasses.

"So . . ." He drags it out. "Mandy's cute. Another one of your conquests?"

His voice is gentle, but I have to convince the spines that want to dart out of my skin to lay flat and friendly. Defensive first is a habit I'm trying to break. He's not making a joke like I'm so hideous and repulsive it's surprising anyone would want me. He's just teasing, talking. Still, I know my cheeks are flushed.

"Nope." I don't have to say anything else because Mandy's back. I hand over a tenner and get almost the same amount back, so I know she's shouted my pint for me. I clatter a couple of quid into the tip jar, dodging her attempt to pull it out of my way.

Grant leans an elbow on the wet bar top, but he instantly regrets it and recoils. His heel slips, and he flails his free arm, saving himself from a tumble but sloshing his beer over himself. Mandy and I both cackle, and she turns to the next customer before he has a chance to recover.

"Smooth, bro," I tell him. Seeing him make a tit out of himself over a girl has cheered me up immensely.

The opening band is still playing: a guy on a soulful guitar and a woman with a plaintive, crying voice. We find a spot wedged next to a pillar—one of the advantages of being a regular is knowing the best spots. We'll be able to perch on the rail when the pit pushes forward to get a better view over the pulsing crowd. The singer croons about pieces of a person being stuck inside her rib cage, and I fall for the band hard and fast, letting the words wash over me.

Grant bounces his head along to the music, getting into it but not truly plugged in. I can feel him thinking. He whisper-shouts in my ear as the trailing last pure notes of a song shiver through the air. "Does Mandy get breaks?"

I laugh at his brazenness. "Yeah, she usually goes out back to smoke, though. She should have one at nine."

Mandy always has one at nine. We've hung out during it a few times ever since she grabbed my hand and tugged me along with her, exhorting me to be her "fake fella" to get someone to leave her alone for her break. I didn't mind. She has an excellent line in band T-shirts, so I knew we'd have stuff to talk about. I wonder what she'll think about Grant running into her outside. He's kind and nice to look at, and Mandy's last boyfriend was a massive prick, so I think it's a step up, even if she does have a couple of years on him.

The band strikes up again, and I finish my beer. Grant goes for the next round while I guard our sweet spot, and we stay there until the Wild Claims have set up, slammed through two of their faster numbers, and strummed the opening chords for one of their big hits. The crowd surges, and I throw the rest of my new beer down my throat so I can slide through the rail, blood pumping. Grant follows me into the pit, and the seething mass of bodies welcomes me into the press. A crowd surfer gets lobbed too hard and comes down heavy, boot crushing my ear. Pain skitters through my nerves, lit up and sparkling. I laugh and taste blood from somewhere. It might not even be mine. Elbows in my ribs and hands shoving me back as the pit sways and throbs. Grant's keeping up, both of us staying on our feet. He grabs my neck for balance, pulls me around. We dance-jump-shout-fall-stand-vibrate as part of a shapeless, formless mass, and my brain finally goes blissfully quiet except for the music.

Grant misses Mandy's break and doesn't care. We tumble out into the warm air at gone midnight. I'm happier than I've been in weeks. Years, maybe. Beer fuzzing the sharp edges but not dulling them completely. Music filling my veins, my lungs. A friend at my side. And I think Grant might be a normal friend, one that doesn't come with a remote control set to my chest, who doesn't need a manual for me to understand what he wants from me. He's simple. So far, anyway. There's no game here. My heart soars with it when he slaps me on the back.

"You need a ride?" He's four or so beers in, and my doubt must show on my face. He laughs. "My sister's picking me up outside Dirty Joe's. She can drop you."

"Sure she won't mind?"

"Nah, Gracie's all right."

Dirty Joe's—officially called Joe's Bar and Grill—flashes neon at us. Grant leads the way to a red Nissan pulled illegally into a bus stop. He swings into the front seat, and I climb into the back, having to push a bunch of baby toys and junk over into the middle.

"Ah, sorry, didn't realise Grant was bringing a mate." Thick London accent, even more so than Grant.

"No worries, thanks for the ride."

"Where to?"

I manage to click my seatbelt into place past the weird plastic objects that are determined to stop me. I'm buzzing with joy. Here, inside me now, is evidence that I can carve out a place for myself with or without the people who shape or break me. I have to choose who I want to be, and what I want for myself. I don't want to go home. I don't want to be alone. Resolute, I ignore the compass in my heart that points to him, him, him.

"Denevue and Third, please."

AFTER

12

IT'S A SONG. It's my song.

The paper crumples in my grip. Hidden behind Danny's poster, close to his bed, as if he kept a part of me close even while throwing the rest of me away. It's the heartbreak song I started writing in my head on the way back from the park after Danny told me it was over. It's his handwriting, and he's written it out carefully, in nicer lettering than he ever uses for school. How did he have this? I rack my brains, scanning the words, and realise it's an old version, one I must have ripped out and abandoned.

I imagine him snagging a balled-up piece of paper from my backpack or from the floor where I'd dropped it. Smoothing out the crumpled paper and reading it. Copying it out. Taking his time with every word. My hands are trembling when I turn the photo strip over. My face smiling broadly leaps out at me. Gloss's too.

I don't know how he got these pictures of me and Gloss at the mall on our shopping trip. I look so young and happy in the picture I can't look at it. Gloss's face is creased, as if maybe that's where a thumb has pressed to hold the sheet, all the better to look at me.

There's a strange taste in my mouth. Here, at last, is proof that Danny and I were real and not a story I told myself in the dark. He hid these scraps of me behind his stupid naked lady poster. Why? To torture himself? Or to remember?

With exaggerated care, so as not to drop anything, I tuck the two pieces of me back in their envelope and inhale. Exhale. Inhale. Exhale. Always remember to breathe, Max, everything starts with breath. Without breath, we are nothing.

My heart is aching and breaking and shaking inside me, like I've swallowed a volcano of pain. I stare at the envelope, holding it in both hands, until my phone buzzes in my pocket, making me jump.

> Wellness check

It takes a few minutes to have steady enough hands to reply to Grant.

> check check

> u comin back soon?
> We got 🍕

> if you + M+M don't mind I think
> I might go for askate, clear my head.
> Danny's dad was a lot

> s'cool, but don't go awol ok?
> we got enuff to b stressed abt

> yep

With that decided, I hit the riverside path at a run. When Ridgepoint is entirely behind me, I realise I'm heading back to the water.

Back to where Danny and I budded and bloomed.

do you remember when
you took my hand
and promised me
i wouldn't sink
i sank, i sank, i'm sinking
it's easier to pretend
than to spend
another moment
fighting
i fought, i fought, i'm fighting

you took my hand
pulled me to land
i thought that you would understand
you threw me back
a heart attack
you stretched my body
on your rack

the demons came
they saw my shame
they told you only i'm to blame
better hope you never misbehave
yeah better hope you never misbehave

i watch you spin
your saint's a sinner
the line between

gets ever thinner
ever wonder where i've been?
remember that it's all a dream

if you took my hand we could go back
just take my hand we can go back
reach out and trust me take me back
or i am simply gonna snap

BEFORE

16

GLOSS ANSWERS THE door on my tenth knock. She opens the door, looks me over with a bleak, unreadable expression and then walks back inside. But she leaves the door open in her frigid wake.

I scrape my shoes off vigorously on the mat, even though they're clean. Skateboarding's good for keeping your soles mudless. Gripless, too, after a while, if you've got to wear them until they fall apart. I'm buying time, like I'm on my way to a guillotine. Gloss curls up in the biggest chair in the living room under a thick knit blanket the colour of storm clouds that match the shadows in her eyes. Something's brewing. Tears lodge in my throat, and I stand in the doorway, uncomfortable. If I want this to be easy, I should apologise—but I'm not sure how, or what would come out if I did. But if I want her back, want us back, I have to reach out to her. I know she won't, and I'm okay with it. I can be brave for both of us.

She watches me. I've seen her stare down adults until they huff and walk away, losing a fight they wish they hadn't picked.

I pad to the centre of the room and sit on the floor, all careful, folded limbs.

"Do you hate me?"

Fuck. I was supposed to say I was sorry, but the question squirms out of my mouth instead. I don't raise my eyes, even when I hear the chair shift. My feet are bare and knobbly. Hair filling in on the big toes. Bald ankles, white and vulnerable-looking. She's going to walk out of the room and shut the door behind her, I know it in my bones. My stupid ankle bones.

Soft fingers lift my chin and then slide into my hair. I melt against her thigh, grateful beyond words for the physical contact. The scent of strawberries washes over me. My eyes are wet. She runs her fingers through my hair, leads me to the sofa and sits. I'm on my knees, curled onto her leg, pressed against her tights.

Eventually, I look up at her. She graces me with a kind smile. It inflates my ribs.

"I'm sorry for chasing you down. I was worried about you." I force the words out. I am sorry. I wish she'd had her phone, but I shouldn't have decided she needed me and charged in after her. I realise I probably owe Mike an apology too. Urgh.

"I don't belong to you, Max. Not like that."

Words rise up in me, but as always, they get stuck in my throat, wedged behind my traitor teeth. We belong to each other. I belong to her, so why can't she belong to me?

"That's not what this is, Max, baby. Not what we have. I love you, and you love me. But for me, sex has nothing to do with love. I don't want to fuck someone I care about, ever. I like to flirt and tease and play, but it's not romance. It's never romance for me. I'm not built that way. You are. You deserve romance."

She's firm with it, but the boundary is a relief as well as a disappointment. An edge, finally, to what we are together. Friends, then. Close, like Liam is to her. Family?

"I'm sorry too, Max," she continues. "I'm sorry you're hurting, and I'm sorry I'm not enough for you the way things are."

"You're enough," I promise.

I don't tell her about the beach. I keep that for me. Well, me
and Danny. I don't want to hear what she'll have to say about
it. If nobody else knows, it can exist outside of reality. If a boy
comes on a beach and nobody hears him, did it happen?

I do tell her how I'd decided to give up on everything
except school, and it's funny instead of sad. I shave in the
bathroom, days-worth of almost-stubble scraping clean off
my cheeks and lips. I only cut myself once, leaving bloody
fingerprints on the tap until Gloss brings me a plaster and
cleans up my mess.

We fall asleep with the TV on, curled up around each other.
She presses her mouth to the back of my neck and tells me she
loves me. I pretend to be asleep until she bites down, reducing
me to giggles and leaving marks I can see in the mirror over
my shoulder when I shower the next day. One day I'll tell her
to stop treating my body like a toy.

When I stop enjoying it.

THE LAST MONTH of the last term of the last year drags by,
exams approaching and the student body torn between exces-
sive cramming and dozing through classes that don't matter
anymore. Gloss doesn't seem to notice it's exam season, while I
have to start carving out time to get things done.

I tutor Grant and we hang out sometimes besides, catch a
few more gigs at the Roxy—he never does get Mandy's number, but not for want of trying. At some point, we start playing
together in the music rooms, pleased to find our voices com-
plement each other. We joke about starting a band. Danny and
I don't look at each other in the halls, and I pretend I don't
spend half the day imagining curling my fingers around his

wrist and dragging him into the single stall washroom to make him talk to me.

Maths is a walk in the park—I could have sat the exam at the beginning of the year without breaking a sweat. English is harder; I have a ton of work to do to make up for my sporadic performance this year, and since Gloss isn't taking it, I don't have anyone to revise with. Essays are much harder for me than poetry, but sadly, that's all I have left. Somehow, it ends up with me and Michelle as default revise buddies, trying to cram in as much as possible in our matching free block. We're edging our way back to a tentative friendship, which would be easier if she'd stop bringing Danny up, asking if I've seen him, if I miss him, if he's talking to me or avoiding me like everyone else.

My music project is almost tied up. I've finalised six of my songs and have to finish the music video. I tried to use stock clips to make it easier to stomach, but none of them are right. In the end, I started using stuff I filmed last summer. I make sure you never see Danny's face or mine. It's all skateboards and surfboards and hands tangled in long grass. Legs flung over each other, shadows kissing on the sand. I mix in shots from Liam's party, and with a few melodic tweaks, the whole tone of the project shifts from bitter and lonely to wistful and longing. Gloss watches me edit on her huge Mac, but she doesn't make me talk about it.

The last long weeks leading up to summer and freedom and future drip away like melting ice cream.

BEFORE

17

THE LAST THURSDAY of school, my exams finished and no more need to even show my face at school, Gloss and I are lounging at the park with Grant, Mike, Lina and Michelle—which has become the norm since Danny started ducking everyone. I asked Grant about it, and he said Danny had a huge fight with his dad. Apparently, it'll pass, and interfering is a good way to get a punch in the face while Danny works through it. I'm supposed to leave him be. The distance helps, but his absence throbs like a missing tooth, and never more painfully than when we're in this park, with his friends, without him. I keep staring at his window behind my sunglasses, pretending I'm on my phone, wondering if he's watching us.

"Do me," Gloss demands, thrusting the bottle of sunscreen into my unready hands.

I drop my phone, and the sunscreen onto my collarbone. "Ow, goddammit!"

I sit up, rubbing mournfully at the injured spot. My tank top strap shifts under my fingers, and I make sure it's arranged just so to hide my binder straps. Gloss had them sewn in half so they're thinner, easier to hide than before, but I'm still hyperaware of them, especially in the summer when I sweat and suffer. Roll on top surgery. If only I could save a gabillion dollars, maybe I won't have to wait for four years on the National Health Service. I only got on hormones because my dad pulled an endocrinologist out of a smashed-up car once. That probably won't happen again, but one can dream. Maybe Gloss will pay someone to cut my tits off for my birthday, and I can join the boys in blissful shirtlessness without shocking the locals. Imagining how people would respond if I decided fuck it, these are boy titties, deal with it, and stripped my shirt off makes me smile.

"What's up, you wankers?"

Danny? For a moment I think I've hallucinated him, but then Mike is on his feet, Michelle's rearranging herself to make room, and Danny plops down next to me as if it's the most normal thing in the world.

The golf ball that has suddenly grown where my tonsils used to be is impossible to swallow. I'm sure I look like a total idiot trying.

"Brosopholes, Brosephs, Brohannigans, Bronies . . . no, wait, that's a *My Little Pony* thing—Fuck!" Mike gets cut off by Danny punching him in the thigh, leaving him hopping on one leg and laughing. "You asshole," he says, thwapping Danny on the ear.

Danny's inches away from me and hasn't even acknowledged my existence—is he going to ignore me in front of literally everyone now? I don't think it's going to work if he does. I lean back on my hands, glowering at him.

"Hey, Maximilian, pass me a beer, will ya? I just finished my last exam." Danny turns the full beam of his smile onto me, and my insides turn into lava. Maximilian is not my name, but it's a lot better than Maxipad, so I'll take it. The memory of him calling me Maxipad is less painful than it used to be, and more ridiculous.

Gloss reaches over, fishes a beer out of the cooler and leans across me to slap it into his hands with more force than strictly necessary.

"Thanks." Danny doesn't even tack on a nickname, which is his version of being incredibly polite and restrained. He sits back, sprawling out with his torso on the grass, and Gloss pointedly arranges herself in front of me. She's wearing only an undone green—forest, Max, it's forest—bikini top, held to her chest while she waits impatiently for me to recoat her delicate skin. It's an excellent distraction from my ex showing up, and I give it my full attention.

I rub the thick white cream in. Her lightly freckled back is sun heated and supple under my palms.

"How come Max gets all the glory?" Grant shades his eyes with one hand, propped up on an elbow. "I'll cream you."

Gloss snorts in a dismissive way that makes us all fake wince. "You couldn't even get the bottle open."

It's not clear what exactly this is a euphemism for, but it's cutting anyway, and Grant clutches his chest, mock wounded. Danny holds out his hand for a high five. I am in an alternate universe as Gloss gracefully takes it. She easily could have left him hanging, but with that high five, it's settled: Danny is welcomed back like he's been here all along.

Michelle rolls over, her chest threatening to escape from her strappy top. "You can do me, Grant."

He chuckles and slicks her shoulders up when I pass him the bottle. Mike laughs at him from his position lying down with Lina propped against his thighs.

"I can't believe I still have another exam," Lina complains.

"At least it's art." Grant reaches for the cooler and grabs a sweating, frosty can of beer.

"True. I've almost finished my piece, anyway." Lina sighs, her eyes closed. She's done something wonderful with her eyeliner today. "I haven't finished my essay thing though."

"Want me to look at it?" Grant asks, popping the lid on his can, and the cool liquid fizzes out, splattering my bare arm. I grumble and wipe it off on my tank. When I look up, Danny's watching me from behind his sunglasses. The weight of his eyes is molten lead, intense enough to muffle the conversation around me. How did we get here? Last summer, this was half of what I dreamed of. Being included in this group, sprawled out in their spot on the blankets and balled-up hoodies, skateboards dumped off to one side. In my dreams, though, it's Danny who's pressing his leg against mine when he moves. Danny whose back flexes under my sunscreen hands.

As though she knows I'm wandering closer to maudlin thoughts, Gloss drapes a delicate ankle over my bare and hairy leg. "Did I get bitten by an ant?"

I inspect her ankle, the shadow dents of grass pushed into the tender skin. "I don't think so, princess," I tell her, and it's supposed to come out teasing, but there's a note of worship in there. Nobody else seems to have noticed. She mouths "Good boy," and I flush, disguising it by rubbing her ankle where an ant definitely didn't bite her.

"At least the party's gonna be lit," Danny says, as if he hadn't disappeared for weeks.

"Uh," Grant mumbles. "About that."

When I glance over, he's doing something weird with his face, scrunched and uncomfortable.

"What?" Mike sits up in a rush, dislodging Lina, who complains about it, grumpily rearranging herself to sit up and then grabbing a hard lemonade from the cooler like it was her plan all along.

"My sister rearranged her trip." Grant picks at the toe of

his Etnies with his thumbnail, squinting at us. "We have to postpone until next week."

"It's the last day of exams tomorrow, Grant. We can't postpone." Danny sounds like his reasonable observation will resolve the issue.

"We can't throw a bender at my house with my baby nephew there either." Grant frowns at him. "It's not like we ever party at yours."

Everyone except Gloss pulls a face at the low blow. Danny glowers and subsides, picking up his can and staring at it moodily as though the ring pull will present an answer to the problem.

"We have to find somewhere to go," Mike exclaims. "I refuse not to party on the last day. It's probably illegal. What about the forest?"

"You don't even have an exam tomorrow!" Grant points out. "We can throw it a week after, it'll be fine."

"People will be gone! Aren't you going to London? And Lina's going to . . . somewhere." Mike rubs his hand over his head.

"Japan," Lina tells the cooler. She doesn't even sound annoyed with him for not knowing.

"We can have it at our place, right, Max?" Gloss chimes in, quiet, but effortlessly redirecting all the attention her way.

Our place. "Yeah, of course." My cheeks are heating, and I pull my shirt up to dab at my forehead like I'm drying sweat off but really just to hide my face for a moment.

"Yeah!" Mike crows, jostling Grant enough he slops pop down his bare chest. He frowns, rolling his eyes and grabs a T-shirt to wipe himself off.

"Hey, that's mine!" Mike tries to snatch it, and an impromptu wrestling match commences. Before they get too riled up, Danny stands, grabs a freezing water bottle from the cooler and empties it over them both. They separate, shrieking, and then turn on Danny as one and dive-tackle him to the floor. I hear the impact with my bones, a dull boom, and Lina yelps and dashes out the way as the tangle of boy-men veers dangerously close to our picnic blanket.

"Wouldn't it be better if they were in their undies?" I murmur, quiet enough Michelle and Lina miss it.

Gloss gives me a loaded smirk. "Pervert."

"Takes one to know one," I tell her merrily, floating on the idea of throwing a party and being here on a brilliant summer day with a group of people instead of by myself. Even if it's a fun-house-mirror version of what I wanted, it's closer than I've ever been.

They break apart, heaving for breath, grazed and rumpled. Danny's hair is standing up wildly, and his ear is bright red. His sweaty chest is outlined with pink marks where the ground clawed at his skin. Mike inspects a bloodied elbow, bending his arm almost back on itself, while Grant nurses a fat lip, grabbing a new can to hold against it like an ice pack.

"You're such animals." Michelle doesn't sound disapproving as she shifts over to pull Grant's wrist down so she can inspect his face. There's a smear of blood on his white teeth when he grimaces at her.

"Better than bitching behind people's backs," he grumbles.

She angles his face from side to side. "You'll live. Kissing might hurt though."

Michelle pats his cheek and tries to inspect Danny's injuries, but he ducks away from her and flops back down on the blanket. He makes eye contact with me and waves his hand in the direction of the cooler. I lean over to grab him a beer and pause, then settle on a fizzy raspberry drink instead. Raspberry was always his favourite. He grabs it from me and pops it open, pulling himself up enough to guzzle half of it down.

The spill of hot pink that trickles down his chin shouldn't be erotic, but it captures me. It drops onto his chest, and so do my eyes. His nipples contract, and I can't tell if it's from the cold droplets or my gaze. I know he's watching me watch him. I can sense it under my skin. A sharp pain in my calf makes me hiss and draws my attention back to Gloss. She waits until my eyes are locked with hers before releasing me, watching me with narrowed eyes. All the reasons I shouldn't be looking at Danny that way flood me, a wash of cold down my spine, and I look away. He doesn't want to be with me. I have to stop wishing for the impossible. I have to stop carving myself open with want.

I glance around, desperate for a distraction. My board is lying in the grass, wheels up. One is spinning, even though no one's touching it. I need to be away.

My trucks are icy in my hot hand as I snag my board, swinging it across my body and over my shoulder, and head for the skatepark without another word.

Classic Max, closing down and running away. I didn't even say "later!" Maybe I can start working on becoming a brooding, silent type instead of an awkward one. With that in mind, I slow down a bit so I'm less in open flight and more walking over to the ramps.

Wheels rumbling on concrete calms me down. The reverberation settles into my veins, replacing the harried pounding of my panicked blood. After all this, how can he still be breaking my heart? It's June now. Last May is when I met him—here, this park, this place. We knew each other from school, of course, but this is where I met him. The real Danny. He watched me on the ramps, bought me a drink when I staggered off, shaking with exhaustion, finished grinding the slurred and hateful words my mother screamed at me into the concrete. He was nervous, picking at the label of the bottle, rolling little paper shreds into balls.

I still want him. I want Gloss too. Between Gloss and Danny my bones are on fire, a heat that won't be quenched. In reality, I know it's not just them—testosterone has changed me so I spend all my time either horny or hungry, but it's hard to remember that when he's in front of me.

I skate until my body is calm and I can think of something other than raspberry-stained lips.

WHILE I WAS on my board, it seems that Gloss finalised plans with the group, because when I pull my phone out of my pocket, it's packed with notifications about the party. There's a busy group chat, a bunch of Snaps, a promo post I've been tagged in on a few stories and an event page. She's even made a document and shared it with me and the elusive Stephanie, complete with a shopping list.

I saunter back over and grab my first beer of the day—it's five o'clock somewhere—then sit on the cooler. It smells like weed, fresh and burning. The Dead South are whistling on someone's phone, and the rhythm catches me so my head starts nodding, my heart settling into the thud-thud of the beat, fingers tapping my thigh.

"You're really good, Max," Michelle drawls, blinking up at me with doe eyes. For a moment, I think she means at music because that's where my head's at, thinking about the way my fingers would move on the frets to pull off that lazy drop swagger tune. Then I realise she means on a board. I also realise she's leaning forward enough to give me a straight shot down her top to her boobs. They're great boobs, but I'm not quite sure how to react. Girls flirting with me is a whole new world, except for Gloss.

"Thanks." I shift, awkward with the attention. Yeah, I'm all right. Anyone with half a sense of balance would be if they spent four hours a day for a few years trying. A shitty home life is good for one thing—if you have to escape from the house, rain or shine, and can't afford a data plan, you get a lot of practice at free activities.

"Did you ever land that three-sixty?" Danny asks. His gaze is fuzzy, and the loosely rolled blunt dangling from his hand is half-burned, stubbed out. There's a black smear of ash on his broad thumbnail.

Gloss drapes her arm possessively over my thigh. My leg hair catches in her watch strap, and I wince-flinch away. She can't have done it on purpose, but it sure feels like she might have. Maybe she's trying aversion therapy. Associate Danny with more pain, Max, you keep letting him come back. Rubbing at the now-bald pink patch right below the thready hem of my faded black denim shorts, I nod at Danny. "Yeah, a month or so ago."

I hold my hand out for the joint, and he stretches up to hand it over. I spark up, letting the smoke trickle out of my mouth. It tastes like promises and sunshine. And skunk, obviously. Michelle leans against my leg, takes the spliff from me after I've barely had half a puff and gives me a sly look through her eyelashes. In a shocking, sudden moment, I know that I could lean down and take her mouth with mine, and she'd breathe smoke into my lungs and we'd kiss. She wants me to kiss her. I sit back on the cooler, too abrupt. I almost fall right off the back, but I manage to catch myself and the tilting cooler, frozen in a moment of balance. If I lean back any farther I'll go right down, but I don't have the leverage to pull myself back. Doesn't that just feel like the perfect metaphor for life as a teen in a world on fire?

Gloss hooks my waistband with two fingers, rings catching on my boxers. She tugs me forward, recentering my weight so the front of the cooler crashes back to the ground. A laugh bursts out of me. After a split second, everyone joins in, and it's not at me, it's with me. I rescue the joint from Michelle, take a puff and blow a ring that Mike punches his fist through.

When the shadows start to lengthen, we smoothly relocate. The kids are gone from the skatepark now, home for dinner and bath time. We're the teenagers people complain about making areas unwelcoming, yelling and pumping our music into the evening air. We're not the only ones, though. There's a gaggle of older teens on the basketball court, and when we walk past, Danny rattles the cage link at them, gibbering like a monkey in a zoo. For a second, I assume that Danny's friends with them, but the looks on their faces proves that's not true. They start towards us, but Grant grabs Danny by the arm and Mike passes him a new beer, and between the two of them, Danny's corralled, to my relief. I'd ground to a halt, staring, but Gloss is ahead, and I jog to catch up, ignoring the guys in the court.

We jump on our boards. I'm tipsy and a little high, enough to smear the world around the edges and make everything hilarious.

We're all showing off because Gloss is filming us and Lina and Michelle are watching. I'm fully engrossed in trying to land the aforementioned three-sixty when Danny runs off his board and up onto the railing, leaning over. "This is our park, boyos. Get fucked!"

My stomach twists. Danny's had a lot of bruises in the time I've known him, and even before, I remember seeing him with more than his fair share of damage. I assumed it was athletics, but the way he's acting reframes those injuries.

There's six of them, rough looking with belligerent expressions.

"Oops, we must be lost." The drawling voice belongs to the biggest of them and he doesn't sound at all like it was an accident. The rumble of wheels fades out, leaving the air rigid.

Danny grunts, pushing himself backwards off the railing and smirking at them. "All at once or one at a time then, fellas. Step right up."

It's his cocky challenge voice, but this time it's not aimed at a teacher or a kid in school. His fists are clenched, and they're big and hard like the rest of him. It's as if a new Danny has been superimposed over the other Dannys I know—the boyfriend, the lad, the athlete. I don't recognise this one, I've never seen him before.

I'm glued in place. I do *not* want to be in a fight, but Mike and Grant are already bracketing him. Two of the boys hop the rail, and Lina flinches back, wedging herself into the corner. Michelle stays where she is, frozen with her hands wrapped around the metal bar. The boys don't pay any attention to her. Gloss has moved to the other side of the ramp, and I catch her eye to make sure she's okay and out of the way before turning back.

If I don't join in, they have double the numbers. My palms itch as I break out in a sweat, salty droplets beading on my upper lip. I'm so on edge I'm aware of the ooze of liquid leaving my pores.

The two boys who jumped the fence—both white, one tall with terrible skin and one short and squat with huge shoulders—swagger up, and the rest of their crew hop the bar and join them, semicircling in front of us.

Danny deliberately gathers a mouthful of saliva and spits on the floor in front of the spotty guy. It looks choreographed as Spots takes a swing.

I have a split second to flee, but I don't, and then Squat is coming for me. I duck away from the first swing but don't manage to avoid the second. A blow thumps into my chest, driving the air out of me. Gasping, I flail wildly, catching his cheekbone and driving his head back. He grunts, and my arms are grabbed from behind. The unfairness of a double attack wipes away fear and replaces it with adrenaline that makes my blood sing.

Instead of resisting the pull on my arms, I throw my weight back, lifting my leg to kick out at Squat. I miss his balls and my shoe bounces off his thigh, but he cries out anyway. Cheater, as I name the one who snuck up on me, staggers backwards. I thrust my pointy elbow out and find a soft place that makes him gasp and loosen his grip.

On TV, they always make headbutting look easy and painless, but when I try to swing my head back into his, I barely skim his jaw. We struggle against each other for a second, and then he spasms and releases me so swiftly I stumble.

Danny's face is twisted in a furious rictus, and as I watch he punches Cheater so hard the blood sprays off his lip. I haven't seen Danny look this angry since Grant's party. Then I'm pulled into the path of a fist, and I have to concentrate on Squat again.

I catch the blow on my forearm and drive my other hand into my attacker's stomach. He barely flinches and swings for my face again, like a boxer. His jaw is tucked in, and his eyes are hard and narrowed under his singular dense eyebrow. I have to give ground, backing up under the flurry of blows, catching them on my shoulders and forearms and unable to hit back. He's grinning, toying with me. I keep waiting for the fear to come back. I can hear the grunts, thuds and cries of the rest of the fight, but I don't know what's happening. I'm too busy with Squat to look. No one comes to help me this time. It's up to me.

My foot lands and slips—I've stepped on a skateboard, my weight making it shoot out from under me. But I've fallen off hundreds of times, too many times to freeze up or waste a second. I catch myself on my other foot, swing my weight up and use my momentum to launch my fist into his chin. It's a good, pure hit, with enough force my knuckles protest.

His jaw shuts on impact, his teeth clacking together. His body goes loose, his eyes out of focus as he teeters. He catches himself and staggers off, running. Running away from me. I took care of myself. Every bone in my body vibrates.

The bruises haven't asserted themselves yet, but I know they're there. The rest of the fight is still raging—one guy has Mike pinned against the fence, swinging methodical blows into his stomach while another holds him by the neck. Mike's going purple, grasping at the forearm around his throat but can't get a grip, his fingers scrabbling uselessly.

Barely thinking, I sprint for him. The kick I aim at the Puncher lands in the back of his knee with the full force of my run behind it. He shrieks and falls hard. I let my momentum carry me up onto the rail and then rain blows down on Mike's captor from above. I don't get any good hits in, but the distraction lets Mike break free, red faced and gasping. Danny's facing off with another guy, who glances around and sees the way the fight is going—one gone, one down, and all of us still on our feet—and dodges out of Danny's way.

They join up, minus two that Grant seems to be surviving, so we're three against three. My shoulders hurt and my eye's swelling up, throbbing in time with my heartbeat. The energy that propelled me through the first few minutes is draining away, leaving me unsteady and weak. Danny's standing close, so close I'm aware of the pressure of his body in the air. There's a manic edge in his posture, a fey energy twitching and zapping, like he's a feral dog fighting a leash. There's a few, frozen moments where no one moves—and then there's a piercing scream.

Grant. My heart swoops. But when I spin around, Gloss is standing over my friend, legs spread. The two guys who were fighting him are rolling around on the floor, clutching their faces. Gloss steps clear of Grant and strolls over to the group of us.

"Have you guys expended enough testosterone to leave by yourselves, or do I have to mace you as well?"

The guys shove each other a bit, trying to front like they're gonna try to take us on again, but a threatening lift of the hand from Gloss sends them running. She places a possessive hand on my shoulder, and it buckles my knees.

My ribs protest the laugh that bubbles out of me, but it feels good, so I give in. After a second of crackling tension, Danny joins in, shoving me hard enough to hurt. Like he punched Mike in the leg earlier, like he's too violent inside to harness it anymore. Maybe now that he's reconnecting, he'll get it under control; maybe Grant and Mike will help him figure it out. It's not my job.

"Fucking Chuck Norris here," Danny chortles. "You drop-kicked that guy!"

"Epic, Max." Mike claps me on the back, and I grin at him, tiredness dropping away.

"Epic, Gloss, more like. Thanks for the artillery support," I point out, because wow, now that I look at us, we're all bloodied and bruised, and I can't imagine a second round would have gone our way at all. My ribs are swollen and hot when I prod at them. My whole face aches.

Gloss squeezes my hip. "You're welcome."

Grant staggers over to join us, holding his nose, which is spewing blood down his front. His eyes are red and streaming.

"Fuckin' assholes," he mumbles through a split and oozing lip.

Lina appears to have made a run for it, but Michelle is perched on the fence, watching us with hooded eyes. Danny lifts a hand to her. For a second, I think she's going to stay where she is, but then she slips down and walks over to us, letting Danny sling his arm over her shoulder. She doesn't join in the laughter that has taken over the rest of us. As we limp back to the main road, she's the only one not buoyed up and silly; even Gloss is buzzing.

"Tomorrow, we party! For it's the last day of exams and the world awaits our glory!" Mike declares to the sky, spinning around, as he, Michelle, Grant and Danny head off down their road.

Gloss holds my hand all the way home, and when she takes the hem of my shirt and pulls it over my head so she can ice my bruises, I don't stop her. Her fingers are careful. The last person who touched me so gently was Danny.

Tonight, though, it didn't seem like there was anything gentle left in him. I fall asleep thinking about that murderous look on his face.

AFTER

13

THE COVE IS quiet, sheltered. A rugged push across a rocky slope keeps the kids and oldies out. Sometimes I find remnants of other people's visits, but not this time. The beach is slick and golden, without footprints, the tide pulled out and leaving the rocks exposed. It's a picture-perfect little beach, the kind Europeans don't believe we have in England. I scramble over the scree and down to the large, shielded triangle of perfect sand.

For a while, I sit, watching the seagulls screeching and wheeling overhead, remembering Danny. If I let my eyes fuzz out, I can imagine him slicing through the waves out there in the water even when it's too calm to surf. He always seemed immune to the cold, but when he came out, he'd angle for me to wrap him in a blanket, and I'd let him sit between my knees while he thawed out in front of the fire. Never again now.

He's gone.

When the sun passes behind the cliff, cold seeps through my jeans, and I light a fire Danny will never warm himself at.

> GRANT
>
> Lina is here n were doin
> a sort of wake fyi. where u at?

I hesitate before responding to Grant's text, torn. Here is the right place to mourn, for me, but I should be with the other people who are grieving.

> I'm at the beach, where Danny and
> I used to hang out. I think you should
> bring the wake here.

I attach an image of the cove, hoping it explains what I can't about this place. Then I drop a pin and tack on another message.

> Bring my car. It has camp stuff in it.
> Not party stuff though.

> MIKE
>
> Party master mike is on
> the case

> of beer

> the case of beer

> GRANT
>
> he's standing on a case
> of beer rn

For the first time, I kind of understand why people like Mike.

IT TAKES THEM about half an hour to find me. I watch as Lina and Michelle pick their way over the rock with Mike's help. He's carrying both their handbags and a cooler but still lets them use him as a handrail. Grant's behind him, lugging the stuff I told him to bring from my car when I sent the directions.

"We brought pizza," Michelle announces as soon as she's close enough for me to hear. My stomach can't decide if it's ravenous or if it's in such a tight knot nothing will fit inside.

I sit like a lump on my piece of driftwood, staring at my hands until Michelle brings me a slice on a paper napkin. She gestures for me to stand and wraps me in a one-armed hug as soon as I do.

"Oh, Max." She leans against me. "How are you doing?" Looking up, she gives me a small smile that makes an answering one twitch on my lips. Almost there. It's good to be with people who cared about him like I did.

She sighs deeply, letting her eyeline drift past me and fall on a sailboat making its way past the cove. "I can't really believe it. I keep expecting him to just"—she waves a hand in the air—"show up."

I nod like I understand, but I don't feel that way. He's gone from the world. The piece of me that he owned is withering away without his existence to sustain it.

"Max! Shell!" Grant yells. Her nickname, given by Gloss, stabs me in the guts. While we were talking, they've laid out a small bar on the rocks. I chew on my cheek. My spotty, flashback memory provides a ream of memories of beers and champagne and shots thrust into my hand and me not even engaging, not even thinking about whether or not I was wasted, whether I wanted them. Gloss at the centre of every scene except one. Me, with blood on my hands and no way to know for sure how it got there.

Making my mind up, I grab a Coke. I'm not going to be my mum. I've been drinking too much. Getting blackout drunk, especially when I'm on meds that don't mix, is dangerous and irresponsible. I'm not going to do that from now on. I want to know what happens to me.

Solo cup in the air, I gesture to the group. "To King D," which is what they used to call him. What the school used to chant at footy matches when he scored, or the swim meets when he'd surge ahead of the competition, slicing through the water like a shark. I've seen the videos, although I never went. Never had the chance.

"King D!" The shout echoes off the rock walls, and the golden predusk sun pops out from behind a cloud, slewing sunlight all over us and making me think Danny heard us, wherever he is now.

BEFORE

18

IT'S KIND OF hilarious how quickly Gloss pulled this end-of-school party together. The music's cranked and it's bumping; there's like sixty people crammed into the place. People are smoking inside, which I wish they wouldn't—but Gloss doesn't seem to mind. She's opened up our bedroom too, which I'm not delighted about. I keep poking my head in to make sure people aren't going through my things. So far, it's just people playing drinking games, cards spread in a big circle. There's strip poker going on atop our bed, two girls and a guy I vaguely recognise as being an art kid. He winks at me when I catch his eye. God, I hope he doesn't fuck them on my bed.

It's weird having this party in my space. I can't imagine having people over to my parent's house, not even friends. I haven't, ever, as far as I know. Maybe when I was really small, but certainly not in my memory. I wonder if I'd have had more friends growing up if I could have thrown birthday parties or invited my class over. Probably not. I was always quiet and weird, with more going on inside than I was able or inclined to express to people.

When I wander through the living room, Gloss finds me again immediately and pulls me into the group.

Michelle slides under my arm and presses against my hip. "Hi." She's breathy and drunk, whisky tinging her breath.

"Hi." I snag the glass out of her hand and take a gulp.

We dance and dance. Nothing else matters. Only this matters. Finishing secondary school not just with a bang, but with friends.

"We fuckin' did it," I yell, crowing at the ceiling, greeted by a chorus of whoops. I grab Gloss's hips, pull her back against my body. "Where's the champagne?" I ask, my lips skating the delicate skin of her ear. Her hair is down, tangled, messy. Beautiful.

She gives me a look, because she knows I know where the champagne is—where it always is, in the wine fridge—but smiles anyway. "Smart boy." And then she's gone, dipping through the crowd.

The bottle she brings is ludicrously big, a novelty item, but the wax seal over the twisted metal cork containing device implies its price. Gloss thrusts it at me, no glasses in her hands. I pop the wax seal and foil off like I've done it before, untwist the wire and thrust the neck away from us all, towards the ceiling. I'm flinched and curled away, peeking with one eye, but nothing happens. Gloss laughs at me, and I roll my eyes at her. Using both hands, I wedge my thumbs against the cork and push. BANG. The cork erupts and so does the liquid, fizzing up and over.

Gloss grabs my wrist and pulls the bottle to her lips, catching the exploding foam in her mouth until she can't take any more, and pushes it towards me. Like a water fountain, I let the fizz fill my mouth, only relinquishing the bottle to grasping hands when my mouth and oesophagus are about to burst. Coughing, I break loose, soaked down the front. Gloss uses my shoulder to dry her mouth on. I give her a look that says, "Really?" and she pecks me on the point of my jaw.

"Go change, lover boy. You're all wet."

"Not for the first time," I grumble at her, recalling slopped drinks and enthusiastic bottle offering. She raises a devilish eyebrow at me and I go tomato red. You could fry eggs on my cheeks. I bolt, her laughter tinkling in my ears.

The embarrassment subsides after a moment, turning to amusement. Gloss is such a demon, wow. I shoulder the bedroom door open, making the card players whirl around to see what's happening. Danny's sprawled against the wall, long legs bent to keep them clear. He gives me a long look. I can't tell what the look means, so I just tug my wet shirt by way of explanation and pull open a dresser drawer, hoping no one will wonder why my clothes and things are in this bedroom. Although I guess there's nothing overtly feminine about Gloss's decoration, just not anything masculine either. If I had been in charge, there would definitely be less white. More band posters, though they'd have to be framed and classy. Maybe I'll get some.

The first shirt I grab is tight-fitting grey cotton. I hope I don't sweat through it, but I don't want to hang around rummaging with Danny watching me like that. I duck into the bathroom without looking at him and yank my wet shirt over my head. I do a shitty job rolling the sleeves, but it's passable.

I spare a moment to rinse my face, tacky with champagne, and rub my thumb thoughtfully against my upper lip. It's prickly. I should have shaved. I grab my razor box from the small cupboard to the right of the sink. Leaving it by my toothbrush should be enough of a reminder to shave tomorrow. I look cute, even with the soft stubble on my upper lip. I grin at myself, flick a mocking salute at the mirror, and head back into the party.

Danny has joined the group on the bed playing poker. As I pick my way through the room, he peels his shirt off. His golden back flexes, and I drag my eyes away, bursting out into the darkness of the hallway.

Gloss is still on the dance floor, surrounded by eager possible partners, everyone wanting to be in her space. She moves past people like she's hardly aware they're alive. I fix myself another drink and join her.

I don't know whose idea it is to go to the park, but it's a good one. The moon is a bleached bone slice in the sky, high and bright. It's late—I'm not sure how late, but it doesn't matter either. It's the last day of school. We've got nowhere to be and nothing to do except this.

Grant and I don't pause our discussion about Black punk through the ages, and Michelle holds my hand even though she's not interested in the conversation. There's about twenty of us between my friends, the music crew, most of the school sports teams and I think a few people have dates I don't know. The energy pulsing around us is wild and vivid, and we paint the air with shouts and laughs. Music beats through the air like reins around us, holding us together. The skatepark emerges out of the summer night, streetlights a bright line in the distance, edging the grass. I don't know where Gloss is, but for once I don't mind. I'm part of this. I'm present, and people can see me. Michelle pulls me towards the ramp. We scramble up, or I do. She slips and slithers down, tries again. Eventually, Grant boosts her from below, and I reach down and grab her wrist to pull her up. There's no way she'd struggle with it if she was sober, and I make sure she's balanced before letting her go. Grant gets pulled into the crowd, laughing as Seana hands him a bottle.

Michelle and I sit with our legs dangling, watching the writhing group passing cans and bottles and joints, jumping up and down and on and off things. I lean back, weaving my fingers together and tipping my head back to look up at the stars. It's a relief to be out of the press of people for a bit. I remember Michelle sitting outside at Grant's house party. Maybe she's like me, prone to getting overwhelmed. I'll ask her another time.

The horizon is hazy with heat, the last faint tinge of dusk long gone, but stickiness still visible in the electric lights of the city. When I look straight up, at the sky is washed with silver by the powerful crescent moon, a scythe in the sky. A killing moon.

Michelle puts her handbag under her head as a pillow, which can't be comfortable because it has a big buckle. She looks at me with huge eyes. Her lipstick is smudged, and her cheeks are pink.

"Hey, Max," she slurs, pressing her thigh against mine.

"Yeah?"

Michelle takes a deep breath. "Danny's such a waste."

My whole body tightens.

I reach for lightness, try to close the conversation and not let it show how much the wound still hurts when it's poked. "What do you mean?"

Michelle doesn't say anything, but the silence is odd, loaded and dangerous. There's an unyielding brightness in her eyes, a question on her lips.

"Michelle?" I don't know what I'm asking for. For her to tell me I'm imagining things? That the ice in the air is all in my head?

"He's an idiot. Treating you like this. He could be happy, and he's just . . ." She waves her hands in the air, weaving a spell with her fingerprints dragging stardust through the night. "Choosing not to. I tried to make him see that."

She's thready and unfocused, not really taking to me

anymore at all. The coldness coalesces in my stomach. What did she say to him?

"What did you do?" I demand, sitting up, pulling my feet up from the ramp and grabbing my knees, protecting my underbelly. Out of the corner of my eye, I see Gloss part with the dancing group at the bottom of the basin.

"I just told him, you know. You're a boy, and he's fucking you, and he's gay." She shrugs. "Sometimes we want people we can't have. That hurts more than anything, but he wants you and you want him. The only person standing in his way is himself."

Words crowd my head and refuse to be ordered into a response, just denial and disbelief and confusion battering at my skull, mixed with booze and weed and knives. Michelle puts her hand on mine where I've knotted my fingers together, white hills of bone blazing with tension.

"I figure that's why it fucked him up so much when you came out. Like, if you were a girl, even a butch punk one, then he wasn't gay if he loved you. And I think he did. Love you, I mean. But you're a guy and he's gay, whether he likes it or not." Her voice has sharpened. Her eyes pin me down.

It's too much. I don't want to hear any of this, but my throat's in a vice and my bones are made of lead, fused to the ramp.

"Loving Danny is a nightmare. I'm glad I grew out of it," she says, leaning in and laying her head on my shoulder. She's wearing bright pink shoes with grubby white soles, and a memory hits me—pink shoes swinging from a sink in a bathroom, behind Danny's knees before he slams the door in my face.

AFTER

14

IT GETS RAUCOUS, as you might expect for five teenagers on a beach holding an impromptu wake. Before I forget, I fire out a text to my dad.

> Gone to beach with Grant and somefriends. Probs won't be back in town tonight, ok?

I keep my phone in my left hand while I hunt through the cooler. A notification comes through. I've been tagged in a post on Insta.

DevonDMan • **Follow**
Ridgepoint

Liked by **Braiden** and **156 others**

DevonDMan Will swim for you at Nationals, buddy, I know ull be watching ☮

#neverforget #themanthelegend ... more

View all 29 comments

Grantus_abeat
Wtf man take this shit down

> **DevonDMan**
> wym?

MikePTank
Bro

ShellyGolightly
RIP Danny ><

AndySalazaaar
Can't believe this.

BraidenMcgee
brutal news just heard.call if u wanna talk n e 1

SheilaRitter69
Anyone know what appened?

HellHayesNoFury
Is Danny dead? Is this a joke?

SonnyBlackmore
I remember hanging out with Danny all through elementary school. We fell out a few years ago but he was such a good dude. Can't believe he's gone. Legit devoed man. Devo.

SerenaMilawi
uwu miss u

JonasCook
Pour one out son

WillowShields

No offence but if there's a killer on the loose and no one is telling us anything that's messed up. I was at that party and everything was ok when I left. Now it's all over the news that Danny's been killed? What the F*

AintIGoodwin

R.I.P big man. See u on the other side of the last wave

HarvGogo

#Neverforget

> **Grantus_abeat**
>
> That's not what that means, asshole

HarmonyChase

Love the sinner, hate the sin. God will protect you now, Daniel

KasimbFlippin

I bet it was Max Foster's new psycho gf

> **UrBoyRitchi**
>
> Seconded! Did you see this?
> www.londondaily.co.uk/april/2022/girl-dies-was-it-murder?!
> She killed her sister, and now she's done for Danny.
> Making it look like it could be a suicidie.

>> **KasimbFlippin**
>>
>> We were right bruv they've gone and copped her

>> **JonnnaThan**
>>
>> It didnt look like a suicide tho did it,
>> they said it was murder right away.
>> They arrested Max, did you know?

KasimbFlippin

1) that dork wouldn't
hurt a fly and 2) they
let him go bc it was his gf

LovelyGirl86
@MusicMaxxx

Thanks for tagging me on this shit, LovelyGirl86, whoever you are. Millie wasn't well, Gloss had nothing to do with
her sister dying. She can't have.

A text from my dad pops onto the screen before I click
on the link to noted trash paper the *London Daily*. It's for
the best; I don't want to read anything they have to say,
but the headline itches in the back of my mind as I open
the message.

Ok. What should I do with this guy?

Then he sends a picture of Liam at the fire station entrance.
What? He must be here for Gloss, to visit her maybe. Why's
he with my dad? Maybe he's here to kick my arse—I promised
I'd take care of her, and instead she ends up in jail.

There's a papery brush behind my ear, making me jump. I
reach up as I spin around to face Michelle. My fingers brush
rolled paper in a familiar shape. A joint, unless Michelle's
started twisting the ends on her rollies. I leave it there, behind
my ear.

"Hey, Max. Come dance?" Michelle leans into me, her eyes
sparkling. A dance party—Lina and Mike giving it, while
Grant barely sways—has kicked off.

"Be right there," I mutter, distracted.

Dad calling.

He knows phone calls make me anxious. However, in the scheme of things I currently have to be anxious about, answering the phone doesn't even rank a grimace.

"Hey?" I mumble.

"Hey, Max."

It's Liam. He sounds like I feel. Like the world has fallen out from under him.

"What are you . . . Why are you with my dad?"

"Reporters are at my place. I wanted . . . I don't know. She called me this morning. Said she was sorry. I didn't know what she was talking about until the vermin turned up to ask me what I thought about Gloss . . . I couldn't stay there. I . . ." There's a door-closing noise, and the chatter of the fire station cuts off. Liam sighs, voice rough. "You're the only one left in the world except me who knows her."

There's a long pause while I do a terrible job being someone anyone would want to talk to, racking my brains for words to say.

Liam doesn't seem to mind. "They said . . . They said Gloss killed her. That she killed Millie. That she was never really ill." His voice breaks.

I'm filled with memories of Gloss's rigid self-control, that predatory stillness in her face. The way she menaced that cashier who misgendered me. But then there's the look in her eyes when we left Grant's party. Is it possible I could be so wrong about her? A cold, slimy sensation fills my tummy, crawling outward through every limb.

Have I been wrapping myself up with a killer?

I shiver. Did I seem like a perfect scapegoat, cowering at the back of the maths room?

This isn't a conversation to have over the phone, and I can't leave Liam on his own at the station. "I'm gonna send you a map."

BEFORE

19

"MAX."

Gloss's voice douses me, and I come up gasping for air as if I haven't breathed since Michelle started talking. Gloss is standing at the base of the ramp, shoes dangling from her index finger.

"Come here."

Her order snaps through my body, loosens my joints. I slide off the top of the ramp and slip-sprint down, having to leap a sprawled-out leg in the hollow of the bowl before skidding to a halt. Momentum carries me past Gloss, which gives me a second to try to figure out what my face is doing. Nothing good, that's for sure.

"You okay?"

I turn to her. She cups my cheek with one warm hand, thumb pressing right where the tears are going to run later, when I'm alone. A wretched, angry knot in my stomach demands a change.

"What've you got on you?" My voice is rough, ragged. I'm shredded. He's gay, he's gay, he's gay. I knew it, but I hadn't made sense of it in my own head yet. Why couldn't he have trusted me? I pick Gloss's free hand up and hold it to my other cheek so she's cupping my face like a baby. My skin is freezing, and her fingers brand me, ground me.

"E, a little molly. There was coke earlier." Her eyes are big and deep enough to fall into. I want to fall into her and forget everything else. "You think you'd be talkative on coke?" she asks.

"I just wanna feel good." The words bubble over, spill out of me, my guts all soft and pink all over the floor.

"I want that too, sweet boy."

She leans up and kisses me on the forehead, a blessing. A spell.

A moment later, a hard pill is against my bottom lip, and I open for her thumb. She swipes it over my tongue. The pill spreads bitterness in its path. I wash it down with a sweet pink drink grabbed from a hand. The squawk of protest barely penetrates my ears. I lay my hands, larger, boy's hands now, on Gloss's tiny waist.

"Dance with me."

She sways easy against me, smelling like warmth and sweat and sunshine and summer. Like love. I lick her neck because it's right there against my mouth, and she giggles and squirms away from my face without breaking free. Body to body. Other people join us, dancing in the belly of the fishbowl, music low and throbbing under the swell of voices and bodies.

The stars are bright and I'm a ghost made of glass and lightning. I've shattered so many times I'm nothing but splinters, stuck into the soles of these feet, under the quick of these nails. I need to be melted down and made strong and whole, and Gloss is the forge I should liquefy in, becoming orange and violent. I want to be a sword—a boy that is sharp and vengeful, who cuts down his enemies like wheat. I want to be Galahad, pure and gallant, unsullied. I feel like I have fingerprints all over me, blue-blushed memories of Danny's hands cupping and holding me, shielding me.

The hole in my chest is yawning open, even with Gloss trying to hold me together. She can't do it alone. I have to grab the sides and pull and mean it. I have to shut Danny out of my hollow centre before he kills me. He was never supposed to be in there. The drugs fill my shoes with glitter and canvas. I paint circles behind my dancing feet, washed away on an ocean of hands and mouths.

Gloss knots her hands in my hair and pulls me down to her lips. We kiss, silly and sliding, laughing and slick. It doesn't mean anything. Nothing means anything. There's only the night and the howling. I bark at the moon, and other wolves sing with me. I don't know if I'm snarling or smiling. I don't care. I pull happiness out of the air and stuff it down my throat. I gorge myself on Gloss's lipstick and her breath on my tongue.

She wraps her fingers around my wrist, around my tattoo. It doesn't hurt, even when she digs her nails in.

"Why me, Gloss?" Brave enough now to ask the question I never asked Danny. I have to half shout it into her ear so she can hear. Her hair tickles my nose, reminding me of slow Sunday mornings and only rolling out of bed for pancakes.

She pulls back enough to press her forehead to mine, standing on her bare tiptoes. She nips my bottom lip with sharp teeth. I hiss but don't pull back.

"You reminded me of her. On the first day."

I don't need to ask who. It strums through the air around us. I reminded Gloss of Millie, who she couldn't protect. From illness, from her parents. I wonder if it should bother me that the echo of a dead girl brought me here, to her.

"You saved me." I push the words into her mouth with my tongue.

"I did, didn't I?" She throws her head back and spins, hair sheeting out around her and sparking scarlet magic in the distant streetlights.

"I hate everyone except you," I tell her, and I'm serious around the edges but laughing on the inside. Because I don't. I love them all and I want them to love me. Everyone in the whole world.

"Good job I found you then."

She dives in to scrape my tongue with her teeth and whirls away, yanking me along for the ride. I step in a cup and trip, stagger-stepping my way to the edge. Gloss pulls me up onto the railing, iron in my belly as we lean over, looking out at the field and the city.

Blue lights are my first warning, flashing on the side of the church tower, then the siren fades into reality.

"Coppers!" I yell it, swinging down, staggering. Gloss jumps on my back, and I slide my hands under her sweaty knees. We gallop into the dark evening, followed by baying teens. The police car whizzes past on the way to the park, probably called by one of the houses that faces onto the close. Maybe Danny's dad. I wonder if he went home. I can't see him in the mess of people. I hope he didn't do anything stupid and get arrested.

We're all laughing as Gloss beeps us into the lobby with her keycard. Jimmy, the night guy, is reading a book behind the desk, and he narrows his eyes at us before calling the lift. Gloss and I jam inside with whoever can fit. We've lost people on the way, and maybe they'll come back, maybe not. The night is still ours; we're still here. Gloss slides her hands under my shirt at the neck. She's on my back but leaning against the mirrored lift wall now. She'll tip Jimmy in the morning and he'll forgive us.

We are money and magic, and no one can hurt us.

AFTER

15

I WAIT FOR Liam at the turnoff. My secret cove is not so secret now. I should have known Danny would change that too, like he changed everything else. A meteor bursting through the universe and rearranging space junk like me as it passes.

He's out of the car as soon as he's parked. There are no tears on his face or in his eyes, but his round face is drawn like he's been weeping.

"Did she really? Did she kill someone?" Liam sounds like a child, and it makes me step forward, opening my arms in an invitation he takes immediately. He's warm and solid, his firm strength gives out against me so I'm half holding him up. His weakness makes me stronger. Grief-stricken, he shakes his head against my shoulder, his breath hot on my throat. I'm taller than he is, and a sudden protective urge has me gathering him close, squeezing his broad shoulders as if it will change anything. *Someone.* Liam doesn't even know his name, doesn't know anything. Did Gloss kill Danny?

Could she?

"How did you find out?" I avoid the question clumsily,

because how can I say that if she didn't, then there's no one left but me who might have?

Liam pulls back, sniffling. His curling hair catches the red warmth of an inchoate sunset. He's not beautiful when he cries. It makes him look young and lost. "The fuckin' newsies started hitting up my social. Vultures. Digging up all that stuff about Millie, saying it was Gloss. That she killed Millie." He takes a big, soggy snuff of air, turning his stricken face to the sky. "They think she fucking set the whole thing up. *Poisoned* her. Three years she was in and out of hospital, Max." He trails off, gasping.

It's so, so awful I don't know how to breathe.

"She said she'd make Danny leave me alone if she had to." My voice is wavering. "She killed him because he hurt me. I didn't take care of her."

Liam's face quivers as much as his voice does. "You're not responsible for other people's choices." He's staring sightlessly past me, his long eyelashes spangled with tears. "Millie once told me I had no idea what she was capable of."

In the silence that follows his words, music starts to throb, echoing over the headland. They must have really cranked Grant's speaker. The smoke from our beach fire dances to the beat, a faint wisp against the neon-streaked sky.

Liam clears his throat with a wet, catarrhal sound. "Sounds like a party?"

"More of a funeral."

"Is it . . . Can I come? Or . . ." Liam looks around abruptly, like he's just noticed he's driven out to the middle of nowhere to ask me if I think our mutual friend is a killer. Verdict: unclear, leaning towards yes.

I bite my cheek hard, the edge of hysteria threatening. "Sure. I came to Millie's wake, didn't I?" There's a wild note in my voice.

He flinches. I shouldn't have mentioned her, even if he did. Tucking my hair behind my ear reminds me there's a joint there, and I grab it with the relief of a drowning man reaching for a life raft.

"Here!" Too loud this time, but Liam doesn't wince. He takes the joint with a puzzled expression, like he's not quite sure what it is. Then he looks back at his car. Oh. "Don't worry, we'll sleep it off. Speaking of, I should grab blankets and stuff . . ."

I start walking backwards towards my car, which is better than sprinting into the distance, I guess. I'm a terrible runner, anyway.

Liam blinks owlishly and then follows me, lighting up.

BEFORE

20

THE LIGHTS REFLECTING in the mirrored walls of the lift are too bright. I have to squint.

Grant is half holding Mike up, who's clutching his knee and grimace-grinning, and there's blood leaking through his fingers. Gloss rubs circles with her nose on the back of my head, her breath ruffling my hair.

"Dude, you okay?" I ask.

Mike hauls himself up using Michelle's shoulder. "Yeah, toasted my knee, but it's cool."

"Drink up, party boy, you'll barely feel it." Lina offers him a half-empty Solo cup, and Mike downs it.

The bell chimes, and we bundle out of the small space and back into the flat, giggling and breathless. The only music still playing is coming from the bedroom, muted and distant. The fading sound of sirens streams from the open balcony doors until it's lost in the humid night.

People are sprawled around in the living area, and I have a dislocating sensation of realising I left my house with all these people in it. People I know. They could have looked at anything. And then I see that the only thing being inspected is each other. There's a small group on the balcony that looks like they're watching the road and smoking. The art guy has a girl on each arm of his chair, and I think they're the same ones from earlier, but I can't be sure. One is shirtless, her lace bra and dangling necklaces the only items covering her upper half.

Finally, I let Gloss slide off my back, and she wobbles, grabbing my bum either for balance or for fun. She gives me a shit-eating grin. I'm panting too hard to return it. The long run with extra weight, wasted, provided a solid workout. I have a moment of violent, vicious gratitude for this body of mine, this trans body that's seen me through pain and trauma. The body I've wanted to rip free of, it's carried me here. To her. It's strong and changing, bending to my will. It's not so bad, this body of mine. I can make this house a home.

Danny's lounging in a chair across the room, watching me with glazed eyes. I could talk to him, but it would be pointless. We're both fucked up, and there's always tomorrow. Tonight, we can pretend.

Lina strolls in from the kitchen with the huge, empty bottle of champagne. "Who wants to relive Grant's thirteenth?" She's standing half-cocked like she might fall over, the floor leaning under her bare feet. Michelle squeals and beelines forward, grabs the bottle and plops down on the floor cross-legged.

"We're too old for spin the bottle," Mike says, holding a cold can against his injured knee. Part of me wants to fetch him a first aid kit, but the rest of me is flying. I've kissed two people in my life, Danny and Gloss. Spin the bottle? Really? Kissing does sound nice.

"We're too young to care what we're too old for," Danny says with a voice like a rusty knife.

The circle fills in. Grant plops down next to Michelle and leans his elbows back on the edge of the fireplace. Lina sits, joined by Helen and Willow from maths, the art kid and his plus two, Devon and a few of the swimmers. The group on the balcony don't come in, and I stay leaning on the barrier between the kitchen and the lounge, straddling two spaces, not sure where I belong.

Danny looks right at me. Tilts his chin at the circle. My stomach flips over, and I take a step forward before I think. Gloss is pulled with me and slides her hand into my back pocket possessively.

"Sure you know what you're doing there, lover boy?" she whispers.

"No." Do I ever know what I'm doing? I sit down next to Grant. Gloss folds herself down next to me and inspects her nails. Mike beams, thrilled by the addition of Gloss to the group, and Danny's eyes are heavy on my throat. I hide in my beer bottle, taking a long, slow swallow. Gloss puts her hand on my knee, digs her fingertips in. It grounds me, small points of pain making little stars in my skin, pinning me to the carpet. I exhale. It might have been a while since I last did that. My skin is oversensitive, and my thoughts are murky and hard to chase.

Danny's gay. That's what Michelle said. That he's gay and the reason he hated me so much for so long is that he thought I could be the proof he wasn't. It makes a twisted, sad kind of sense, and I want to tell Gloss, but I'm not sure I could be quiet enough inside to find the words.

The bottle spins, and Michelle kisses Lina, a small, quick peck that gets a few jeers and boos. Lina spins and catches Devon. They make out enthusiastically until Mike kicks Devon in the arse. Devon gets Grant, and they both make a gross face before kissing lightly, then Devon puts his hand on Grant's face and goes back in for another. Grant scoots backwards, laughing, to grab the bottle.

"Ooh, Danny and Grant," Michelle announces. The two boys put in the bare minimum effort and the maximum disgust, scrubbing the backs of their hands over their mouths and making exaggerated vomit noises.

"This is the gayest game I've ever played," Grant says, disgruntled. "Danny, for fuck's sake, spin a girl."

Danny does spin a girl, and that girl is Gloss. She beckons him in and doesn't relinquish her hold on my leg when he crawls across the circle to press his mouth against hers. It's a quick brush, and Danny doesn't try to chase her when she pulls away. His eyes flick to me and away again as he backs up and regains his spot and his beer while ignoring the many wolf whistles.

"That's more like it!" Mike whoops. "Gloss, you're up."

"I can't believe you made me play this children's game, Max." Gloss spins, and the bottle lands on me as she says my name. She sighs dramatically. "It's so much less fun when you're being told what to do."

"For you," I joke, "you don't have to play." But she's already crawling into my lap. She straddles my hips and snakes her hand around my neck until she can make a fist in my hair and tug.

Instead of answering, she bites my lip. I hiss and open my mouth for her. We kiss slow and erotic, tongues sliding. When she pulls away, I might make an embarrassing noise. She kisses me on the nose and climbs out of my lap. "But I like to win."

I don't have enough blood in my brain to respond, so I just grunt and snatch my beer up, fanning myself. Everyone laughs with me, not at me. When I lean forward to spin the bottle, I feel in my hand that it's going to land on Danny. I freeze, panicking. I don't know how to kiss him, especially not after that kiss with Gloss. Not after what Michelle told me. My heart chokes me as I send the bottle hurtling around.

As it turns out, my panic wasn't necessary, because it lands on Michelle. I scoot over to her, shy and hiding behind my shortened fringe less effectively than I used to be able to do.

Our noses bump when I move in, awkward, like neither of us know how to kiss. I'm seeing double, which might explain it. Her breath smells of sweet cocktails. Her lips are chapped and dry but sticky at the same time. She licks at my mouth, but I pull back, my head lurching from the movement. It should count, though. Our lips met, that's a kiss, and it was longer than Danny and Grant's, so it's not like anyone can give me shit for it. I need to sit down.

Grant nudges me in the ribs good-naturedly when I sit back on my heels in my circle spot, flopping against the wall so I don't have to hold my own body up for a moment. Michelle spins and gets Danny, who sighs in seeming exasperation.

"No need to sound too pleased about it," Michelle says lightly. "For that sigh you can get your tight arse over here."

"All right, take it easy," Danny grumbles and stands up, plodding around the circle to kneel next to Michelle.

"Don't I always." She loads it with double meaning and tilts her head, making Danny lean in and take the kiss she's offering.

It looks like Danny tries to go for a quick peck, but he winces and stays close for longer, the kiss getting deeper. When he pulls back, there's tightness around his eyes that I don't like.

He scoots back across the circle and grabs the bottle, looking as if he wants to end that interaction as fast as possible. He spins, and the bottle glides around twice in full circles before juddering to a halt on me. If I didn't know better, I'd say someone put their hand on it. Gloss, in the side of my vision, might be glowing.

Our gazes lock—the click is almost audible, hovering at the edges of my ears. He gives me a soft, lopsided grin, and there's none of the fear I expected in his gaze or in my chest.

He comes to me. I knew he would. Gloss's hand is hot on my thigh, and she doesn't move it, not even when Danny's exhaling on my lip and waiting for permission. I lift my chin, slow, so slow, molasses poured through my veins instead of blood; I'm made of sweet, hot honey. He kisses me, the seam of his mouth pressed against my lower lip, faintest hint of suction, light scrape of teeth. His stubble is sand against my cheek, my philtrum. My mouth has never had so many nerve endings. There's no tongue, no sex, but so much heat, and in the far distance—drowned in an ocean of blood rushing in my ears—someone whoops.

I expect the kiss to break because Gloss does something Glossish, like digging her nails into the tender skin of my thigh. But the kiss ends in its own time. We pull back at the same split second. It's the sweetest, purest thing. Danny hovers an inch away, then his eyes slide sideways, and he moves back into his place. It feels like the entire circle exhales, shudders. I'm blinking, dazed with wanting.

"Man, why don't you just come out already?" Mike sighs, reaching over to pat Danny on the thigh. "We love you, dude, it's all good."

Danny's whole face breaks in a complicated way. Sunlight busts through the clouds in his eyes like he's real and whole and ready for one, blinding second.

And then it ends.

I've seen the flatness in his dull-iron eyes before, but it's never hurt so much. There's a splintering, shattering sensation in my chest. He looks right at me. Gloss squeezes my thigh so hard it'll bruise, and it's the only thing stopping me from disintegrating.

"I'm not fucking gay." He spits it, but there's no emotion in the words, just a roaring emptiness.

I hate him, thick and hot and angry. What's so bad about

being gay when you could also be happy? "Gay enough to sleep with me."

I barely realise I've said it. I didn't mean to, not really. My mouth is numb and stupid.

Danny's eyes land on me. The "how could you" is stamped so clearly on his face he doesn't need to say it. "Yeah. Tell them as well, why don't you? Come on, Michelle." He's on his feet, as suddenly as if he's teleported.

Michelle doesn't look at me as she obediently gets to her feet and follows him out of the room. Towards our bedroom.

AFTER

16

WHILE LIAM AND I were talking by the road, the others seem to have made good use of their time. Mike is no longer wearing a shirt or jeans. He's doing cartwheels that are quite impressive, undermined by the fact his black boxer shorts have neon hotdogs all over them. Grant appears to have found a hat on the beach, because I'm pretty sure he didn't have a straw bonnet on when we arrived.

"This is Liam," I announce once we've made it over the rocks. Mike finishes his gymnastics with a flashy somersault, landing just a metre away from us.

"Liam." Mike says the name slowly, with narrowed eyes, and my heart sinks. None of them know him. Why would I bring a stranger to a party? I barely even know them. Why am I so weird? We probably should have left together. But this is my beach.

"You in mourning, Liam?"

"Always," Liam replies solemnly, and Mike nods, taking the answer at face value. Liam offers him the joint, and Mike accepts it, then offers his fist. Liam bumps it, and apparently, that's that.

"Great spot," Liam observes, looking around at the rocky space. The tide is coming in now, covering the rocks up and leaving just the golden sand and craggy, sheltering walls.

"Max found it." Grant claps me on the shoulder, and my heels slip in the sand. He looks so absurd in his straw hat I forget for a moment why we're here.

"Dope." Liam kicks his shoes off then shimmies out of his jeans, leaving him in loose, plum boxers and a plain maroon tee. "I wanna put my feet in the water."

"An excellent plan, mon new ami!" Mike does a truly awful French accent. "We should go skinny dipping! Danny loved to feel the water in his pubes."

I cough, caught between a laugh and a cry of instinctive fear.

Skinny dipping. I'll never be just a normal kid, doing normal kid stuff. Guess I'll sit on the beach and watch. How can I do that without being a pervert? I should leave.

Mike doesn't miss a beat. "But of course, everyone should feel free to keep a top on for the good ole pube water experience with dignity."

Blinking, I consider his words. He thought about me. It's not dark and the water is pretty clear here. I don't even swim by myself until after dusk when even my pale body disappears under murky water. This T-shirt isn't ideal, though. It's long enough when stretched down, but what if it looks like a dress? Will I look like a boy in a dress—acceptable, if not my jam— or a girl? "Is the pube part really necessary?"

Mike spreads his hands expansively, "Hey, man, I don't make the rules."

It seems a lot like he does make the rules, but also, I'm possessed by want. I want to fucking do this wake properly, with my friends, who are totally fine with me wearing a T-shirt if I want to. And who don't care that I was suckered in by a murderous siren.

"I'm keeping my shirt on too." Lina sidles up and into Mike's arm. He snugs her close.

"You do you, Leens! What the fuck, I'll daffy duck it up too."

Mike dances back and pulls off his boxers. He whoops as he runs naked across the cove to his clothes. He yanks his T-shirt on, which is short enough we all see everything he has going on anyway, as he gallops towards the water.

"I gotta admit"—Grant takes a puff on the joint—"Danny would think that was fuckin' hilarious."

Then he starts unbuttoning his fly. Michelle and Lina confer quietly, then walk towards the water, shedding their shoes, and step out of their shorts just before they get to the wet sand.

"Daffy duckin' it is," Liam agrees affably, delicately turning to the water before pulling his undies down, exposing a round gold bum for a minute before his T-shirt drops back down.

Well. If everyone's doing it.

I'm the last one in, but when we float in a circle, heads together, Michelle holding one of my hands and Liam the other, I am so deeply in my own body that the sadness ebbs. Looking up at the bruising sky, the slender arc of moon glowing despite the shadow cast over it, I am myself.

BEFORE

21

I HOVER. MY body is between events. Everyone is looking at me. There's a full range of expressions, from Lina's mild interest to Grant's open *O* mouth.

Then a laugh explodes out of my chest in a huge bark, shattering the ice-strung air and washing over everyone, reanimating the room. I clap my hands over my mouth to stop the sound. Laughing hurts so much I wouldn't be surprised if the wetness hitting my palms turned out to be blood. Gloss rubs my back, and Grant moves around the circle and grips my shoulder, squeezes gently. Mike loudly starts talking about the rugby game that was already thoroughly discussed last night.

I laugh and laugh. I'm waiting for it to turn into tears, but it never does, just rattles dark out of my chest and into the cave of my hands. Brave, bold Danny, golden boy, too afraid for words. I always thought it was me that hated myself, but compared to that, I'm my own best friend.

That kiss. That kiss, though. It's impossible to deny that kiss. And yet he is. Again. Over and over again. I deserve to love and be loved by someone who'll hold my hand in the skatepark and kiss me in front of my friends and look at me only with sunshine and never turn his back on me like Danny just did.

In that moment, I'm free. My chest stops trying to laugh my lungs through my nose, and I take a deep, gasping breath. I throw myself backwards, arms splayed and head thumping gently on the plush carpet. Gloss leans over me, haloed by the streaming streetlight pouring in through the window. She's worried, her face scrunched and desperate, more messed up than I've ever seen her.

"I'm good!" I tell her, and I mean it, relief tangled around the words. "I'm good."

She narrows her eyes at me, eyebrows pinched together. I sober, although not literally because I am still very high and drunk, and all things considered, maybe I'm not actually good, but it sure feels like I am right now.

"Really, lover. I'm good!" I push at her shoulder with one hand because she's too close to really see. She goes, but unwillingly, and Grant kind of hovers at the edge of my vision. I hold my hand out to him. His is big and warm when he closes it around my knuckles and pulls me upright. During my small collapse, the party has redistributed, scattered around. Game over. The balcony doors are open and inviting, breeze ruffling the curtains.

"Let's go outside," I decide and head for the open air, not looking to see who follows me.

On the balcony, there's a cooler full of melted ice and floating cans. I snag a Coke and open it. The cool fizzy bubbles are perfect spooling down my throat, and I sigh in appreciation, flopping down into a chair that could use more cushions.

Grant's hovering in the doorway, and Gloss pushes past him and leans on the rail, and then he follows her out. No one says anything until Grant clears his throat.

"You okay?" His hands won't still, fiddling with his cuffs.

"I think so," I reply, and Grant snorts.

"Gloss?" he asks.

Her hands are knotted on the metal railing, eyes gazing unseeing out over the park.

"When?" She turns her lasers onto me. I don't need to ask what she means. Eels squirm in my belly.

"The night you lost your phone." I raise my chin, meeting her gaze head on.

"You seemed different," she murmurs. "I thought it was just me."

"Everything else is you." I'm earnest, hoping it's enough.

Grant has one foot inside and one foot outside. He can't decide whether or not to leave. It's sweet of him. As though he could protect me from Gloss, or Danny, or anyone. When people are inside you, no one can protect you.

"Do you guys mind if I . . . sit, by myself for a bit? I'm fine, I swear. I just want to write." I need space to think, to escape from Gloss glaring at me. I project as much I really am fine, honestly, for real and true, into my voice and face as I can manage.

"You're not going to do anything stupid." It's an instruction, not a question, and Gloss moves closer to me to punctuate it by digging her nails into my neck.

"No, ma'am," I tell her very seriously, because I've been in that place, where it's hopeless and dark. I don't live there anymore.

"I want you to go inside." Gloss's thumb traces my jaw, and Grant keeps himself busy with the cooler. "If you need to be out here, I want someone to stay with you. Is that okay?"

"Just let me in your folks' room. I'll sit in the armchair. Like Sherlock Holmes. Promise."

Everyone is noisy, and I want to think quietly for a bit. I have a lot of thoughts spiralling around each other, and I need to tease through them.

"I can kick everyone out," Grant chimes in, not looking at us. "It is four A.M."

I glance through the window into the living room. "Everyone's still having fun." Even Danny, in my room with Michelle, except he's not having any fun at all, and if anyone goes in there it'll be another fight. I'm sure Grant would go and try to kick him out if I asked, and I'm equally sure Danny would relish the opportunity to beat the shit out of someone even if it was his best friend. Best to leave him be, hiding his shame and self-hatred in Michelle.

"Okay," Gloss decides. "Text me if you need me."

"Always." I stagger to my feet, the balcony lurching under my socks, and traipse indoors. Gloss's parent's room always has a museumlike quality, too clean and too empty. I eye the unsmiling man and woman who watch me from a gold frame on the mantle. It's their favourite wedding picture, or so I'm told.

The four-poster bed that would be at home in a historical house dominates the wall furthest from the door. Flopping down, I roll onto my back and take a moment to wonder if my overheated body is going to leave sweat marks on the cream duvet. I don't know why Gloss's parents are so obsessed with white.

My shoulders sink into the pillows, and I'm supported enough that I can still see out of the large French doors to the surrounding balcony. The room spins, and my brain swirls with it. There are words on the tip of my tongue that don't want to be said but want to be written. I dig around in my tight jean pocket and haul out my small notebook. The stubby pencil tucked into the elastic is barely long enough to hold, but it does the job. I flip the book to the nearest blank page and start draining myself onto paper.

AFTER

17

LYING BETWEEN A softly snoring Liam and a warm, somnolent Michelle, exhausted to my bones but unable to sleep, my body ratchets tighter and tighter. I'm creaking with tension, trying not to disturb anyone. On the other side of Michelle, Lina sprawls against Mike's chest, and Grant is rolled in a blanket by himself against the rocky wall. I can't sleep. I can't even lie here. I am a kettle boiling. The steam has built up inside me, and I need to scream.

I extricate myself inch by inch. I can do this one thing for them and let them sleep while they're able to.

Dark night envelops me. Instead of taking the more clearly beaten track back to the road and my car, I turn right and scramble upwards over the rough, unforgiving edges of granite. The headland protrudes over the water, so if you lie down on your belly, you can dangle your head off and scream into thrashing spray and open air. The crashing waves underneath drown out all the rest of the sound in the world. I kneel, then lie on my belly and inch forward. Under me, the waves howl and roar. Over thousands of years, these water shaped this cliff; it's also washed the last traces of blood out from my nails where scrubbing them hadn't. There's a metaphor in there somewhere. Or a song.

I'm chaos inside. Everything has shaken out of place, and I can't shimmy it back in. Maybe nothing will ever fit where it used to. There's salt on my lips, cold spray freckling my face, and my scream gets lost, blending into the mighty force of nature below.

When I roll over, Michelle is sitting less than five feet away, watching me. I almost leap right off the cliff in shock. Her smile holds an affectionate edge that pulls at me, and I'm swamped with gratitude that she came to find me, instead of letting me isolate myself up here. Talking to her, or even being quiet with her will help more than screaming myself out. Michelle sits down beside me on the rim of the world, then leans back and takes a deep breath of sea air. I pull myself up and settle next to her, gazing out over the black water.

Moving grass tickles my hand, and I glance down to see Michelle edging closer until our little fingers brush.

"What are you doing?" I blurt. I'm genuinely confused. It's like she wants to hold my hand but isn't brave enough to go for it.

She looks up from under her lashes and shrugs. "I figured with Danny and Gloss both . . . maybe we could finally explore our chemistry."

My brain does the record scratch. "You like me?"

"Of course I do, Max. I don't just sit on people's laps if I don't like them. I've always liked you. Remember how close we got over summer?"

She sounds sincere. I grimace, trying to find words to explain that I couldn't start a new relationship right now, even if I wanted to. I'm grieving.

Michelle fiddles with her phone as she watches me. Her

face is more thoughtful than nervous. The light ricochets off the black and diamanté phone case she's had as long as I've known her.

Like an overlay, the memory comes to me—a hallway, a silver mirror flashing in her hand.

BEFORE

22

THE MUSIC COMES out of me in gouts, like blood spurting onto the pages. I wish I had my guitar, but I'm messed up and my writing looks like tangled threads, which doesn't bode well for playing. I leave notes to myself for the rhythm, but I know I won't forget it regardless. It's a throb, a heartbeat, a wave washing on the shore. It's a song about letting go and moving on. I pace around the room, unseeing.

Eventually, spent, I collapse back into the embrace of the cushions of the bed, breathing like I've run a marathon. I'm obsessed by what I've written. It's stuck in my head, a circling shark, even now I've put it down on paper. I wonder how long I've been in here. It could have been hours, but when I glance out of the windows, dawn is still spreading rosy fingers over the balcony. Time warps and twists for me when I'm writing even when I'm sober, and right now, I'm definitely not sober. When did I come in here? The world fades out for a few minutes, and when I come back, my muscles are sore, and my neck is screaming. I need painkillers.

I stumble on tingly pins-and-needle feet to the bedroom door. The flat is hazy, drifts of smoke and music and words mixing into each other. There are people in the hallway. I can't make out their faces, but they're kissing.

A shadow looms without a face. Michelle.

Her silver phone throws light into my bleary eyes, spangling my vision with white stars. She shoulders past me, pale in the ghost glow. She follows the conversation trickling on apricot light from the open lounge.

The door to my bedroom gapes into a dark, silent room. Either Danny has passed out, or he's left. I'm surprised to find the idea of walking in on him sated and sweating doesn't sting. I kissed him goodbye. He could have chosen me, over and over, and he never did. Well, I choose me. I choose happiness and people who care enough about me to do it right.

My heart is light as I slip into my room. There's no one in there, and I head straight for the bathroom to grab ibuprofen from the cabinet. I wash them down with cold water from the tap, gulping thirstily and filling my belly. I sploosh water on my face, touching my fine stubble with the pads of my fingers and remembering I'm supposed to shave. The case is where I left it, on the side, to remind me. I reach out to tap the lid with a finger, and weirdly, the top shifts. It's not been pinned in place properly. I lift the lid to realign the lip and stop with the box half-open. It's empty.

My treasured razor isn't in its case.

It's been taken, but by who, and why? It's not so expensive that it's worth stealing.

The only reason to take my razor is to hurt me.

Danny. In my reflection, my forehead is tightly knotted, my face scrunched in outrage. All the joy I was floating on pops and vanishes, leaving me incensed. He can't stop treating me like I don't matter. That's all I want. Just some fucking respect.

I storm out into the bedroom, about to barge into the living room and round up a search party, but before I do, I see shadows moving on the balcony.

The latch slides under my clumsy fingers, but I manage to pop it up and slide the door open. Danny's alone, and he has his back to me, but I'd recognise his shoulders any-where. God knows I've spent enough time staring at them out of the corner of my eyes in class. His white T-shirt glows in the half light. He's leaning on the balcony rail, and his shoulders are shaking. He's crying, I realise, a wave of derision rising up in my throat and blending with the sharp taste of rage that burns my tongue. In that moment, I'm glad he's crying. He deserves to hurt. He's done enough hurting himself.

"Danny." I know the pain he's in, the familiar shape of self-hatred. He needs to get over it. Like Mike said. No one cares, Danny. The words won't come out because I know people do care, but I'm so angry with him, so endlessly angry for throwing us away when we could have been beautiful.

He staggers towards me, drunker than I thought. He drops to his knees faster than I can catch him, and it startles a little laugh out of me.

It dies on my lips.

There's something wrong. The light breaking over him shows me his face is stricken, and his eyes aren't full of tears but staring blindly. I can see the sunrise reflected in his blown pupils. There's a stain down his shirt, spreading dark and red. Wine? My brain won't process what I'm seeing, but the salt smell in the air isn't Danny's ocean scent. It's metal-lic and animal. I'm shaking as I lower him to the balcony with strength that comes from refusing to drop him. Sunlight glints in bloody orange from a wet slick under his chin. I scream then. Loud and ragged. His beautiful face is waxen and starkly lined.

I've found my razor. It's buried in his throat.

AFTER

18

"YOU HAD HIS phone. At the party. I saw you with it. You took his phone . . ."

It was you.

Gloss didn't kill Danny. She didn't do it. I didn't either. She confessed to save me because she thought it was me. My ribs are constricted and solid, metal instead of marrow and muscle. I can't feel my lips, but I hear the words they're shaping. "It was you." My voice isn't my own. It's a plaintive cry.

Michelle recoils. Her face goes white, eyes hard. "It was an accident!"

"They arrested me! Gloss is in prison!" I can't stay still, leaping to my feet and bouncing five paces forward and back.

"It's not my fault they thought it was you, and then she was stupid enough to say it was her." Michelle spits it, a cat with teeth bared. "I figured they'd assume he did it himself." Michelle laughs a small harsh laugh that makes every hair on my neck stand up. "He was waving that razor around like a crazy person. It could easily have been him. It was an accident!" Her voice gets higher. "I thought he was going to hurt me! I just grabbed his arm to stop him."

She's standing now too, and I'm aware of the cliff edge so close the updraft from it is yanking at my hoodie. "Aren't you even a little bit glad he can't hurt you anymore?" Her voice peters out, and she takes a step towards me.

"No!" I deny it hotly. "No. Not at all. Because he's dead." My throat's tight, my head spinning. "Are you?"

"You won't tell anyone, will you, Max? Gloss has all those lawyers, all that money! She'll be okay. If they . . . If they put me away, who's going to take care of my family?" She steps closer, reaching out for my hand.

"Michelle . . . you have to come forward." I back away from the cliff edge, but she's between me and the path. "You have to tell them what happened. It'll be all right. It was an accident." I'm trying to reassure her and myself. I'm a tempest inside, but all of me is focused on one shining fact, the only one with Danny dead. Gloss is innocent. I'm innocent. My eyes are stinging, and my hands are shaking, but they're not covered in blood, because *it wasn't me who killed the boy I loved.*

It was Michelle.

"They won't believe me! I'll get some shitty public defender, and they'll nail me to the wall!" she wails, clutching her bag closer to her chest, watching me with those unnerving eyes. The coldness in them doesn't match her words.

The facts sink in, all of it. She left him on the balcony to drown in his own blood and walked back through the party, his phone in her hand. It's like I've never seen her before. Shaking her head, Michelle paces. Her face is feverish, and her eyes gleam silver like the moonlight on the ocean.

Even if killing him was an accident, leaving him there to die alone wasn't. Letting me get arrested or letting Gloss confess wasn't. Taking his phone wasn't. There were so many moments where Michelle could have made different choices.

"I'm going to call the police. I'm going to go to my car and call the police. It's over, Michelle."

I can't even look at her anymore, don't want to look at her, so I drop my eyes as I push past her, towards the path that leads back to my friends.

Lightning hijacks every nerve and muscle in my body, radiating from my lower back. An involuntary cry forces its way out of my throat. My knees hit the ground hard enough to clack my teeth together. I topple sideways, writhing, jerking uncontrollably until I go limp. Michelle looks down on me, a thoughtful frown on her face. There's a black rectangle sparking blue light in her hand. A taser. She fucking tasered me. My brain is confused and foggy, my limbs responding slowly, as if they're underwater.

Michelle crouches over me. "Max, if you move, I'll hit you again, okay? You can get anything online these days. Gloss may be a mace girl, but I'm really good with a taser. You would be too if you had to deal with my mum's boyfriends."

Staying very still, I try to control my breathing. "Michelle, what are you doing?" It comes out ragged and shaky.

She grabs my feet and starts to untie my left shoe. Before she gets the knot out, I twist my body desperately, trying to pull away from her and get out of reach of her handheld weapon.

Electricity ends me, pauses me, until my body starts again with a shuddering inhale that hurts like knives in my chest. Michelle has pulled my arms behind my back and is tying my wrists together.

"I sort of wanted to kill him. I think I have for a while. You should understand that. He had two people right in front of him who would have done anything for him. Most people don't even get one, Max. And here we were, both of us. And did he care? Did he treat either of us with any respect? No. He didn't deserve us. He was a selfish, stupid little boy, and now that's all he'll ever be because he couldn't fucking control himself." Spittle spatters on my cheek, and she crushes my jaw into the clumpy ground, speaking into my ear. "I'm glad he's dead. There was a moment when the blade was so close to his neck and I thought about saying 'be careful.' I opened my mouth to say 'be careful,' but instead I told him it was me who outed him to his dad, not you."

She grabs me by the hair and yanks. I try to resist, but she twists, and I have to move with her or lose my scalp. "He didn't like that, but how long can you cover for a guy who treats you like shit? What did I get out of it?" She drags me, writhing and yelling, across the clifftop. It's rough going over the rocks without my hands to balance, and I trip a dozen times. Michelle prods me on, threatening with the taser. There's no one to hear me screaming. That's why I loved this place.

I close my mouth.

I'm bleeding in an exciting variety of places, my jeans ripped and my shoulder bruised from a nasty fall. "What are you going to do? Run away? They'll find you."

Michelle grinds to a halt on the grassy path back to the road. I can see the hedge. My car is maybe twenty metres away. If I can get a head start . . .

Before I so much as tense up, Michelle cracks me across the ear with the body of the taser. A star explodes in my skull, and I go down hard. It's staggering how much it hurts.

"I'm not going to run away, Max. You are. Tragic teen,

dead ex, lover in jail. No wonder you want a fresh start. How long before anyone even notices you're missing? You think there's traffic cameras on this road?" She grabs the waistband of my boxers and forces me up with a wedgie, taser still in her other hand. "I'm willing to bet not." I'm thrust towards the gap in the hedgerow.

"I'm not . . . I'm not going to run away, Michelle." I try to say it gently to get her to come back to reality.

Her laugh is shrill and high and awful. "Oh, Max."

And I realise she doesn't expect me to run away. It's what she expects everyone else to think when I don't go back to the beach or come home.

Among all the things she's horribly wrong about, she's right about one thing. No one will be that surprised if I'm gone and they can't find me. I've left before. How could my dad understand that even with Danny dead, even earlier today when I thought Gloss had killed him, that things are different for me? I have roots now. I've grown roots with Grant, with Gloss, with Mandy. Hell, even with Mike, who skinny dipped in a T-shirt so I could be included.

I'm not who I was: a boy who cowered away and froze and never made a choice.

My charge takes her by surprise. I aim low, hunched over with my hands tied behind my back and all my weight thrown forward. I'm off balance, no way to save myself or stop myself from crashing into her. Her stomach compresses under my shoulder, the air exploding from her mouth in a huge gasp. Her hands fly backwards, and the taser spins up, out of her grasp and into the darkness. I land on top of her but don't stick around. She gasps again as I propel myself upwards using my legs and bound hands, wildly off kilter. As soon as I'm even partially upright, I dash for the car.

She's right behind me, her feet thundering. She wasn't

down for long, but I make it to the stile. Rather than waste time trying to hop up with my hands tied, I throw myself face-first over top, the wooden bar crashing into my thighs and arresting my fall enough that I manage a sort of belly flop over the top and onto the ground. Skateboarding taught me to take a nasty stack and get the fuck up before another skater came down on top of me. It takes every ounce of strength I can muster to force myself back to my feet, but worse is coming than a flying board and a rolling teenager. I dare glance back.

Michelle already has two hands on the top of the stile. Her face is set and solid, the moon painting her an unforgiving white.

Looking costs me time and balance. I'm flagging, pain and a stitch teaming up to force me to stop. Did she find her taser? I can't fight her off with my hands tied. I'm struggling to get the leverage to run, let alone kick.

Stumbling forward, I careen towards my only hope for salvation.

I don't lock my car at the beach, too quiet to worry about, and I told Grant to leave the keys in the visor.

With too much momentum to catch myself, I curl to brace for impact, offering my uninjured shoulder as a sacrifice to my car door. The collision slaps the breath right out of me, but even as I'm gasping, my fingers scrabble behind me for the handle.

My lovely trash pile doesn't let me down. The handle pops first try, but Michelle is bearing down on me. She's clutching a huge piece of wood, one of the long sticks people lean up by fences after using them as walking poles. She swings for me as I shrink backwards, pulling into the car like a turtle into its shell to avoid the door bouncing back on its hinges. The wood crashes through the window, sending sparkling shards of glass spin through the air like snowflakes.

Hands still tied behind me, all I can do is kick out with my legs as she grabs the door and jerks it wide open. I'm lying on my hands, on my back, wedged into the front passenger seat. My hands scrabble at the central console, searching.

My fingers close around cool metal. My multitool. I would never have found it if I didn't keep my car more organised these days. Michelle thrusts the end of the stick down towards the junction of my thighs—there's no time to dodge. I scream when it lands, the blow deadens my thigh muscle, but it could have been worse—the silicone padding of my soft packer has protected my groin. Desperately, I try to work the tool open, pinching the tender skin under my wrist with the hinge. Michelle pulls back, yelling, but I can't hear over my brain screaming at me to concentrate on freeing my hands.

The stick flies towards my face, and I perform a last second superhuman contortion to avoid it. The weapon rebounds off the edge of the seat and into the horn with a piercing blast. In the split second of Michelle's jump at the noise, the multitool snaps open. I grasp with useless, short nails for the knife dent.

A faint whistling noise is my only warning. Michelle's face is twisted as she stabs the stick towards my throat. I'm wide open. She's got me.

My knife flicks open. It's razor keen thanks to my dad's tool checking habits. It slices through the shoelaces digging into my wrists as if they're not even there, and then I'm moving.

The pole slaps into my hands. I hold it. Every muscle in my body—every hard-earned muscle that I fought and sweated and begged doctors for—tenses, forcing the weapon back in incremental steps. When she loses her grip, it slips back fast through her hands, and the far end of the pole hits her between the eyes with a meaty thump.

She drops like a duvet from a washing line, going down so easy I don't even hear her land over my harsh breathing.

After checking she's not dead, I call my dad.

NOW

DAWN IS BREAKING by the time I've finished explaining what happened, wrapped in a silver emergency blanket and my dad's arms. He hasn't let go of me since he got to the lay-by to find me sitting on the ground, counting Michelle's breaths with her in the recovery position next to my car. She was coming around as the ambulance loaded her up. I saw her hands moving.

The stick is where it fell, on the ground, but I folded my multitool up and put it back in the car. The jagged border of glass makes a vicious mouth of the broken window. I wonder how much it will cost to fix. Does my car insurance cover attempted murder?

Rimmett promised that an officer would be watching her, that they would make sure I knew she was okay. Because I made different choices than she did, she'll survive this gruesome weekend. Not like Danny. He's dead, and he'll never have a chance to be who he could have been, to grow up and away from the stony, loveless soil he was born in. There's an ache in my chest, but it's changed shape because I don't have to shut

Gloss out anymore; there's someone in this world who loves me enough to do anything for me, even confess to murder.

There are still two police cars blocking the overgrown road. Liam's car's trapped, but I haven't seen him. I have to find him, have to tell him it wasn't Gloss, was never Gloss. That she was protecting me from the consequences of a crime I didn't commit. If I hadn't remembered Michelle holding Danny's phone, she'd be driving home with the others now, wondering aloud where I'd gone to while knowing exactly where I was. I shiver, cold fingers dragged down my spine. For all the times I've thought I wanted to die, when it came down to it, I fought with everything I had to stick around.

"Are you sure you won't come to the hospital?" Rimmett stands, small and hunched, watching the ambulance bump over the beach track towards the town.

"I'm sure." Covered in bruises, my wrists worst of all—the ties dug in cruelly while I struggled against them—and running on empty, desperately in need of a handful of ibuprofen and a vat of coffee, but sure that the hospital isn't where I'm going. "You'll let her out, right? Gloss? That's where I'm going, and I'm not leaving until you let her come home with me."

Rimmett looks me over with an utterly exhausted expression on his wan face and then shrugs. "What the hell. I'll give you a lift to the station."

ONE YEAR LATER

"SHIT."

I swear as I bump my guitar case, hard, against the door, and it slips out of my hand. It's pouring, and water is streaming down my neck into the collar of my shirt. I manage to reorganise myself enough to squeeze through the red painted doorway and into the pub. The warm, wood-panelled room isn't busy, but a few people look around in mild interest at the noise and swearing.

"Here, I got you." Liam dashes forward, a cloth in his hand and hair in his eyes. It looks like he's been moving furniture in preparation for the evening crowd. He's sweating lightly, dewy on the forehead and temples. It suits him. He grabs the guitar off me while I get through the door and crack my neck, grimacing at the cool slide of wetness. "Good day?"

"All right." I grin at him, patting my pocket. "Think I made about forty quid before the bloody sky opened on me."

"Oh, so you'll be chipping in for rent this month then," Liam teases easily, leaning his hips on a nearby stool. He's still painfully handsome, and these days, there are fewer shadows in his eyes. I like to think that's due to his excellent new room-mate and how cute I am.

"Hey!" I reach out like I'm gonna ruffle his hair with my superior height, and he ducks out of the way, laughing. "You know I'm almost caught up."

"Yeah, yeah, I know. Between tutoring and busking, I'm surprised you have time to help me out in here." Liam straightens up and saunters across the creaky wooden floorboards.

"You know I always have time for you." I follow him across the floor, grimacing at the sensation. The London pub-venue is the kind your soles stick to unless you're Gloss—human Teflon. She texted me earlier to say she'll be here around eight. Trust her to miss the hard work. But then, even if she was here, I can't imagine she'd be much help. Being forced to do manual labour is treated as an outrageous assault upon her person-hood. And I skipped the furniture rearrangement part too, so I can hardly talk.

"Grant's in the back, but you towel off before you go in my nice, clean office." Liam throws a tea towel at me, and I ruefully try to sponge the worst of London's weather out of my shaggy hair. "You might wanna just take those off and throw them on a radiator in the hopes they steam out some before you go on . . ." He waggles his eyebrows at me over his shoulder.

"Perv," I tease him, but my hoodie is dripping from the sleeves and hem, and it's far from comfortable. "Gimme a pub shirt."

"Twenty quid, mate!" he says but pulls one down anyway.

"Put it on Gloss's tab and tell Grant I'll be right there if he wants to start setting up."

I whistle on my way to the bathroom, ducking into the men's without even a second's hesitation. I don't even go into the stall to pull my soaked hoodie and T-shirt off. The three-month-old scars from my top surgery are thick, vivid horizontal lines. I have a cover-up tattoo appointment booked in for when they're faded down. It took a while to come up with the design, but Liam helped by taking photos of all the elements, and then the artist managed to combine them into a killer chest piece. Skateboard, pen, paper, music, guitar, fire engine—for my dad—lipstick print for Gloss, road signs for where I grew up and a half dozen other defining symbols. It's my "I'm still here, and healing, and whole" piece.

The T-shirt is tight and clingy, and I roll my eyes at myself in the mirror, then try to finger comb my messy hair into the semblance of an appropriate style for playing on stage. Grant and I were gonna jam tonight—he's crashing at mine and Liam's place on the way back to uni in Canterbury—but Liam's opening act broke her ankle this morning.

My shoes are noticeably squelchy as I head back through the main room to the back, but there's not much I can do about it. Grant's sprawled in Liam's chair, leafing through the music I printed off for him before dashing out the door to make a living wage this morning. Liam's leaning against the desk, typing on his laptop.

"Hey, dude, ready to sound check?" I grab my guitar from its leaning spot in the corner.

"For sure." Grant gets up and grabs his bass. "You look . . . wet."

I grimace at my damp legs and soaking skate shoes. "I feel wet."

Liam snorts, and I poke my tongue out at him, turning and heading for the stage. It's more of a small raised area that usually holds more tables and chairs, but Liam had a carpenter friend of his cut the railing to open it up, and it worked really well. With the sports screens off and a couple of stand lights pointed at the wall, it makes a nice, intimate space with great acoustics. I can't see any rock bands wanting to play here, but for open mics and mellow singer-songwriters, it doesn't get much better. He's lined up several good names already, even though he's only been manager for a few months.

Grant follows me up, and we position the lights and my stool how we want it. Grant will stand, plugged in to a small amp and pulling up to a standing mic when he wants to sing. I'll be in one spot, exposed to the crowd. A few more people have come in since I arrived, and the main floor is starting to bustle with people finding spots to sit and ordering drinks from the bar.

Gloss arrives in her own little bubble of atmosphere, as always. She's chic and sleek in a designer raincoat over a plaid suit that manages to be feminine and authoritative at the same time. Her transparent umbrella patters water on the floor as she folds it up and shoves it into the umbrella bucket. She blows me a kiss when she catches my eye, and I grin, resisting the urge to pretend to stuff it in my pocket because there are a lot of strangers watching me and it would be nice if they didn't immediately discover what a huge dweeb I am.

We finish setting our stage up, run a quick sound check, and then I hang my guitar on a wall stand since we have a little time before we're due to start. Gloss has staked out a corner table in a nook with a good view of the stage. Her white coat is spread out on the other chair, making it clear that she doesn't want anyone to join her. She could give out classes in how to stop single men from encroaching on your space and time, but she's too busy learning how to change the world.

"Hey, gorgeous," I greet her, leaning down for her kiss. She presses red lips to my cheekbone, and I know now there won't be a stain. Her lipstick is way too expensive for that. She smirks at me and tugs the hem of my shirt when I straighten up.

"That is an extremely camp look for you, love."

I growl, but I'm kidding, and she knows it. The skintight black shirt is giving me a bit of a femme rock and roll vibe, but I think I'm pulling it off. "I got soaked, and Liam misjudged my size."

"I see you didn't demand a larger one." She has me there. I shrug in acknowledgement. Hell, it wasn't that long ago I couldn't wear tight shirts without my binder being noticeable. I can wear skinny tees if I like. "Want some eyeliner to go with that vibe?"

"Sure." I sit down on her raincoat and lean my chin on my hand while she digs around in her handbag.

"Black, gold or silver?" She holds up three pencils.

"So prepared." I choose the gold.

"I used to fuck a Scout leader. He'd be so proud. You're gonna look so pretty," she crows, pulling the lid off a black pencil, and I wrinkle my nose at her in mock irritation.

"I am pretty."

"He is pretty," Liam agrees, appearing through the growing crowd. "Ooh, eyeliner! My fave!"

"We know," Gloss and I both reply at the same time and giggle. He's always trying to get us to let him do our makeup.

"Do you want some, Grant?" Liam calls over to Grant at the bar, who has one foot up on the brass foot rail and is flirting with the bartender. He definitely has a thing for bartenders.

"Some what?" Grant gives the punk woman behind the bar a last, cheeky grin and then makes his way over to us with two beers in one hand and one in the other. He plops them down on the table and shrugs at Gloss apologetically. "Sorry, didn't know you were here."

"I don't drink hops anyway," she snarks, grabbing my ear to angle my face into the light. I follow her rough hands with the ease of practice and the glow of knowing that her affection is violent and dominating. I like it.

"Want some eyeliner?" Liam asks, grabbing a beer and taking a swig. "Thanks for the hops."

"I'm all right, thanks." Grant shakes his head. "Maybe I'll experiment some time when I'm not about to get on stage."

"That's the spirit!" Liam crows delightedly. "I have a silver that would look divine on you."

"Divine is what I'm always aiming for." Grant taps me on the shoulder. "Come on, pretty boy. Let's get this party started."

"Hey, it's my bar." Liam pokes Grant in the ribs. "You're not the boss."

"It's ten past eight." Grant raises an eyebrow.

"Oh. In that case. Get the party started, pretty boys." Liam flaps at me, and Gloss hisses at him like a cat as she smudges the eyeliner under my eyes and gives me an approving look.

"Okay, now you may go."

"Thanks, Your Majesty." I take a welcome swallow of beer from the cold, sweating bottle as I get up. "Pray for me."

"Just sing to me," Gloss tells me, pinching my bum as I turn towards the stage. "You'll be wonderful."

I yelp at the sharp fingers and frown at her over my shoulder before stepping up onto the raised dais and heading to grab my guitar.

The lights are bright in my eyes, and sweat is forming under my pits at the idea of all the people watching. My hands are slippery, and my full beer bottle slides out of my hand and thunks onto the floor when I try to set it down by my chair leg.

"Evening, folks." Grant's melodious voice rings over the mic, and I relax and sit down, adjusting my own mic stand and pulling my guitar into my lap. "I'm Grant, and this is Max, and we're gonna be playing some of Max's original music for you this evening. How're you all doing?"

There's a couple of whoops and a smattering of light applause, but Grant isn't fazed by the weak response. "All right,

buy us a beer after if you like the sound of us. Don't forget to
tip your servers."

I think about saying something, but nothing comes to
mind, so instead I find Gloss's eyes through the haze of lights
and face, and she smiles at me. Liam's off, behind the bar
again or doing some other managerial shit, but I know he's
there for me as well. I shift my fingers, find my chord, and
start to play.

Sunlight darts in through the window above the door and
flares off the mirror behind the bar, spilling gold all over my
hands.

> *you and i curled in the safety of the deep leaf shadows*
> *our mouths lodestones, forever drawn to each other*
> *and the bottles i snuck from my mother's kitchen*

> *our bare skin touched*
> *i discovered electricity*

> *the summer lasted forever*
> *it was over in seconds*
> *your love anointed me*
> *gold and made me precious*
> *made me believe i am worth*
> *something*

> *am i worth something?*
> *i have been a lost boy since before i was born*
> *stuffed into ill-fitting skin*
> *but when you looked at me*
> *i knew myself*
> *for the first time*

our days were long and hot, thick with confessions
secrets
wishes
and when we walked away from each other
both of us looked back
every time

you told me you wanted to tie yourself to me
i said i'd rather be tied to you
and your laugh was music that spawned a dozen songs
ideas swimming up water, against the current of your kisses

i never said thank you
or goodbye
but i hope you knew
everything
i never said

Acknowledgments

FIRST AND FOREMOST, the thanks go to my wife, Marie, without whom my entire life would be a shambles. This book has been a labour of love, hate, joy, rage, misery, melancholy and a whole bunch of other emotions. It's the rawest thing I've ever written, and the book I have struggled with the most. It's been through four (Covid!) years, two agents, six rewrites, and now it finally exists in the world. Through all that time my wonderful partner has believed in this story, and believed in me enough to keep me going.

To the many others who have thrown their belief, time and energy into this novel, I am deeply grateful. To my delightful agent, Stacey Kondla, and my incredible editor, Alexa Wejko, I am indebted. Stacey, without you this book and my writing career would have been shelved in 2022, I cannot express how much you changed my path, and I don't know where I'd be without you. Alexa, working with you has been a blast, you saw right to the bones of this story and showed me how to pull them out (gross bone metaphor intended!). Thank you for your tireless dedication to finding the right paths for these complex characters/utter disasters.

The whole Soho team deserves all the appreciation! Thanks to everyone behind the scenes I didn't get to know! Thanks to Rachel Kowal, for working on the details; Janine Agro, thank you for your impeccable art direction. Thanks also to Lily DeTaeye for her care and work as my publicist. My gratitude to amazing copy editor, Adam Mongaya. I'm so, so sorry about my fractious relationship to commas, you are a champion and a scholar. I owe you a beverage if you're ever in the 'Couve.

From the moment I saw the cover of this book, I fell in love. Erin Fitzsimmons, you are a magician, thank you for capturing the essence of this story so perfectly.

To my dreamy collection of friends around the globe, in no particular order, my love and gratitude! Leah Tottenham for the tea and sympathy; Lianna Teeter for the yells and the cozy; Meryl Wilsner, who has the hugest heart, Mish Maune, my partner-in-smirk; Sinead Stinson, who brings the chats and the smarts; Jo Grimditch, who always believes in me and also cracks me up; Karen and Dom Melanson-Chong, thanks for the games and giggles; Ali Hewitt and Peter Michaud, the best bocce-beer pals you could ask for. Kate Cash from tents to islands you're a champ and I love and appreciate you; Rebecca Skye, you may be the kindest soul alive I'm so glad we are pals now; Jillian Christmas, friend and perfect neighbour, ty for the saunas, the frybread, the gossip and the help. Dylan Carothers, thanks always for the mermen; J Scott Coatsworth and Cari Z for the support, celebration and commiserations and finally Alix Anttila, perfect bestie, for Literally Everything.

To those who stepped in and read the incoherent earlier drafts—Sara Codair, Lori Griffin, Sam MacNeil, Meryl and Dylan (again!), and anyone I may have forgotten because I have a brain like a sieve. Thank you for wading through the plot holes and dramatics as I found my way through the swamp.

Thanks also to my dear family, near and far—Mum, Dad, Alex, Dave, Ari, Sefi, Anne, Eva, Kyle, Kimbal, Loralee, Gavin, Yossi, Tony, your support means everything. Thanks for always being there.

The greatest thanks to the youth I work with, the youth who trust me, the youth who reach out to me and the youth who grant me the privilege of helping them navigate this world. Thank you